What HAMLET SAID

TERRY MORT

McBooks Press

Guilford, Connecticut

McBooks Press

An imprint of Globe Pequot, the trade division of
The Rowman & Littlefield Publishing Group, Inc.
4501 Forbes Blvd., Ste. 200
Lanham, MD 20706
www.rowman.com

Distributed by NATIONAL BOOK NETWORK

Copyright © 2019 by Terry Mort
First McBooks Press Paperback Edition 2022

British Library Cataloguing in Publication Information available

Library of Congress Cataloging-in-Publication Data available

ISBN 978-1-4930-6194-5 (paperback) | ISBN 978-1-4930-6499-1 (ebook)

∞™ The paper used in this publication meets the minimum requirements of American
National Standard for Information Sciences—Permanence of Paper for Printed Library
Materials, ANSI/NISO Z39.48-1992.

To Sondra, the best and the bravest

Chapter One

"What kind of name is Bruno Feldspar?"

"Fictitious."

He thought about that for a moment.

"You mean, made up?"

"Yes. Made up."

He smiled and seemed to relax. We had something in common.

"Me too," he said. "I'm not really Rex Lockwood." I wasn't surprised. "I'm really Jimmy Hicks, but the publicity department thought it wasn't romantic enough. I guess maybe it ain't, when you come right down to it. Besides, they thought the papers might make fun of it. You know, 'A Hick Named Hicks.' Stuff like that. And worse. Besides, I'm from Idaho, so that added to it."

"I understand." Lots of words rhymed with Hicks.

"They were going to call me Ramon Zapata, but I didn't really have the look of a Latin lover. I looked pretty bad with a pencil mustache and pointed sideburns."

"Most people do."

"Huh? Oh, yeah. Right. Plus, I'm blond. There ain't that many blond Mexicans or Brazilians or South Americans. They tried a dye job, but it really didn't look so good. Sort of like I was wearing a patent leather bathing cap. So they settled for the All-American angle. That's what they called it. Besides, the Latin Lover bit is starting to get old. But you can call me Jimmy, if you want. I'd rather you did. My friends all do, not that I have that many out here. This is no town for making friends, if you know what I mean."

"I know what you mean."

"And I still haven't got used to being Rex. Even after two years of it."

"Okay. What can I do for you, Jimmy?"

He studied his hands for a moment. I couldn't tell whether he'd learned that move in acting class or whether it was genuine. Initial impressions were that he was entirely genuine, but you can't ever be too sure with an actor. On the other hand, lots of people in the business would say that Jimmy Hicks wasn't really an actor. Just another good-looking boy with long eyelashes.

"I got a problem," he said, finally.

I nodded reassuringly and didn't bother even signaling the obvious. Guys without problems don't contact private detectives or come to their office. Guys who do call you are seriously worried about something. And generally they have a good reason to be. That goes for women, too. Maybe more so. I knew that firsthand.

"It's about a woman," said Jimmy.

"Shocking," I said, mildly. Following Gary Cooper's advice in *The Virginian*, I smiled when I said this, just to take the sting out of the sarcasm. Jimmy seemed to be a nice guy, a kid really. He was old enough to vote, but probably hadn't yet. And unfortunately for him, as I learned, the word "guileless" fitted him like old shoes. I could see the headline on the cover story—"Hicks from the sticks gets his dick in a fix." I could hear *Hush Hush* magazine panting and slobbering just outside Jimmy's cabana door. Figuratively speaking, that is. But if I knew them, and I did, it wouldn't be long before they were there literally, notebooks poised to write the story, or their version of it, seasoned with smut and smirks. Somebody would tip them off. Then there'd be cameras waiting for that precise moment when the subject looked either ridiculous or guilty. "Close enough is good enough" was their unspoken motto when it came to facts. Truth was something else—sometimes useful and colorful, but not essential. Like paprika.

"So... it's about a woman," I said, prompting.

"Yes." He paused. "Ah... people say you can be trusted. Ethel Welkin gave me your name." I wasn't sure, but I think he blushed a little.

Good old Ethel, my pint-sized mentor and occasional afternooner, wife of a big-time producer and prime mover in Hollywood. Ethel was the one who'd dubbed me Bruno Feldspar, when it seemed possible that I might make it in the movies. I didn't, for a number of reasons, but I got known by that name around town, and there were reasons why a *nom de guerre*, even a dumb one, was worth keeping.

"I'm probably the most trustworthy guy in Hollywood," I said. "But you and I both know that isn't saying much." Another smile, this time to indicate that we were on the same side, just two honest Midwestern guys trying to get by in Gomorrah West.

At this point in these conversations, there's almost always a long pause. The "client" takes one more look at the fix he's in and tries to decide if it's really as lousy as it seems—whether it's lousy enough to spill to a stranger. He's wondering whether he can tell it without looking like the damned fool he knows he is. Confession may be good for the soul, but it's hard on what the French call your *amour propre*. And it's worse if the client happens to be a cowboy star like Rex—the hero who always ends up with the adoring girl and a dead bad guy in the final reel—the hero who drinks sarsaparilla and rides alone, except for his faithful old sidekick Soapy. Rex/Jimmy may be naïve, but he'd been in Hollywood long enough to know that certain news can wipe out a career, whether the news is strictly factual or not. Some guy in Washington once said that the only thing that could ruin a politician's career was being caught in bed with a dead woman or a live man. But that wasn't true in Hollywood. Either one could turn you into an untouchable—the Hindu kind. But only if the word got out, of course. The purveyors of the word made their money by writing stories that sold papers and fan magazines, or by not writing those stories in exchange for envelopes of cash. Rex had made two well-received pictures, but they were only B westerns. His prospects were good, but he wasn't a big enough star yet to be absolutely sure the studio boys would go into their pockets and out of their way to protect him. Worse, Rex's image was as clean as his Stetson and as white as his horse Blanco. (Real name Ned.) And that made him a perfect target. The gossip-mongers would be thrilled to get some dirt on him. They knew their reading public wanted to believe only one of two things about their screen idols— either the best or the worst. In between didn't sell. And the worst stories were the best. There's nothing quite like a little vicarious sin. You get a little frisson, and no one presents a bill for it afterwards. Well, that's no scoop.

So I sat there letting him decide whether to drop his pants or not.

He reached into his pocket and pulled out a picture—a standard eight-by-ten glossy publicity shot. It was a woman, of course. A girl, really. You've heard of the "It Girl." This was the "Not It Girl." She was pretty enough, but her looks were nothing more than ordinary, and her ordinariness was accentuated by too much makeup. Drag a seine net through any soda fountain in America and you'd capture one or two. She was trying to look sexy, but didn't—more like she was getting ready to ask you for a stick of gum. It was clear that whoever had taken this amateurish shot was in a hurry to get it over with so that he could get to his other job, delivering Chinese takeout.

The picture said her name was Lulu Marquessa. I believed the Lulu part.

If this was the girl causing Jimmy's problem, my respect for him went down a notch. Surely he could have done better.

"I guess I drank too much," he said, as if reading my thoughts. "I guess I was drunk."

"That'll happen. Cause and effect." Well, at least that explained something.

"We met in a bar. She told me she was an actress but hadn't had much luck yet. A few auditions. The usual brush-offs. She knew who I was, she said. She'd seen both my pictures. She thought maybe I could help her." He shook his head as if wondering at the mystery of it all. "I don't mind saying I was a little flattered. I'd never met a perfect stranger who'd seen my movies. Most of the 'meet and greets' with fans were arranged by the publicity department to get photos, you know? Half the time, I thought those fans were just paid extras."

He was half right about that.

"But this girl seemed to really like me. Made me feel good, you know?"

I wondered—was there anything about Jimmy's story that was the least bit original? Would we ever get to it?

"Anyway, things went on that way for a while. And then she asks me if I'd take her home. So I said sure. I guess you know what I was thinking."

"I guess."

"So we get to her place. It was just one of those cheap apartment buildings on a side street in Santa Monica. You know, kind of Spanish-looking. Or Mexican. And we go upstairs and you know what happens next, I suppose, you being a private eye and all. And afterwards I say good night and drive on home. She asked me to call her in the morning, but I didn't. Next day, I get a call from a guy who says he's her manager. He's all upset, but he sounded phony. You know?"

"Yes. I do know the sound of phony."

"Anyway, he tells me she's underage. Says one of the studios is grooming her to be their next ingénue. You know what that means?"

"Yeah."

"I didn't. But apparently it means underage."

"How much did he want?"

"He didn't say. He said he'd be in touch."

"Probably wanted to let you stew a while."

"I guess in your business you'd expect that. It sure as hell surprised me."

"Let's just say this isn't the first time something like this has happened."

"Do you think it's a... shakeup?"

"No, I think it's a shake*down*."

"That's what I meant."

"I know." I looked at the photo again. This girl was no more underage than Madame Curie. "Did the guy leave an address or a phone number?"

"Yes. I wrote it down on the back of the picture."

Acme Management. Acme? Really? The address was some back street in San Pedro. Not exactly the high-rent district. And there was a phone number.

"Can I keep this photo?"

"I wish you would. I sure don't want to ever see it again. Do you think you can... take care of it for me?"

What Hamlet Said

"Not only do I think I can, I *know* I can."

"Whew! That's a relief. Ethel said I could rely on you."

"In this case, Ethel was right. Don't worry about a thing. I'll be in touch."

He smiled, and I could see what the studio saw in him. He was a handsome kid, of course, but he had that sort of honest, aw-shucks thing that Gary Cooper had and that the studios were forever in search of—and rarely finding. The way Jimmy looked and moved, even a camera couldn't have found a trace of cynicism or phoniness in him, and the camera doesn't miss anything. It's the one thing in Hollywood that's absolutely honest.

"I don't know how to thank you."

"Just say 'thank you'—when the job's done."

"Don't I owe you something?"

"I get twenty-five bucks a day plus expenses. This should take a couple of hours. You can either buy me a fancy dinner or a week's worth of BLT's at Schwab's. That'll square it."

Jimmy didn't know it, of course, but I was doing this as much as a favor to Ethel as anything. I was going to see her later at the Beverly Hills Hotel for one of our occasional lunches followed by an afternoon romp, and it would make her happy to know that I was taking good care of one of her new protégés. She had done lots of favors for me, and I was happy to do something in return. Besides, I liked Ethel. For a five-foot woman built like a fire hydrant, she was a pretty good bed partner, as well as a very good and very useful friend. She might not be all that well constructed, but she was very well connected.

Chapter Two

"Did you take care of my new star's problem?" she said after we were finished.

"No, but I'm going to, later this afternoon. I didn't want to head all the way out to Pedro and be late for our lunch."

"That was sweet of you."

"That's me. Ask anyone."

"Is it as straightforward as it sounded?"

"Yes. Grade school–level extortion. Nothing to worry about, so far as I can see."

"I thought so. Poor Jimmy. He was so scared. I thought about sending one of Izzy's studio security boys to take care of it, but they think being subtle is when you don't use a blackjack. That can cause problems, if things get out of hand. You, on the other hand, my dear, are the soul of discretion and subtlety."

"I don't even own a blackjack." That wasn't strictly true. I did own one, but I didn't know where it was. In a drawer somewhere, I guess. Next to a spare .38, probably under the socks. "But I told him not to worry and that I'd take care of it."

"Thank you, dah-ling." Ethel liked imitating the affectations of the female stars, especially the Eliza Doolittles who came over here fresh from selling fruit in Covent Garden. With work, they were able to drop their cockney accents and acquire refinement from some pansy dialog coach. That all made Ethel smile. Quite a few things did. She was an amiable soul, as long as you treated her right. Otherwise, it was a different story.

"So—how did you like the new one?" asked Ethel.

"New what?"

"You know. Don't be coy."

"Number sixty-two?"

"Yes."

"Just as much as the first sixty-one."

"Good," she purred. "I was doing exercises all week to be ready." Ethel was a dedicated student of the Kama Sutra. She said there were sixty-four positions, and she had tried them all. Not all with me, but we were working toward that goal. Or she was, anyway. It was all nonsense, if you asked me. Someone once said number so-and-so was just like the one before it, only with your fingers crossed. After all, there were only so many things you could put somewhere, and only so many somewheres to put them. But if she wanted to do research into the matter, it was all right with me. She had other galloping partners, of course, not counting Izzy, her husband. Most likely, Jimmy Hicks was either next in line or had already been to the buffet. But I was one of her favorites. And you wouldn't think it to see her dressed, but she had quite an attractively sturdy figure under it all. I mentioned fire hydrants before; but if you look carefully at your average hydrant, you can see some aesthetic qualities. If you try, that is. Besides, Ethel had been good to me and was still being good to me, and it was no strain at all for me to be good to her one afternoon a week, on average. I did wish she'd cut back on the garlic bagels, pickles, and pastrami at lunch, maybe save them for afterwards. But, as Voltaire said, "perfection is the enemy of the good." Actually, he said "the best is the enemy of the good," but I think he meant to say perfection.

"I could tell," I said. "About the exercises, I mean."

"Could you? Could you feel the contractions? I never know when you're telling the truth. Most times I just assume you aren't. It's easier."

"You know what Mark Twain said—truth is a valuable commodity; we should be economical with it. Or something like that."

"That's one reason I like you. You're educated. A nice Presbyterian college boychick."

"More like the college of soft knocks. But I read a lot. And I stopped being a boy about fifteen years ago. Maybe one day I'll convert, so you can divorce Izzy and marry me."

That brought one of Ethel's trademark guffaws. It was somewhere between a honk and an epic snort.

"That'll be the day. But you wouldn't have to convert, dah-ling."

"That's good. I'm too old for a bris."

"And you'd have to have more than two hundred bucks in the bank."

"I'm safe, then." Actually, I had quite a bit more than that in the bank—about five years' worth, if I was as economical with the money as Ethel thought I was with the truth. The less said about where it had come from, the better. Ethel, of course, knew all about that, too. Or some of it.

"Yes, you're safe. Besides, I like Izzy, and I like the life. Flatbush was never like this. Speaking of Flatbush, are you going to Manny's party this weekend?"

"Wouldn't miss it."

"Are you bringing your beautiful lady?"

What Hamlet Said

"Under normal circumstances, she'd be bringing me. She's the star. I'm just the boyfriend. But I'll be there by myself. She's on location. In Yuma."

"That's right. I forgot."

They were shooting another of those Foreign Legion pictures in the California desert just across the river from Yuma, Arizona. She was playing a White Russian princess who'd been kidnapped by the Bedouins. Lucky Bedouins.

I started to get out of bed.

"Where are you going?"

"I thought I'd head out to San Pedro before the traffic gets bad."

She pouted—made what the French call a *moue*. "Oh, you have time for number sixty-three, don't you?"

"Do I have to stand on my head or something? I'm not sure I'm up to that. Besides, the old tennis elbow..."

"Nothing like that. It's fast and easy."

"Well, all right. But make it snappy, woman."

"That is precisely the idea—and precisely the right word... dah-ling."

You could describe her grin as either roguish or sinister, depending on the lighting and camera angle. Either way, it was part of her charm. Another part was her complete lack of interest in anything beyond these occasional afternoons. In exchange, she'd do whatever she could—and that was a lot, since she was so well connected—to help me and mine in our careers. A nice lady.

* * *

San Pedro was the home port of the Pacific Battle Fleet. There were rumors about maybe moving the fleet to Hawaii, and the local people were nervous about that. The town made a lot of money from the Navy. Sailors don't earn much, but there's always a lot of them, so it all adds up—and they all want the same simple things.

11

Local merchants didn't have to worry too much about the variety of their inventory. If it came in a bottle, that was good enough. As for the local women—well, they were there and they were friendly, and that's basically all that the Navy asked for.

Some of the fleet were out that day. You could hear the big guns pounding away at the islands they used for target practice. They were getting ready for the next big war. It was sure as hell coming. You could smell it. Maybe we could stay out of it. I hoped so. But if we couldn't, I hoped the Navy got in plenty of practice beforehand. They'd need it.

The town had a pretty exotic blend of foreigners—Mexicans and Italians, of course, and a few Japs who kept to themselves but made people wonder, what with all the tension in the world. Their cousins back home were currently burning China to the ground, so it made you think. And surprisingly there were quite a few Croatians. I guess they mainly worked in the shipyards. My stunning girlfriend, who went by the silly studio name "Yvonne Adore," was on her way to becoming a big star. But when I met her in Youngstown, Ohio, she had just been off the boat from Croatia and married to the pathetic owner of a diner next to the steel mills. She worked there waiting on steelworkers who came off shift or who'd been laid off, and she was just about the only thing that brightened up their days. She'd been sort of a mail-order bride who quickly realized that the price she'd paid to come to America was a little higher than she'd expected. But the marriage and the arrangement didn't last long, because her sad little husband got run over by a city bus, and that gave Myrtle, as she was then, free rein to ride to California with me. I introduced her to Ethel, who rarely made mistakes when it came to judging star potential. And she didn't make one with Myrtle. It helped, of course, that Myrtle was even more beautiful on film than in person, and that was saying something. And she had the most alluring, sultry voice, with just the right amount of accent. She put Garbo in the shade, at least as far as I was concerned. And a lot of people agreed with me. Plus, she had a better figure. We lived together much of the time in a beach house in Malibu; and if you're wondering whether I say prayers of thanks every night, well, yes, I do. On my knees, even though, as Ethel said, I was a Presbyterian, originally. Anyway, now and then Myrtle and I would come to Pee-dro, as the locals pronounced it, because there was a Croatian bakery she liked. It was one of the few places in LA where you could get an authentic bread, called *pogacha,* and real apple strudel. So I knew the town. And I knew a few of the characters who hung around the waterfront bars. One of them was a master forger who came in handy now and then. He could have gotten rich and lived the high life, if he wanted to risk making U.S. currency. But he didn't. He always said it wasn't curiosity that killed the cat, but too much ambition. He stuck to making passports and work papers for the Beaners and the Nips. The market was plenty big enough for him, and nobody really seemed to care all that much. So it was really low-risk forgery.

Acme Management's address was on a seedy side street. It was more or less residential, meaning there weren't any service stations or warehouses on that particular block. The two-story houses were close together. Every one was taller than it was wide, and they all were dark-colored because their siding was asphalt shingle material —the kind that comes in big rolls. It was a neighborhood for first-generation immigrants or second-generation losers. I had second thoughts about parking my Packard convertible on the street in front of Acme's address. I didn't expect to be long, but it doesn't take a professional much more than a few seconds to make off with a car like that. And there weren't any urchins hanging around that I could bribe not to steal my hubcaps. There was no choice but to park and take my chances. I figured I could always replace hubcaps, but if someone ran a key along the paint just for the hell of it, it would ruin my day.

I rang the doorbell. The guy who opened the door was wearing a dingy dress shirt that was straining at the middle buttons and a hand-painted tie featuring a palm tree and a hula dancer. He looked like the Before picture in a Geritol ad. ("Tired Blood? Here's the answer.") He didn't need a shave, because the three dabs of toilet paper on his face showed he'd done it already. But the rest of him needed real work—a year's worth of good exercise, sunshine, and green vegetables. But I'll say this for him—he was careful with his hair. It was brilliantly slicked, and I remembered Jimmy's comment about patent leather. He stood in the doorway and didn't seem inclined to ask me in. That was fine with me. This wasn't a social call. But even standing on the porch I could smell the odors coming from inside the house—fried pork chops and cigarette smoke.

I smiled genially.

"Mr. Acme, I presume."

"Huh?"

"I see you're getting dressed for the prom, so I won't take up too much of your time."

"I don't need no insurance. Or Fuller brushes. And I don't want to get to know Jesus." He had a pretty heavy accent. It was familiar.

"That's lucky, because I'm not selling anything. This is the office of Acme Talent Management, isn't it?"

"Who wants to know?"

"You see anyone else standing here?"

"Smart guy, huh?"

"That's right. Well, Mr. Acme, you have an odd name. For a person. What's the first name? Alphonse? Maurice? Dumbass?"

"Smart guy, huh?"

What Hamlet Said

"You need new material, Alphonse. Here's the deal—I represent Mr. Rex Lockwood." I could see that the name registered, and he did not like this kind of quick, in-person response, especially when the guy making the call looked and dressed like he came from the part of town where money was made. And where it stayed. "You made a threatening call to my client. Yesterday. Remember?"

"Your client?"

"Right. Rex Lockwood."

"What of it?"

"What of it? Here's the 'what of it.' That was the poorest excuse for a shakedown I've ever heard about. Now, granted, I haven't been in the business more than a couple of years, but I can't believe anybody ever made a more pathetic effort. You get the blue ribbon."

"Oh, yeah?"

"Yep."

He marshalled his thoughts. He looked at me and then looked past me at the fancy car I had driven there. He was calculating the odds and not liking the way they added up.

"She was underage," he said, defensively. "He took advantage of her."

"'Took advantage of her'? What is this? A Victorian novel? But I will give you one compliment—your mother looks really young for her age."

"What?"

"But she can't pass for an ingénue, Alphonse. Or any kind of gnu. Those days are behind her. So I suggest you put your dreams of a quick buck back in the cigar box next to the dirty pictures and forget you ever had this idea."

"Yeah? What if I don't?"

"Bad things happen to good people. They also happen to bad people. Especially two-bit hustlers in Hawaiian neckties."

"You threatening me?"

"Nope. You ever go to the movies?"

He thought about it.

"Maybe."

"Well, I'm like the scout who goes ahead of the cavalry and locates the Indians. I don't bother threatening the Injuns. I just go back and tell the army where they are. Then the cavalry comes up and kicks the shit out of them. Fade to black. So think of this little meeting today as life imitating art—we're playing the scene that comes just before the last scene."

"What's that mean?"

"That means if we hear from you again, or even see Lulu again, the cavalry's going to beat you till you won't see the white for the black and blue. For starters. They might be tempted to do it anyway, just on principle. But I'll put in a good word for you, since you have such good taste in ties."

He thought things over.

"Suppose I call the cops? Tell 'em you've been trying to strongarm me. I got rights."

"Go ahead, Alphonse. Most of the cops are on our payroll. They'd be very interested to hear you explain about your rights. They might even offer you a place to stay for a few nights, while you recover. And by the way, the only cops who aren't on our payroll are the ones who'd like to be. They're just waiting until there's an opening."

"You saying the cops are all crooked?" Did I detect even the slightest glimmer of irony? Was it possible Alphonse was not a complete moron? I was curious, but then I realized it didn't really matter.

"No. I'm saying they're hard-working Americans with two jobs just to make ends meet. But working two jobs makes them cranky."

What Hamlet Said

"I'll bet," he said sourly.

"Bottom line—you'd be smart to forget this whole thing. Do yourself a big favor and go back to reading the want ads. Leave the shakedown business to people who know what they're doing."

He looked at his shoes and shuffled. Then he made a good decision and gave up.

"It was worth a try, I guess."

"Well, no one can hate you for that. Not every idea works out. I'm sure Edison had a few flops."

"It wasn't my idea. It was Lulu's."

"I'm also sure you read the Bible, so you know that Adam tried that excuse too. Didn't work for him either. You were the voice on the phone. That makes you the Indians."

"I told Lulu it wasn't going to work. But she kept after me."

"They can be persistent."

"She gets an idea in her head and she won't let go."

"Women! Can't live with 'em. Can't live without 'em, except during the week. Right, Alphonse?"

He grinned a yellow-toothed grin.

"You're right about that."

"So, are we clear?"

He stood there looking chagrined.

"I guess," he said, finally.

"Good."

"You won't, ah... send the cavalry?"

"Not this time, Alphonse. I feel that you have learned a valuable lesson and are a better man for it."

"My name's not Alphonse, by the way. Or Acme."

"That a fact? Well, the truth is, I don't really care."

"And Lulu ain't my mother. She's my girlfriend. She don't live here, though. Lives in Santa Monica."

"Well, there's no accounting for taste, is there?"

"I guess not."

"Nice doing business with you."

I left him standing on his porch. The whole thing took about five minutes, and even counting the drive out there and back, I figured I'd only earned a couple of BLT's. But as I said, I really did this for my pal Ethel.

Chapter Three

The next morning, I drove to my office feeling pretty good about taking care of things for Jimmy. He seemed like a nice kid. I'd called him the night before and left a message that everything was all right and that he should forget the whole thing. His answering service took the message and said they'd pass it on. He'd be relieved. The old Duke of Wellington was threatened once with something salacious, and he just said "Publish and be damned." Well, there weren't many in Hollywood with either the juice or the brass ones to pull that off. There were a few, but only a few, and they were all the brightest stars, of course. The big female stars were the toughest. They were broads, in the best sense of the word. They had to be to get where they were. Everyone else was in Jimmy's boat and stayed awake nights worrying that their indiscretions might see the light of day, suddenly appearing like toadstools after a rain. They worried about other stuff too, like how long it would be before someone finally woke up and discovered the con. The fig leaf of the *artiste* would fall away and reveal the limp noodle of the fraud. They all had a little voice inside their heads saying "Surely they aren't going to keep paying *me* that much for doing *this*. Surely they're going to find me out." Chronic insecurity was a communicable disease. Almost everyone had it. One of my writer friends said that in the dark soul of America, it's always three A.M., or something like that. I don't know about the rest of America, and I wasn't sure that Hollywood was even part of it, but I was sure that when three A.M. rolled around in this town, it lingered. And a lot of people were lying in the dark staring at the ceiling.

As far as I was concerned, that was more than okay. Guilt feelings may have pretty much gone out of fashion in this town, but nervousness had taken its place, and nervousness paid better than guilt because it never went away. There were no priests to offer absolution. *Ego te absolvo* didn't work on the yips. The pervasive feeling in the air was that everything was so fragile. A breath of wind could bring it all down. Of course, everything boiled down to either love or money, and in this town both were like handfuls of mercury.

So it all made for good business for a private dick—so good, in fact, that I didn't have to take the sleazier cases. There was no sneaking in the bushes and taking pictures through a motel window, no following some guy named Lance into a steam room. I was able to specialize in high-class neurotics and white-collar stuff. Now and then I'd have a brush with the mob and the cops. But that was okay. In this town you couldn't avoid either one. Besides, I didn't want to avoid them. Some of them were my friends. And speaking of now and then, now and then I'd even get to work on a genuine crime.

Like today.

My office was in the Cahuenga Building on Sunset Boulevard. It was a standard outer reception office and inner private room. Both rooms had an oak décor that reminded you of the post office. On my office wall were a Barbasol yearly calendar and a Winslow Homer seascape print that I got for fifty cents at a garage sale. The more I looked at it, the more I thought I'd overpaid. Not that I didn't like

What Hamlet Said

Winslow Homer, you understand. It was just that the colors were faded. Well, Southern California sunlight will do that. There were quite a few people walking around who suffered from a similar condition, although I guess it was time and the business that had done the fading, not the sun. The calendar was free, of course, courtesy of my barber.

I opened the office door in a fairly good mood. My part-time secretary, Della, was typing away at something. It probably wasn't work-related—not my business, anyway. She ran an escort service in her spare time, and that most likely had some paperwork associated with it. Plus she said she was writing a crime novel about a smartass detective in LA. I don't know whether that was true or not. Della only told you what she thought you needed to know— about anything. She was married to a retired chief petty officer who was now running a water taxi to the gambling ships outside the three-mile limit. His name was Perry, and he did things for me too, now and then, when I needed someone who had his conscience firmly under control and on a short leash.

Della looked up when I hustled in.

"You again!"

"Greetings, loyal employee," I said. "How's the novel going?"

"I'm having writer's block. But I'm working through it."

"You know what Hemingway said about that."

"Nope. What?"

"Nothing important. Keep me posted on your progress. Any calls?"

"Sergeant Kowalski wants you to call."

"What'd he say?"

She looked at me like a nanny regarding an idiot child.

"He said to tell you to call him."

"Ah. That clarifies it. Anything else?"

"The studio called and wanted to know if you were interested in starring in *Gone With the Wind*. I told them you were busy."

"Good. I'm too good-looking for that part."

"I didn't tell you which part it was."

"No matter. Anything else?"

"That's all, Chief." Della got a kick out of calling me Chief, for some reason. She was twice my age, smoked Pall Malls incessantly, and had a shade of red hair never before seen in nature, or anywhere else. We were good pals. Perry, too. In fact, I got along with Perry better than she did. At least that's what she said. "You like him," she'd say. "That's the difference."

"Oh, there's one more message. Your sweetie called. She said it was hot out there and to be sure to eat right while she was away. She also said to say she misses you."

"And who could blame her?"

"You must be getting payback for being some sort of saint in a former life," said Della, "because I can't think of anything you've done in this life to justify having her."

"You're forgetting that little matter you and Perry helped us with. Something about a body."

"Aside from that."

"Aside from that, I have to agree with you. I don't even remotely deserve her. But I hope she doesn't find out for a while."

"Does she know about your occasional afternoons with the producer's wife?"

"Up to a point. She 'knows' it's just a sociable business lunch, and we leave it at that. And just between you and me, that's really all it is. No more important than that. As you very well know."

"Yeah. I do know that."

I went into my office and made the call. I left the door open. There weren't many—or even any—secrets between me and Della.

What Hamlet Said

At least I couldn't keep anything from her. She, on the other hand, was another story.

Kowalski answered on the first ring.

"Homicide. Kowalski."

"Ed, it's Bruno Feldspar."

"You still using that stupid alias?"

"It's not an alias. It's what the French call a *nom de guerre*."

"Yeah? Nom de bullshit's more like it."

"Ed, you have no couth."

"It's been said before. You know an actor by the name of Jimmy Hicks, nom de bullshit Rex Lockwood?"

"You must know I do, or you wouldn't have called me."

"Nothing gets by you, does it? How do you know him?"

"I just took care of a very minor matter for him. Some lowlife in Pedro tried to shake him down for going to bed with his girlfriend— the lowlife's girlfriend, that is. Her name's Lulu Marquessa. Not real. Actress."

"Former actress. Current inhabitant of the LA County morgue. Real name as yet undetermined."

Uh-oh.

"What happened to her?"

"Shot once in the forehead. Forty-five or forty-four-caliber bullet. Ballistics is checking. Not much of a hole going in, but you wouldn't want to turn her over."

"Where'd they find her?"

"On the beach, not far from the Santa Monica pier. Looks like she was killed right there. No one reported hearing the shot, but you know how that goes. We figure it happened around three A.M."

There was that number again.

"What about Jimmy?"

"He was seen with her at the Hide and Seek Bar and then at her apartment building going into her rooms to play hide the salami. You might tell him that if he wants to go incognito, he should leave the Stetson at home."

"He was recognized."

"Yep. By five different people in the bar and the super of the apartment building. Your boy must have been laying off for months, 'cause he sure made up for lost time. More dead Trojans than in *The Iliad*."

"A classical reference. Impressive."

"What? Surprised we read Homer at the Police Academy?"

Kowalski actually was one of the new breed of cops—a college graduate. But he had to downplay that with most of his peers on the force. When those guys heard someone mention Homer, all they thought about was a ball flying over the outfield fence. So Kowalski had to seem more hardboiled than the rest, which was really no problem for him. He came from a family of cops and knew how things were done. He just also happened to have a scholarly bent. That was something we had in common. I never made it to college, but I read a lot.

"Sounds like Jimmy put in an impressive performance in the sack," I said. "But he's only a kid. Remember those days? Making love all night, sleeping for an hour and then going fishing?"

"All I remember is the fishing part. Anyway, we'd like to talk to him, but he's nowhere to be found. We checked his apartment, and it looks like he hasn't been there for a couple of days, at least. I thought you might know something."

"No. Sorry."

"You're not handing me some client confidentiality horseshit, are you?"

What Hamlet Said

"No. He's not officially a client. I was just doing a favor for Ethel Welkin. She's professionally interested in the kid."

"What about the boyfriend in Pedro? What's his name?"

"I didn't bother to find out. He called Jimmy using his company name, Acme Talent Management."

"Original. What's the address?

I gave it to him.

"Well, if Jimmy gets in touch, you know what to tell him."

"Yeah, I do. And I will. How's Lois, by the way?"

"Gaining weight."

Next I called Ethel's home number. Her maid answered.

"Mavis? It's Bruno. Is Ethel there?"

"Hiya, honey. Whatcha got on your mind? This ain't Wednesday."

"I know. This is business."

"Oh. Well, she's out by the pool with cucumber slices over her eyes and nothing else but a hand towel covering your old Kentucky home. I'll tell her to pick up the extension."

"Hello, dah-ling. Calling for number sixty-five?" She sounded halfway through the morning Bloody Mary.

"I thought there were only sixty-four. But the fact is I'm trying to find Jimmy. I thought you might know where he is."

"Why, no. What's the matter?" She had the instincts of a panther when it came to sensing trouble.

"The cops are looking for him."

"God! What now?"

"That girl who was trying to shake him down turned up dead the next morning. And he seems to have disappeared."

"Damn! Not good. Not good at all." She thought for a minute. "What about the papers?"

"I don't think they have the story yet. There's not much to report."

"That's the worst kind. Leaves lots of room for creativity. I better call the publicity boys. They can start collecting stones for the wall."

"Let me know if you hear anything. I might be able to help. He seemed like a nice kid."

"You don't know the half of it."

She hung up, leaving me wondering what she meant by that last remark.

Chapter Four

The next day was Saturday, and out of curiosity I drove out to San Pedro. I figured it wouldn't hurt to check in with Acme Management again and see if Alphonse had anything useful to say about the murder of his client and girlfriend. I also wanted some apple strudel.

It was another perfect Southern California day. Blue skies, seventy degrees, the mountains to the east in perfect profile in the clear air. Add in the beach and the ocean and you'd have to ask yourself why anyone would ever live anywhere else. Then again, there was San Pedro to balance things off. The Navy had come back into port, and although it was only ten A.M. the sailors on liberty were out and about and the bartenders were hard at it. Whenever I saw this, I had to laugh about something Bret Harte said about a young Mark Twain. Twain was about to leave town for some reason and Harte said "the early morning bartenders would miss his bright smiles." So too with the sailors, bless 'em. If there was a war coming, let them use the time they had now in any way they chose. Let them smile at the morning bartenders and let the bartenders smile back.

I parked in front of Acme Management's house/office. I took a look around and didn't see any potential thieves, either big or small.

There were no lights on in the Acme house and when I knocked on the door, expecting a strong whiff of Alphonse and pork chops, nothing happened. The house had the distinctive look and feel of being empty. I knocked a few more times, but there was no response, no rustling noises inside. The windows all had shabby curtains pulled over them. The curtains looked like thin dish towels and I could almost see through them. I could see well enough that there was no movement inside, no shadowy figures creeping around or running out the back door. I glanced up and down the block again. No one was stirring.

Well, I thought—what's the worst that can happen? I got out my junior detective piece of stiff plastic and wiggled it in the door jamb. It opened easily. It was a cheap lock, unsurprisingly.

The main room was empty except for a metal desk and steel filing cabinet, both of them Navy surplus. I opened the drawers in both, and they were all empty. There was a lingering odor, all right, but nothing "fresh." It was the same story in the kitchen and the bedrooms upstairs. No dishes in the sink, no unmade beds. No furniture of any kind. Nothing. Acme Talent Management had either moved or gone out of business. What was it King Charles I said when he tried to arrest five members of Parliament? "The birds have flown." If I remembered correctly, those same birds flew back with an army and ultimately cut off Charles's head. I'm sure when he'd asked himself what's the worst that could happen, he hadn't thought of that. But the Acme birds, or bird, had definitely flown and it didn't look like he or they were ever coming back. Coupled with Lulu's murder, this disappearance made for an odd coincidence. Detectives aren't supposed to believe in coincidences. Those were for Dickens novels.

I thought I'd better call Kowalski and tell him about this. I tried the phone on the desk, but of course it was dead. Turned off. I drove to our favorite bakery to kill two birds with one stone, speaking of birds. The owner, Josip Vranic, went by Joe. He welcomed me like a cousin, told me the strudel was fresh from the oven, and lent me his phone.

"Homicide. Kowalski."

"Ed, it's Bruno. Acme Management has flown the coop. Their office is cleaned out completely."

"I know. We checked last night."

"Impressive. You boys are working long hours."

"Your tax dollars at work. Any word about Jimmy Hicks?"

"No. I told Ethel Welkin, but she didn't know a thing. Do you have anything new?"

"Not much. But I'm giving you a merit badge for checking in, even though we already knew Acme was gone. It's a good habit for a smartass shamus who wants to keep his license."

"That about describes me."

"There is one thing. You know all about the movies. Let me ask you—those guns they use. I know they fire blanks, but are they real guns or just plastic models, like cap guns?"

"I'm pretty sure they're real. They couldn't get the sound and smoke with a toy."

"Oh, I thought they could add the sound later."

"Well, yes. I guess so. Why?

"Just because when we went through Jimmy Hicks's apartment we found his gun belt, but the holster was empty."

Uh-oh.

"How do you know it was his?"

"Now you sound like a defense lawyer. Who else's would it be? Stands to reason that a real-life cowboy from Idaho would have a six-gun laying around where he could get to it in a hurry. And by the way, do you happen to know where Jimmy's apartment is?

"No. The only time we met, he came to my office."

"That must have been a special treat for him. Did Della offer to arrange a date for him?"

"I don't think so. She doesn't mix business with business."

"Well, his apartment happens to be in Santa Monica—just down the street from the former Lulu Marquessa, but in a better neighborhood. We're still trying to find out her real name, by the way. All her personal stuff is missing. And we have no record, no prints on file, no relatives wondering what the hell she's gotten herself into this time. The photographer who took her publicity picture got paid in cash. Never saw her before."

"And no phone call from the distraught manager?"

"Nope."

"How about the actor's union?"

"Never heard of her. She has achieved almost unimaginable status in Hollywood—complete anonymity. Keep in touch."

I put the phone down. At that moment I remembered just seeing Gary Cooper's latest, called *The Cowboy and The Lady,* in which Merle Oberon plays the rich girl masquerading as a maid and Coop plays a cowboy called "Stretch." It struck me—not for the first time —the difference between the movies and real life. Happy endings versus the real thing. It was a banal, common, ordinary thought, I know, but inescapable just then. Coop would never shoot the girl and leave her in a sandy heap on the beach. Neither would Rex Lockwood, I guess. But would Jimmy Hicks? That might be a different story.

"Bad news?" said Joe.

"For somebody. Not me, especially."

"That's good. Sit. Have some strudel and coffee. Good for you."
By which he was not paying a compliment, but offering the same

What Hamlet Said

advice he heard every day from his plump wife, Magda—"Eat. Eat. Good for you."

I sat down at one of the two tables he kept in the front of the bakery for his friends. They'd come by most mornings and gossip. The tables were covered in red-and-white–checkered patterns to honor the Croatian flag, even though Croatia wasn't a separate country. It was a very reluctant part of the country called Yugoslavia, which had been invented after the last war and held together by almost nothing and constantly straining against the lines in the map. Take a half dozen male wildcats and one female in heat and stick them in a cage, and you have Yugoslavia. Croatia and Serbia were the two big cats and they both wanted the female. That's what Joe and his pals said, anyway. Personally, I knew very little about it all. But I did know Joe knew what he was talking about. And on nights when I was very lucky, I slept with Myrtle who talked Croatian in her sleep and called me *miljenik* and *dragi,* which were Croatian for "darling." So I was predisposed to her point of view. And she hated the Serbs as much as Joe and his buddies. I don't really know about Joe's reasons, but I understood Myrtle's. She had brought them with her from "the old country." I also knew all the Slavs—Croats, Serbs, and the rest—had many fine virtues: piety, loyalty, willingness to work hard, and a talent for hating. Not necessarily in that order. They were also good at strudel. The funny thing is, the Croats and the Serbs looked alike, spoke the same language, and liked the same foods and what have you. The only difference I could see was that the Croats were Roman Catholic and the Serbs were Greek Orthodox, which seemed like a poor reason for murderous hatred. But it was not any of my business.

Joe came over with two large mugs of coffee, sweetened and creamy. He also brought a platter of strudel and two plates and forks.

31

"Magda says good morning. She would come out, but she is busy making *pogacha*. How is darling Mirta?" That was Joe's name for Myrtle.

"She's in Yuma, Arizona making a movie about a White Russian princess who's been captured by the Arabs."

Joe made a sour face. "Bah. Russians." Joe didn't care for Russians. "Arabs! Bah!" He didn't like them either. "Turks on camels. Who writes this silliness?"

"Guys from New York."

"Bah. What do they know?"

"They know what sells."

"Well, that is something, anyway. That is something worth knowing. And we are all very proud of her. Of course."

"Of course."

"You and she are... together?"

"As much as possible."

"Good. I like you."

"I'm glad."

"How's the strudel?"

"Heavenly."

He nodded at my grasp of the obvious. "The Navy boys are back. What do you think? Will there be war?"

"I hope not. But I think it's very possible."

"I hope not, too. My boy Nicky is just nineteen. He is learning the business. And you should hear him play the accordion. It would make you want to dance the polka."

"He must really be good if he could do that."

"If war comes, he will surely be called. Maybe he should join the Navy. Be a cook. Cooks don't fight."

"It's worth thinking about." I didn't mention that Navy cooks go down with a sinking ship like everyone else. I didn't have to. I had the feeling that Joe knew a lot more about fighting than I did. He had the look of someone who'd been there. I didn't know where, exactly, although I could guess. Joe never talked about that part of his life, which was another indication that he knew things.

"I tell you one thing—there are plenty of people in my country who would be glad to see the Germans come into the Balkans. Yes, it's true. The enemy of my enemy is my friend. Who said that?"

"I don't know."

"Well, whoever said it was right. But I tell you something else— all these Japs around make me nervous. You think they ever come in and buy anything, maybe say hello, have a little talk like civilized people? No. Never. I don't like them. They are sneaky. Keep to themselves. They watch the Navy boys. Take pictures. And they are Hitler's friends. That I do not understand. He talks big about the pure German race and pushes the Jews around, and yet he is pleasant to these yellow people. How can he like them? It is all very confusing."

"The enemy of my enemy is my friend."

"Yes, I suppose you are right. Have more strudel. Eat, please. Good for you."

And it was at that moment that I placed the accent of Alphonse of Acme.

Chapter Five

That evening, I went to a party at Manny Stairs's house on the beach in Malibu. The house was finally finished after lengthy delays. The roof seemed to be the primary problem, but now everything was in perfect shape. It sat on a small hill overlooking the sea. To the south you could see the shoreline of LA and environs, and at night the lights sparkled against the surface of the sea, almost as brilliantly as they do in the movies. It was a heavenly place that was usually filled with beautiful people and a few others who weren't so beautiful but knew how to make money.

Manny Stairs had been the second most powerful producer in Hollywood, after Thalberg. Then Thalberg had died suddenly, leaving Manny at the top of the heap. I had done a little work for him in the past, and he remembered and included me whenever he had one of these soirees. I guess my role was to be part of the local color, the hardboiled detective that the movie people were fond of fictionalizing. Except I wasn't all that hardboiled, didn't carry a gun and didn't like to wear a hat. Nor did I smoke. By movie standards, I was really unqualified. I did own a trench coat, but it only came out when it rained, and it almost never rained in LA, as everyone knows. And when it does, you need rubber boots for the mudslides. Of course, the fact that "Yvonne Adore" was my girlfriend was the real reason I was included. Manny wanted to keep his rising star happy even if it meant humoring her improbable affection for an LA private eye who had no redeeming qualities—at least none that Manny could discern, except for reasonably good looks and a minor gift of gab. In Manny's business, those qualities were a dime a dozen—no more than drugstore commodities. I knew all that. I didn't mind. When I first came to California, I had made a halfhearted try at the acting business. It was Ethel Welkin's idea— she of the gymnastics persuasion. But I soon learned acting wasn't for me. If you ever see the movie *Cimarron* (which won Best Picture that year) you can catch a brief glimpse of me as the third wagon driver to the left in the big land-rush scene. That was my only role, and they didn't call me to the stage when they gave out the Oscar. That was when I became a P.I.

I pulled up outside the beach house and gave the car keys to the houseboy, who happened to be a Japanese. Manny called him Mr. Moto, because he couldn't remember the guy's real name, which had quite a few syllables in it. Apparently Mr. Moto didn't resent the nickname, but then again you never knew with these Nips. I was as down on them as Joe Vranik, because I had read about what was going on in China. They had just gone on a killing spree in Nanking. Reports were sketchy but enough to turn your stomach. All their smiling and bowing over here couldn't cover that up.

I walked around the house to the patio. The air was cool and perfect for what I was wearing—my white ducks and blue blazer. They say you're not supposed to wear white after Labor Day, but that didn't go in Hollywood. There were too many yachts. I was not trying for the nautical look. But others were, including Manny, whose outfit was exactly the same as mine, except he had a captain's hat perched on his bald dome. His yacht, *Action!*, was an oceangoing masterpiece, all gleaming white and polished mahogany and glistening glass and brightwork, so I guess he was entitled to the hat. But I remembered the old joke about the Jewish mother who said to her son who also had just bought a boat and a hat—"To you you're a captain, and to me you're a captain, but to a captain you're no captain." Neither was Manny, but he was a big-time movie producer with a stunning wife, and he knew how to spend his money and enjoy it. And he spent a lot of it. So he wore his yachting costume, and if you didn't like it, you knew what you could do with it without Manny having to tell you.

Manny's wife, whose name was Catherine Moore, saw me arrive and came bouncing over, all three dimensions symmetrical and in perfect harmony. She wrapped her scented arms around me and nuzzled my ear. We had what they call a history.

"Hello, Sparky," she said in a fragrant whisper.

"Hello, Catherine. You look like you smell good all over."

"I know. And do you know what?"

"What?"

"I do."

"Is it possible that you're even more beautiful than the last time I saw you?"

"When was that?" she said with mock curiosity.

"Last week."

"Yes. It's possible. Do you like my dress?"

It was a dress in name only. In reality it was a silvery, diaphanous rumor, the kind of thing the goddesses wore on the Grecian urns. It covered her just enough so that your imagination was free to roam. The rest of her was color-coordinated, for her skin was creamy white, her eyes the color of darkest jade, and her hair silvery blond and arranged in tumbling falls. She had none of those tight curls that looked like helmets and made the girls seem untouchable. Catherine always looked touchable.

"The dress is lovely. But it doesn't do you justice."

"Smooth talker." She took my arm, tucked it against her breast, and looked up at me coyly. "Remember that?" she said.

"Who could forget?"

She put her head on my shoulder and led me toward the patio. "All our old friends are here. I made Manny invite them so it wouldn't just be Manny's boring business friends."

"How are you and Manny getting along?"

"Oh, you know Manny. He only cares about two things, money and schtupping. I let him take care of the schtupping in the morning before breakfast, so that he goes off to work with a smile on his face. Aside from that, he doesn't bother me. And it only costs me fifteen minutes a day. Sometimes not even that long. It could be worse. He adores me."

"And who could blame him?"

"I know. He's as devoted as a Peke. I've sort of gotten used to the fact that he's so short. I've told myself that there's advantages to that."

"Really? What are they?"

"I don't really know. There must be some. It doesn't matter, anyway. We're married, and I'm set. Beats working in an insurance office. And he doesn't worry about what I do all day."

"Should he?"

"What do you think?"

That insurance office was where I'd first tracked her down. She had a job there based on her looks and nothing else, but it was a dead end and besides she had come to LA to be an actress. As the French say, *quelle surprise*. One day she took a tour with a busload of other tourists through Manny's studio lot. He saw her from his office window. Not only was she a knockout, but she was a dead ringer for Manny's first wife, who had been a big-time star and had died of an overdose in a cheap motor court out in Joshua Tree. The guy she was with was a local goombah who called it in and then took off before the cops and medics got there. The news that chivalry wasn't dead hadn't reached him. Or he had misunderstood. They had registered as Mr. and Mrs. D. Bumstead, so there was no way to trace him. I knew who it was, but I wasn't supposed to. And it was healthier for me not to mention it. The death was reported as a heart attack, which I suppose it was, technically. For three years Manny mourned her, and when he saw Catherine Moore he was instantly in love all over again. He couldn't believe what he was seeing. When she disappeared with the tourist bus, he lost track of her and hired me to find her. So I did. He wasted no time pursuing her, and she wasted no time accepting his jewelry. He was desperately in love; she wasn't even a little bit in love, and in fact didn't really like him much, but could put up with him in exchange for the benefits. So she married him. Theirs was not a new story in this town. Or any town, for that matter. It's like the old song "Love For Sale." Some deals last longer than others, but the principle is the same.

"Was I wrong?" she'd say, as if she cared whether anyone cared. Then she'd flutter her eyes innocently and laugh and show me her newest bauble. More often than not it was a diamond or pearl necklace, which let her bend over and also show her breasts, which were quite simply flawless. She and Manny had been married now for almost a year, and he was still smitten, so I guess she was treating him well enough to keep him wearing out a path to Cartier. Maybe she would figure out some way to use his lack of height to their mutual advantage. If anyone could, she could. But as long as he could see over the display cases, she could live with it.

What Hamlet Said

Of course, I was—or at least had been—half in love with her, but so was everyone else who knew her—including the man who walked up just then and joined us.

"Hello, Sparky," said Catherine. It was her all-purpose name for the men she liked; we were a fairly large fraternity.

This particular Sparky took her hand in continental fashion and kissed it, then raised his own hand in a dramatic gesture. He had obviously been drinking, but that was normal with him. "Here will I dwell, for heaven is in these lips, and all is dross that is not... Catherine."

"Smooth talker," she cooed. "A little something of your own?"

"Marlowe's Faustus describing Helen of Troy. But appropriate for you. Hello, Riley, old sport."

"Hello, Hobey."

I should explain that Riley Fitzhugh was my real name and all my friends called me that. "Hobey" was a writer who lived at the Garden of Allah Hotel along with a half dozen other writers who were refugees from New York and London and had come to Hollywood for the money and the action. They hated themselves for selling out, but not enough to stop taking the money and the action. I rented a cabana at the Garden. It was my official residence. I liked the party atmosphere, and besides, the studio didn't want me to overdo cohabitation with "Yvonne." They had turned her into a White Russian virgin, and they didn't need me being conspicuous. They felt it might lead to gossip that they'd just as soon not have to deal with. Besides, they were thinking about marrying her off to one of the up-and-coming male stars. It would generate lots of gushing magazine coverage and simultaneously obscure the fact that the guy would rather troll for sailors in San Pedro than spend time with actual women, except on the movie set, where he had no choice. Whether anything would come of those marriage plans remained to be seen. I had mixed emotions about it, naturally, but understood it really didn't mean anything. My Myrtle/Yvonne thought nothing of it, for she knew it would amount to a few photo sessions and that would be it. They might not even go through an actual legal ceremony and just fake it for the cameras. And if the guy had some sort of miraculous conversion and tried something with her, she knew how to handle herself. The "divorce" would then be announced a year or so down the road. The explanation to the fans —and the assignment of guilt—would depend on which one was the bigger star right then. There wasn't much doubt about who that would be, though. The guy was as light as air, and she was light and shadows and mystery and beauty. Besides, she had natural talent, whereas he had only a pretty face—another Woolworth-level commodity in this town.

But to return to Hobey. He used to be a famous writer back in the Twenties. He had a glamorous wife and a glamorous life, but it all came crashing down, along with his literary reputation. The Roaring Twenties gave way to the Depression, and no one was interested in flapper stories anymore. So, like a lot of writers needing cash, he came to Hollywood. He had some success, but not the kind he was hoping for. He left the wife back east and fell in love out here a few times. Falling in love was one of his talents, or afflictions, depending on how you looked at it. Things never worked out, but he wasted no time moving on to the next dream girl. Anyway, he adopted the name "Hobey Baker" after his idol at Princeton. The real Baker was a star football player and big man on campus who was killed in the war and so fitted the role of tragic hero perfectly. "An athlete dying young." So when this "Hobey" came west, he decided to adopt the name of his romantic hero, since he hated his real name and hated his real self, both of which he associated with failure. It was his way of pulling the curtain down on the truth. But it was a thin curtain and everyone who knew him saw through it. He knew all that, too. He was a smart guy and proof that brains and talent don't always add up to success. Lady Luck generally has the biggest say in that. Sometimes the only say.

He was pushing forty and looked a little seedy from the usual causes, but he dressed like a prep school teacher—tweed jacket, flannel trousers, white button-down shirt and knit black tie with horizontal orange stripes, white bucks properly scuffed. Usually the tie didn't make it much past the middle button of his shirt. To say he was a disappointed man would understate the case, but he also had an unquenchable belief that things could turn around, if he could only get some money together and if he could only ever finish the novel that he was endlessly working on. I liked him very much and hoped he'd somehow make it. But I didn't have much confidence that he would. He once told me he'd gotten the idea for his novel from me and from Manny Stairs, but he hadn't mentioned it since. I didn't ask, because when things were going badly, he didn't say anything except that things were going badly. And when he had good news about anything, he shared it with everyone and anyone. Like now.

"You seem pretty chirpy tonight," I said.

"That about describes the situation! You've heard they're planning to make *Gone With the Wind*? Of course, you have. Who hasn't? Well, I am going to work on the script! Ta da!"

He struck a pose and beamed.

"Hey! That's great news," I said. "Congratulations!"

"Good for you, Sparky," said Catherine sincerely. She and Hobey also had a brief history. He was feeling so low one night around the pool at the Garden that she had taken him to bed as a kindly gesture. You might say she was a wife with a heart of gold.

"Thank you. In all modesty, they have made a wise choice in hiring me. I'm itching to get started. You know Hedda, don't you?" He gestured toward his latest girlfriend, who went by the name Hedda Gabler. She was standing there as if trying to remember something. She was a journalist, at last report, doing gossip columns for *Hush Hush* magazine.

"Pleased to meet you, I'm sure," she said. I had met her before, but she apparently didn't remember. She was attractive, of course, in a Flatbush kind of way. Not my type, but Hobey liked her.

"How's the writing business, Hedda?" I said. Hedda Gabler wasn't her real name, of course. Her agent had picked it out. Whether he had a sense of humor or just liked the sound of it was a question not worth answering.

"Not so great. The bums gave me the ax. They said it was too much trouble to edit my stuff. You know?"

"Her style is all her own," said Hobey. "Ask her to define a sentence and the odds are she'll say 'twenty years to life.' You don't find that level of creativity on every street corner. But it's a challenge for a run-of-the-mill hack editor."

"They said if they were going to have to rewrite that stuff themselves, they didn't need me to bring them coffee. They already had somebody for that."

Hobey took her hand and kissed it. "Your talents were wasted at that magazine, my dear."

She smiled vacantly at the compliment. "I'll say. So, what's it take to get a drink around here, anyway?"

"Follow me," said Catherine.

"Okay," said Hedda. And they went off to the corner of the patio where the bar was.

"She's dim, but she's decorative," said Hobey to me. "Very good for morale."

What Hamlet Said

"Too bad about losing her job at *Hush Hush*."

"Yes, I suppose so. But no ménage can exist very long with two writers of genius." He smiled his pleasant ironical smile. "She's applied for a job as a Miss Lonelyhearts for one of the dailies. She has the perfect temperament for it. She could spend all day reading distressing letters from people in appalling and heartbreaking difficulties and never be affected. Other people's misery just bounces off her. Almost everything does, now that I think of it. Her advice wouldn't be worth much, but the people who write to Miss Lonelyhearts are usually beyond help anyway. I'm fairly fond of her."

"How does she feel about you?"

"Hard to tell. She is entirely self-contained and self-absorbed. Almost uniquely so."

"What's the old song—'It ain't love, but it'll have to do.'"

"'Until the real thing comes along.' Words to live by. I think that's a Sammy Cahn song. Have you noticed that most of the great songwriters are Yids?"

"There's Cole Porter." Speaking of "Love For Sale"—that was one of his, I think.

"He's the exception that proves the rule. But I like him anyway. There's no better songwriter. Bit of a pansy, though. Not too surprising. He went to Yale." He smiled benignly.

"So, tell me about the new job."

"I'm very excited about it." That was not surprising, either. He got excited easily and whenever there was a new project. It was only after he'd worked on it for a while that he became discouraged. He'd been hired for a lot of movie scripts but was fired just as often and pretty quickly. He always tried to make a frothy bit of nothingness into a tragic romance, and his male characters always seemed to end up becoming versions of himself. If the studios let him, he'd try to turn Popeye into *Wuthering Heights*—which, by the way, I heard they were in the early stages of making. Hobey would have been right for that job, but he didn't get it.

"Have you read it, by the way?" he asked.

"The book? I started to. I'll save the rest of it for my golden years."

"The purest bilge, if you ask me. Can bilge be pure, by the way? It's wastewater, isn't it?"

"I couldn't say. Ask one of the captains around here."

"Well, no matter. If they follow that book faithfully and make Scarlett the focus, it'll be a flop for sure. But I have an idea that Rhett is the key to the story. He's the romantic egoist, always searching for the love of his life. He believes that Scarlett is the one, only to find out that she isn't. It's the perfect arc of the hero—searching, finding, losing. Do you know Yeats's 'Wandering Aengus'?"

"Vaguely." I didn't, but didn't want to risk a lengthy side trip of explanation.

"Well, it's the same sort of story. Don't you agree?"

"Sure."

"Plain as the nose on Durante's face. This movie's going to be a winner."

I could see where he was going with this, and sadly I knew that his work on the picture would be brief. They hadn't bought the rights to a blockbuster novel just to turn it into 'The Sorrows of Young Werther, Part Two.' But at least he'd get a couple of weeks' worth of paychecks. Besides, he was happy now, and the situation was perfectly in line with his world view that happiness was always fleeting anyway, so this experience would be no different. It would in fact confirm his overall outlook on life. There would at least be that satisfaction to accompany the failure.

What Hamlet Said

"It sounds like you're on to something," I said, encouragingly. "How about a drink?"

"That sounds like *you* are on to something, old sport. Lead on! Excelsior!"

We wandered over to the bar through the crowd of well-dressed men with little or no hair discussing business, and other well-dressed men with gleaming hair who were chatting up beautiful women in expensive couture, if that's not redundant. There was a small combo playing the aforementioned Cole Porter tunes—'Night and Day,' 'In the Still of the Night,' and so on. Lovely stuff. The whole patio seemed to be suffused with exotic and wonderful scents. Chanel perfume and sea breezes. The sun was going down and casting a red glow over the party, and it all gave you the feeling that nothing in the world could possibly go wrong. At least not here. No God with his eye on the ball would allow anything to spoil such a perfect scene. Or way of life. Now that I thought of it, that's what they all believed at the beginning of *Gone With the Wind*—Scarlett and Ashley and the rest.

Hobey spotted Manny Stairs in the crowd and made a beeline for him, after first getting a drink. Hobey never let an opportunity to talk to a producer get by him, and so he was widely regarded as a pest. His formerly high literary reputation had impressed the moguls at first, for they went by what they read in the papers, not by what they read, themselves. But the thick ice on which he started skating years ago was gradually melting, for his name was no longer mentioned in literary circles and publications, and the moguls were starting to think he was old news. And, in fairness to the moguls, he was. They had no interest in literature, but they could read the tea leaves of popular culture better than a gypsy with second sight. The best-seller lists and the Broadway box-office receipts were the indicators of taste that mattered—that and their own box-office receipts, which naturally were the most important of all. They may not have a seat at the Algonquin Round Table, but they didn't need or want one. They were the producers. They bought the people who sat at the Algonquin, put them in a Hollywood office, paid them conscience-numbing amounts of money and told them to start typing. And that's why the producers were here on this lavish patio being served Russian vodka and caviar and lobster and Champagne, while the sun set over the Pacific, and their elegant yachts rode serenely at anchor, just offshore. They *produced*, in more ways than one.

I spotted another friend standing off to the side. It was Dennis Finch-Hayden, known as "Bunny" to all and sundry. He was a professor of art at UCLA who was busily cutting a swath through the legions of bored yet wealthy wives in Hollywood and, occasionally, in New York. He was a tall thin Englishman who was more elegant than handsome. The buttons on his suitcoat sleeves actually buttoned, and he wore a gold signet ring on his pinkie. Neither was an affectation. Needless to say, the ring was small and the crest genuine. He had straw-colored hair, a beaky nose, and pale blue eyes that were almost always merry. His usual expression seemed to say that he had just seen a new example of human absurdity and was thoroughly delighted because of it.

"Bunny! What ho, as Bertie Wooster might say."

"What ho, indeed. Hello, Riley. You're still going by Riley, I assume."

"For the foreseeable future."

"I would like you to meet Amanda Billingsgate. Amanda, this is my friend and occasional colleague in the art world, Riley Fitzhugh."

Amanda was a tall, tastefully dressed woman somewhat past thirty. Well-preserved is the term people use when they are not being kind, but she had not reached the stage yet where artifice was important. She was still quite lovely and wore very little jewelry, understated perfume and a simple black dress that showed off her blond hair and figure very nicely. She had very dark brown eyes which were unusual with blondes—at least in Hollywood. There was something about her coloring that was alluring. She reminded you of butterscotch. She smiled when Bunny mentioned the word "colleague." Until then she had not seemed interested.

"How do you do," she said in a refined English accent. "Are you in the art business?"

"Only occasionally," I said.

"We were just discussing Monet," said Bunny. "Riley has done some work with Monet forgeries."

"Are you a forger," she asked, "or a sleuth?"

"Sleuth, I'm afraid."

"It sounds exciting."

"It can be, I suppose."

"Are you an all-purpose detective, or a specialist?"

"A specialist. I only work for clients who can pay me." I smiled. I didn't want her to think I was a smartass. She was attractive, after all, and my motto with attractive women was—you never know.

"And when someone asks you how you like your Bourbon, you say 'In a glass.' Am I right?" Her smile was charming. It almost seemed genuine.

"I try not to use other people's material, except as a last resort," I said.

"Very wise. I suppose you must carry a gun."

"Not usually." I was about to say that carrying a gun in a shoulder holster spoiled the cut of my jacket and that wearing one on my belt dragged my pants down. But while that was nothing but

the truth, I thought it might sound a little, what's the word—
epicene.

"Do you have a card? I might have something of a confidential
nature that needs looking into." Was there a flicker of slyness in her
expression? A hint of double entendre? "Something that needed
looking into?" Was it my imagination? "In fact, I was going to ask
Bunny if he knew anyone who was reliable."

"Of course, I would have recommended you, old boy."

"And no one who knows me would blame you," I said.

I gave her a card. My business cards were particularly elegant, if
I do say so—embossed letters and numbers on heavy pasteboard.
They were done by Blinky Malone, a printer in San Pedro who also
did very good work in forged immigration papers, driver's licenses,
and government ID cards.

"Bruno Feldspar?" she said. "I thought your name was Riley."

"*Nom de guerre*. It's sometimes convenient."

"It's a dreadful name. Almost as silly as 'Bunny.' I hope you
don't mind my saying so."

"Not at all. I agree with you."

"Really? Couldn't you think of something else? Lawrence of
Arabia? Marcel Proust? Lancelot du Lac? I can think of dozens I like
better."

"It's a long story."

"It must be. Well, I may call you. I'm not sure my little problem
is worth looking into." Again the pause, the flicker. "But it might be.
Let me think about it."

"I'd be happy to hear from you." That was true enough.
"Speaking of sleuthing," I said, "I wonder if I could stop by your
office someday, Bunny. I have a question or two for you. Not worth
talking about here."

What Hamlet Said

He raised his eyebrows, obviously interested. "Why not Monday? The wretched students are still on break. Any time in the morning."

"Good. Monday it is."

Just then, we heard someone playing the piano. It was Hobey, singing one of his favorite comic songs about a dog. People were making sour faces, but he wasn't noticing. High spirits and gin were fueling him.

"Oh, dear," said Bunny.

"Yes," I said, gloomily.

Chapter Six   ,

Sunday's supposed to be a day of rest, so I rested. I sat around the pool at the Garden of Allah and watched the writers emerging slowly, one by one, from their cabanas and rooms. Individually and collectively, they were advertisements for the dangers and disadvantages of strong drink. One of those Russian artists who specialize in Socialist Realism would never use any of them as a model for the sturdy proletarian worker. They had neither the inner glow of political enthusiasm nor the outer glow of physical health. Muscle tone was a dim memory from a half-forgotten youth. And that went for the women too, including a dumpy brunette with bangs who was the presiding cynic of the crew. She shared that honor with an equally dumpy man who had not yet made an appearance that morning and was quite possibly breathing his last at that very moment. Or wishing that he would.

About a half dozen of these artists gathered around the outside bar and began the grim work of restoration. I remained stretched out on a chaise, feeling smug and virtuous because I didn't have a hangover and had done nothing the night before that I couldn't remember.

Hobey came down a little while later. He didn't suffer too badly from hangovers, because he had a surprisingly low tolerance for alcohol. He drank steadily throughout the day, but in small amounts—just enough to keep him in a constant state of mild exhilaration or creative depression. So, physically he wasn't too badly affected the next day.

He sat down on the chaise next to me.

"Mornin', old sport," he said.

"Morning. Where's Hedda?"

"Upstairs. She doesn't like mornings; and, between you and me, mornings don't think much of her either. She looks her best after you've had a few drinks."

"What's the Cole Porter song? 'You'd Be So Nice To Wake Up To?'"

"Actually, it's 'You'd Be So Nice To Come Home To.' An entirely different sentiment. But in Hedda's case, the song is 'You've Got That Thing.' 'Thing' being left to the imagination. A lesser known tune, but apropos. I'm glad she keeps her own apartment and only stays over with me now and then. I am fond of her, as I mentioned last night, and perfection is the enemy of the good, after all."

"I have heard that. Actually, he said 'the best,' not 'perfection.'"

"Yes, I know. It still fits. An all-purpose sentiment. We can't ask for too much. It might be given to us, and then how could we write 'Ode on Melancholy'? Our cup of sadness would always be empty. What fun would that be?

"Speaking of cups, I feel the need for a gin and tonic. Care to join me?"

"Why not?" I thought about asking him about his performance last night, but decided against it. If he remembered, he'd also suspect it wasn't his finest hour; and if he didn't remember, so much the better.

He went to the bar, exchanged a few words with the other communicants, and returned with two drinks.

"I've been meaning to ask you," he said. "Are you working on anything interesting? I'm always in the market for a good story, you know. Not that I would pay anything, you understand."

If Hobey was well known as a pest with producers, he was equally well known as a nosy pain in the ass when it came to people's private business. He carried a little notebook around and was never shy about asking the most personal questions. I didn't mind, though. After all, he was an acclaimed author—at one time, anyway—and he understood plotting and storytelling. And once when I was puzzling over a problem, he came up with an idea that led to solving the case. So I was happy to share.

"Well, since you ask, I'm involved in something now. It's not really my case. In fact, it's a police matter. A murder. I got involved because one of Ethel Welkin's new protégés is a suspect."

"Oh, good! What's the story?"

So I told him about Lulu Marquessa and Jimmy Hicks and Acme Management and the strange disappearance of Jimmy and Alphonse. He thought about it for a while.

"Very interesting," he said. "When you reduce it to its basics, you have a murder, two missing persons, and a suspicious foreigner—all somehow linked together. Correct?"

"Yes."

"Any idea where the suspicious foreigner is from?"

"Just a guess. The way he talked sounded sort of like a Croatian baker that Myrtle and I know."

"Ah. The plot thickens! The Balkans! Hotbed of blood feuds and religious pogroms for centuries. Hatred and murder raised to the level of art. Or theology. Or both. And to make matters even more complex, they are centers of intrigue and espionage during these awful times of European tensions. Hitler and Mussolini both have their eyes on the wretched area. Spies everywhere. Quite exciting, if you think about it."

"If you say so."

"I'm sure you know that there are many little countries in the Balkans all speaking pretty much the same language and all sounding pretty much alike, although now that I think of it the Albanians speak a language like no other, with obscure antecedents. But they would, I suppose. All the rest of them pretty much use the same words, so when they come over here and learn English, they have the same accents. At least to our ears. So our mysterious stranger might not have a Croatian accent. It might be Serbian, for example. Or Slovenian. Or Russian, for that matter. Yes? Think of the possibilities of intrigue."

"I suppose so. But we're talking about a crime right here, in the U.S. Not some European mare's nest of politics imported to the U.S. It might be a simple case of homicidal jealousy. No politics involved at all."

"That's right. It might be. But far less interesting, don't you think? Better if there's a wider sinister connection to international intrigue. And if so, what is it? That at least makes it more fun to think about than a simple murder or two."

"I get that, of course."

"Care for another drink?"

"Why not? But... any ideas occur to you so far?"

"Lots, old sport. Lots. But embryonic. Ah! Here comes a flock of birds of rare plumage."

I knew that Hobey would now be distracted for the rest of the afternoon, or at least until Hedda woke up, came down, and reclaimed him. For it was the usual weekend influx of would-be starlets, women who had just arrived from the hinterlands. They hadn't learned yet that the writers and bit-part actors who made up the Garden's population had no influence whatever in the movie business and were little more than serfs. These girls would find out the hard way, through disappointment and broken promises. Well, that was the way things worked in this town. But for the time being, they were eager and gay, and they came dressed in bathing suits designed to reveal everything, and the writers were happy to take advantage of their innocence. Even a dashing young private detective had been known, once or twice, to introduce himself and possibly exaggerate his level of influence with the movie powers-that-be. Ah, it's a wicked world. Could I live with myself? I often asked myself that question. And the answer was always the same.

Why not?

* * *

On Monday morning, I stopped at the office before heading over to UCLA. Della was at her desk early, typing whatever it was she usually typed. Invoices to the customers of her escort service, I imagined. Or discreet queries to the same clients asking if they'd like to buy the photographs that had been taken as an extra and unasked-for part of the service. Negatives included, of course.

She had the eternal Pall Mall dangling from the side of her mouth, and her right eye was watering from the smoke.

"Mornin', Chief."

"Top of the morning to you, loyal employee. Any calls?"

"Kowalski."

"What did he want?"

"A tip on the third at Santa Anita."

I went into my office and called Kowalski.

"Homicide. Kowalski."

"It's Bruno. You called?"

"Yeah. Anything new on your end?"

"Not really. How about you?"

"Well, we got a line on Lulu. Her fingerprints turned up in the FBI files."

"Really? Why were her prints on file?"

"Routine immigration procedure, I guess. But she's also listed as a possible foreign agent. Of course, those guys think anyone not descended from the *Mayflower* crew might be a foreign agent. Seems a bit of a stretch to me. How many spies do you know who go around passing out eight-by-ten glossies and showing up for auditions?"

"Truth is, I don't know any foreign agents of any kind."

"Me neither. Lulu's real name, by the way, was Irena Steponovich."

"That's foreign enough, I guess."

"So is Kowalski."

"So's Bruno Feldspar. Any news of Jimmy Hicks?"

"Still missing. No leads. Got anything at all that might be of interest?"

"Just the third at Santa Anita."

"Keep in touch." He hung up.

I drove out to Westwood to the impossibly beautiful campus of UCLA. Unfortunately, the students and especially the coeds, who were also impossibly beautiful, were on some sort of vacation break. It was good to be a student there. Or anywhere, for that matter. I had missed most of that. I read a lot and considered myself what my friend Hobey called an autodidact. But that was no substitute for a careful four-year study of the American sorority girl, her likes and dislikes.

Bunny's office was in the art museum. I was green with envy whenever I visited, because I could easily have lived in that office. The walls were lined with floor-to-ceiling bookshelves, and where there was an empty space there were pictures of Bunny's school days—the cricket team, the Oxford rowing eight, assorted young men standing and smiling with carefree expressions—because they were, in fact, carefree. The furniture was well used but well maintained and had been expensive to buy and would be even more expensive to buy today, for it was all antique. The chairs arranged around a coffee table were dark red leather and the carpet was a well-worn and very old Persian that Bunny's father had brought back from some sort of diplomatic posting. The room smelled pleasantly of pipe tobacco and of Bunny's Labrador Retriever, Tom. It was a St. James's Street club room transported magically to Westwood. I had never been to a St James's Street club, but Bunny told me the décor was similar.

I knocked on the heavy oak door and went in.

"Riley! Welcome. Have a seat. I was just finishing up an analysis of a Rouault pencil sketch. It seems to be genuine. Would you like to see it?"

"Of course." I peered at the few pencil marks on a piece of sketching paper. "Looks good to me."

"I'm glad you concur. Care for some coffee?"

"Sure."

He rang a bell, and his secretary appeared carrying a silver coffee service and a dish of macaroons. She had apparently been waiting for the summons. Tom woke from his slumbers under the office window and sat at attention next to the tray.

Bunny poured out the coffee.

"Milk for you? Yes, I remember that. You know, there are certain people who make a great show of putting the milk in first and then pouring the tea or coffee. They seem to think that it's the thing you must do. And that not to do it is somehow déclassé. Or, worse, middle-class. But the joke is, that sort of attention to minute and inflexible rules could not be more middle-class. The true upper-class person doesn't care about such things and does as he pleases. Do you remember Amanda from the other night?"

"Yes. She was lovely."

"I think so too. Well, she's planning to write a book. A satire, really. About all these little things that one should do or not do and how to do them and not do them, what to say or not say. Should you say duvet or bedspread? 'Take' tea or 'drink' tea? Serviette or napkin? That sort of thing. I think it will be a best seller, even though it will be a joke. The audience for the book won't see the joke, of course. They'll think it's a guide, like Emily Post. But that's the funny part. Americans will devour it. Your people can be such snobs."

"I'll make a point of reading it. And although I'm sure asking this is not the done thing, are you and she...."

"Having a fling? No. Just pals. We're living proof that a man and an attractive woman can simply be friends. It helps that we got that sort of thing out of our systems back in university days. Between us, I mean. Since then, strictly amigos. She's married, but of course that only means as much as one wants it to mean." He paused and smiled. "Do I detect a budding interest?"

"No, just curious." This was not strictly true, and he knew it but let it pass.

"Of course, of course. Well, no one would blame you if anything unexpected should occur. Amanda was quite the girl, ten or fifteen years ago. The London papers referred to her gang as the Bright Young Things. They were a gay crowd in all senses of the word, always running around to nightclubs and parties till all hours. Jumping into fountains, going on scavenger hunts, stealing policemen's helmets. The usual sort of thing. Now she and the rest might be described as the Bright Young-ish Things. They've slowed down considerably. But you wouldn't know it from looking at her, would you?"

"No, you wouldn't."

"She is living here now. Has she called you, by the way?"

"No."

"I think she will. She's got herself in a bit of a muddle. I'll let her explain it. Now then, what's all this you're worried about?"

He sat back, sipped his coffee, and gave Tom a macaroon. Bunny had the most appealing way of giving you his full attention. He told me once that it was the essence of charm. He came by it naturally. I was still learning the art.

"Are you still working now and then with the FBI?"

"Yes." Bunny was a consultant to the Bureau on all matters involving art theft and forgery.

"Have they opened an office here yet?"

"Not my chaps. There's a fair amount of skullduggery in the art world out here, but the real action is still in New York and London. So when there's an interesting case, I usually have to travel. But they have an office here that specializes in the routine sorts of FBI work. Especially now, with tensions so high in the Far East. The Japanese seem bent on making trouble. There are lots of the little yellow fellows scurrying around seeking whom to devour, or at least photograph. You've probably noticed."

"Yes. If war ever comes, there'll be a sudden shortage of gardeners and houseboys in Hollywood."

"True enough. You have to wonder—are they more interested in bonsai, or banzai? Is that too crude a pun?"

"Almost."

"I'm not sure. You know what Dr. Johnson said about such things."

"No, but I'll bet you do."

What Hamlet Said

"He said: *I think no innocent species of wit or pleasantry should be suppressed, and that a good pun may be admitted among the smaller excellencies of lively conversation.* Who am I—or who are you, for that matter—to argue with so great a man?"

"I concede."

"Well, to return to the point, in light of the nervous situation, the local FBI boys have beefed up their counterintelligence staff."

"Do you know any of them?"

"I've met a few. Strictly socially. My contacts back in New York wanted the local agents to know I was around and might be useful in some way or another."

"Would you mind introducing me?"

"Not at all. But would you mind telling me why?"

So I told him about Jimmy and Alphonse and the murdered Irena, a.k.a. Lulu. I also told him what I was thinking about the situation, my suspicions.

"I see," he said. "Rather thin, I suppose. But not impossible in this day and age."

"Yes. And if Jimmy was not the murderer and in fact has been kidnapped and done away with as a cover-up, that would be the FBI's bailiwick, I think."

"Yes, kidnapping is their pigeon, certainly. Well, let me make a call or two and I'll get back to you with some suggestions. All right?"

"Perfect."

"Care for a macaroon? More coffee?"

"Yes. Thank you."

"Mind how you pour the milk."

Chapter Seven

I went back to my office and looked up that quote in *Bartlett's* and was very pleased to see that it was Boswell, not Johnson. Aha, Bunny! Close, but no cigar. I tucked this away for future use.

Della had left for the afternoon and I was sitting in my office with my feet on the desk, wondering what I was doing there. It was a lovely afternoon, and there was certain to be someone around the pool at the Garden, someone either gorgeous or interesting, maybe even both. Then the door opened, and I had the answer to why I was there. It was Amanda Billingsgate.

"I hope I'm not disturbing you," she said, insincerely. "You seem very relaxed."

"Not at all. I do my best thinking in this position. As Hercule Poirot said, you do not have to exercise the body to exercise the 'little gray cells.'"

"Did he really say that?"

"Maybe. Certainly sounds like him."

She smiled, and I stood up to shake her hand. Unlike most English females, she had a strong grip. She was wearing gray gloves, a blue pinstripe, double-breasted suit with trousers, a white shirt, blue tie, and a gray men's fedora. The outfit did absolutely nothing to display her figure, but even so she looked elegant and almost beautiful. The French have a word for the way she looked. I'd learned it from Bunny. They call it *soigné*. She also looked like money.

"Please sit down," I said.

She took a quick survey of my office, then sat down in one of the two uncomfortable oak chairs opposite my desk.

"I see you like Winslow Homer," she said.

"Yes. He's one of my favorites. I was lucky to be able to get it for fifty cents."

She sat there for a few moments looking at me noncommittally.

"Nice tie," I said. "Eton?"

Her expression was not quite "wild surmise," but close.

"You surprise me. Yes. Eton. It's my husband's. But how did you...?

"Our mutual friend Bunny has one just like it."

"Oh, of course. For a minute, I thought you might be a public-school man."

"In fact, I am. But just not the kind you mean."

She paused again. She seemed self-possessed and assured, which was unusual for someone making a call on a private detective. Usually, snooty clients don't start to look down their noses until they get to know you a little better.

"I'll bet you have a pint of Bourbon in that desk drawer, right next to your thirty-eight," she said, finally.

"You've seen a lot of movies."

"Am I wrong?"

"Partially. It's only a half-empty pint. But I do have a stack of new Dixie cups to serve it in."

"I'll only need one, thank you. Dixie cup, I mean. I may need more than one drink."

"That serious, eh?" I got out the Bourbon and cups and poured one for each.

"I'm afraid it might be. But even if it isn't, I think it's poor form to stop at one drink."

"Is that going into your book?"

She raised her eyebrows, as if to say "So you know about that, eh?" She had elegant eyebrows and knew how to use them.

She took the Bourbon and sipped at it. "I like it neat," she said. "Does that surprise you?"

"Why would it?" I looked at her steadily. Her expression seemed to soften, and the forced playfulness, if that's what it was, began to melt away, but only a little. It might also have been aggressive nervousness. I'd seen that before. Or maybe it was the Bourbon. "So... Mrs. Billingsgate...?"

"So ... why am I here?"

"Yes. And what shall I call you? Mrs. Billingsgate is a little formal. But I'll stay with it if you want."

"Has Bunny ever told you why he's called Bunny?"

"Yes. It was something about an evil-minded nanny who disliked him, or something. And the name stuck."

"Well, I am called Pansy, for almost exactly the same reason."

"England must be overrun with sinister nannies."

"There are certainly at least two. I suppose I should say that my friends call me Pansy, but in fact everyone does, including and especially people who dislike me."

"Surely there can't be many of those," I said, gallantly.

"Quite a lot, actually. I don't blame them, really. I can be difficult—a pain in the ass, as you people say."

"You people?"

"Americans, I mean. We say pain in the arse."

"Two countries separated..."

"By a common language. Yes, I've heard that one too."

"What would you like me to call you, then?"

"Amanda. Almost no one does, and I much prefer it. That's why people won't do it, I suppose."

"All right, Amanda. What's up?"

She reached into her handbag and pulled out a photo. It was an eight-by-ten glossy. For a moment I thought it might be a publicity shot. And it was, in a way. But just not the usual kind.

"It's a very good likeness of you," I said.

"Thank you."

"Who's the guy on top?"

"Does it matter?"

"Probably. I assume it's not Mr. Billingsgate."

"The Honorable Freddie? Hardly. If it had been, I would have been yawning, instead of gasping."

"I see. Well, in that case, I assume someone sent this to you anonymously, with a note attached offering to sell you the original and the negative."

"Yes," she said. "He didn't say exactly how much he wanted. He said he'd be in touch."

It really was an attractive photo of two attractive people stretched out attractively on a bed in a very nice hotel room. Amanda was looking in the direction of the camera; she had not yet noticed the man at the window, not yet become alarmed. She was still registering the obviously intense pleasure of the moment. The expression on her face said that the lover, whoever he was, had penetrated her cool façade and exposed a level of passion she usually kept hidden. At least that's how it seemed to me, but then I'm a romantic. Maybe I was reading too much into it, but it's interesting how much of a story a good photograph can tell. The photographer in this instance either had a gift for timing or he was just lucky. A lot of great photographs are really just lucky that way.

The man's face was turned away, but he must have been sharing her delight, for her long lovely legs were wrapped around his waist in a way that suggested the lovers were just on the verge of finishing. And you had the impression that afterwards, they'd take a few breaths, restore themselves from the Champagne bottle that stood in an ice bucket next to the bed, and then begin again.

"So, the object of the exercise is to protect Mr. Billingsgate's illusions." I tried to assume an entirely professional expression. It wasn't easy to do with her sitting there, given the fact that I now had no need whatsoever to wonder what she looked like naked.

"That's part of it, I suppose. Although that's not the main thing. I don't mind telling you that we married under false pretenses. He believed I loved him, I believed he had money."

"*Quelle surprise?*"

"*Quelle* bloody mistake. But the point is, if Freddie found out, it would not be the end of the world, as far as I am concerned."

"And may even be a convenient way out?"

"That has occurred to me. No one thinks much of divorce these days. It's so common. Look at the King. Or former King, I should say."

"The one who fired himself."

"Yes. To marry a twice-divorced woman. Someone said, he went from Grand Admiral of the Fleet to third mate on an American tramp."

"Good line."

"But there's a larger problem. The man on top, as you put it, is Joachim Embs. He's a cultural attaché at the German consulate. *Colonel* Joachim Embs, I should say."

"What exactly does a cultural attaché do?"

"I don't know. Go to parties, as far as I can tell. He's very handsome and quite charming."

"But...?"

"But... the Germans are in a tricky position. Or rather, we are in a tricky position *vis a vis* the Germans. There's a large group of our chaps who don't like them and think there's going to be war. There's another who think Uncle Adolf has got the right idea about a lot of things. They quite like him and his crowd. Our former king was one of those, so that way of thinking is quite respectable in some circles."

"What's your opinion?"

"I don't really have one. I do think it's terribly funny that Hitler goes around talking about the purity of the German race and all that stuff about Teutonic warriors and whatnot, but he and his closest people all look like shopkeepers and sausage makers. Hardly the stuff of heroes. And that moustache. Really? A couple of years ago, we were at an embassy party in Berlin and I met this fellow Himmler. His breath was not to be believed. I simply can't take them seriously, so I don't see what all the fuss is about. And my having it off with Joachim wouldn't matter at all to me or anyone else, including the Honorable Freddie, if it weren't for all this dreadful politics. But some of our chaps are pretty worried about things like espionage. So it wouldn't do, you see, for the wife of a British consulate official to be seen in bed with a Nazi attaché."

"Pillow talk and secrets?"

"I suppose that's what they're afraid of. But to be honest, there's not a lot of pillow talk between me and Joachim... if you follow me. And I can't imagine he'd be interested in anything I know, because I really don't know anything. Not about politics or that sort of thing. But it would look so bad, you see."

"Is he a Nazi? I mean, not all Germans are, are they?"

Terry Mort

"I couldn't say about all of them, but Joachim is one through and through. A true believer. But at least in his case he looks the part. A Siegfried, head to toe, straight out of Wagner. Quite handsome, as you can see. Even his dueling scar is tasteful. Well, you can't see his face, but you can take my word."

"Are you... in love with him?"

"Heavens, no. I don't think I've ever been in love with anyone. But I do like men who are charming or good-looking. I like them best of all if they're both. As I said, he is."

"So, what would you like me to do about this blackmailer?"

"Find out who it is and shoot the bastard. Assuming it's not someone who matters. In that case, we'll have to have another think."

"You know of course that I can't go around shooting people, even if they are blackmailers—even if I wanted to, to please a lady. Naturally, I'd be happy to be of service, if I could get away with it. But I'm afraid that's out."

"What ever happened to the Wild West?"

"This is California. It never was part of the Wild West. It's just the East with better weather and movie stars."

"What about the gangsters? They're always shooting each other."

"That's true. And if you decide to go that route, I can recommend some excellent goombahs. They're not all that good at detective work, though. If you want them to push a button, you have to point out the button."

"Too bad. Well, we'll just have to do it the legal way—at first, anyway. So please find out who it is, and let me decide what to do next. Okay?"

"Of course. I don't suppose you've considered paying him off?"

"Not at all. I don't have the kind of money he's probably after, and neither does Freddie. Besides, it's not the sort of thing one does. If one can help it."

"And the police are out of the question, for obvious reasons."

"Yes. For obvious reasons."

"All right, Amanda. I'll look into it. Often these things are not as bad as they seem at first. It could just be some amateur trying for a quick score. People like that are easy to scare."

"That's reassuring. While we're on the subject of money, I hope I can afford you."

"I'm sure between the two of you, meaning yourself and the Honorable Freddie, you can scrape together my twenty-five dollars a day plus expenses."

"Oh, yes, of course. I can handle that myself, assuming you don't take all year."

"I won't. By the way, why do you call him the Honorable Freddie? Has he done something wonderful?"

"That'll be the day. It's just that he's the son of a lord, and all such offspring use that term. It's called a courtesy title. Doesn't mean anything. I'm one myself."

"The Honorable Pansy?"

"Please. It's quite enough being the Honorable Amanda."

"Quite a mouthful."

"You have no idea," she smiled.

I was about to say that on the contrary, I had a very good idea. But I let it pass.

"Do you mind if I keep this photo? It's the place to start."

"No. But I may blush when I think of you having it."

"Somehow, I doubt it. Care for a refill?"

"I thought you'd never ask. And a fresh cup, if you please."

She had twisted her first cup into a wad. She wasn't quite as cool as she let on. I liked her better for it.

Chapter Eight

After Amanda left, I sat there thinking the situation over. I studied the photo, thinking impure thoughts. There certainly was more to her than that pinstripe suit would have you believe. Lucky Joachim. Poor Honorable Freddie.

The phone rang. It was Bunny.

"I've got a name for you, old boy. William Patterson. Goes by Bill, of course. He's on the counterintelligence team at the Bureau. Offices are in City Hall, third floor, Room 300. Very discreet, I should add. I told him that you were the premier private investigator in LA."

"You know what Mark Twain said about truth."

"Yes. We should economize on it. Normally I would. I also said you were especially well connected with the film business. That always impresses these government types. Then I told him you were on the edge of something you thought might be of interest regarding foreign nationals. He rose like a trout to that one."

"Well, thank you. Is he expecting my call?"

"Not necessary, he said. Just pop round when you feel like it. Nothing formal. He's usually in the office during regular hours. I gather his job doesn't involve much gumshoe-ing and shadowing or cloak-and-dagger. More like research and analysis."

"Many thanks, Bunny. I'll zip over there this afternoon."

"Did Pansy Billingsgate ever call, by the way?"

"Yes. In fact, she came by the office this morning. Just left. Among other things, she said she doesn't like to be called Pansy."

"Of course. Who would? Who would like to be called Bunny? It's just something we must bear for our sins."

"Speaking of sins..."

"Ah! Yes. She told you all about her muddle?"

"Yes, and I would describe it as more than a muddle."

"Of course. British understatement, my friend. You know what Dr. Johnson said about understatement."

"No.

"Remind me to tell you sometime. I'm sure you'll be able to straighten it out for dear old Pansy. And good hunting with our government friends."

I was about to tell him about his mistake with Boswell but decided to save it for a better time.

Next, I called Kowalski on the off chance there was something new regarding Jimmy Hicks.

"Nothing solid," he said. "You?"

"No."

"There is something, although it's probably not connected. An interesting body floated ashore out at the marina. Scared the hell out of a lady having her evening cocktail on the good ship lollypop. The corpse was a young man—mid-twenties."

"Any ID?"

"None. No clothes. And both hands had been removed. Whoever did it was obviously worried about prints. Took no chances."

"Easier than going finger by finger, I guess. How about dental records?"

"If his head ever comes ashore, we'll be sure to check."

What Hamlet Said

"Ugh."

"It's a wicked world. Keep in touch."

For Jimmy's and Ethel's sake, I hoped the kid floating in the marina wasn't our boy. But he was still missing, and that was a worry. Floating bodies weren't exactly a rarity in LA, but they didn't come in flotillas, either.

I went back to studying the photo and wondering the best way to proceed. In my line, I never used photographers like the guy who'd taken this picture. If I ever had to have a picture of something, I took it myself—and, as I may have mentioned, I didn't take cases involving motel rooms or Turkish baths. Or even high-end hotels. But I did know someone who knew her way around that business.

And just then she came breezing through the door. It was obvious that she had lunched on her usual Braunschweiger-and-onion sandwich washed down with a couple of martinis. She came back to pick up something she'd forgotten.

"Hiya, Chief. What are you doing here this time of day, and what's that perfume in the air?"

"Client meeting. As for the perfume, you be the judge."

"Chanel? Reminds me of something Perry almost got me for Christmas one year. He lost the urge when he saw the price."

"Could be. But I'm glad to see you."

"Like the old Mae West line?" She pulled out her Zippo and fired up a Pall Mall.

"Not quite," I said. "Take a look at this photo."

"Hmmm. Nice ass."

"Whose?"

"Either one. I'm broad-minded. New client?"

"The one on the bottom."

"Too bad. The one on the top interests me more. She seems to like him, too." She handed it back to me. "So?"

71

"So, I know that you occasionally use professional photographers."

"We offer a full service, sometimes even when not asked."

"Naturally. So I'm wondering if there's any way you or the guys you use could get a line on who took this one. Maybe even recognize the technique or the finishing process. Or if that doesn't work, just ask around. Whoever took this is sure to remember it and maybe even talk about it. Discreetly, of course."

"If by 'discreetly' you mean showing a copy to all his buddies in his favorite bar, then yes. It's highly likely. Especially one as interesting as this. You don't often get two full-lengths with this amount of detail. She has very nice muscle tone."

If Amanda Billingsgate knew that, she might blush for real. The boys down at Moe's Saloon or wherever might even ask for a copy they could frame and hang in the men's room. It would be a form of immortality through art. But I doubt she'd see it that way. Even one of the formerly Bright Young Things must have some limits.

"Well," Della said, "if it was me trying to track this guy down, I'd start with Flash Gordini. He gets around a fair amount. That's not his real name, of course." She paused and grinned, waiting for the straight line.

"So what's his real name?"

"Flash Moroni. Ha! Rim shot!"

"He's one of your photographers?"

"One of them. He tends to specialize in divorce cases, which, strange as it may seem, usually involve some sort of shenanigans like this. People really ought to know better than to rent first-floor hotel rooms. It makes life too easy for these photogs. They should at least be made to suffocate in a closet for a while and only come out when they hear someone yelling 'YES!' That's their cue to burst out and say 'SMILE!'"

What Hamlet Said

"Where can I find him? In the book?"

"No. He's strictly a word-of-mouth guy. Advertising in the Yellow Pages might not be so healthy."

"I'm surprised he gets enough business that way."

"LA private dicks aren't ever supposed to be surprised by anything. Don't let it get around. I'll lose face. The truth is, he has other interests on the side. Porn, of course, but he's also big in passports and ID cards. He and Blinky Malone are tight. Flash can doctor a genuine official photo to make Fu Manchu look like Ronald Coleman. Or vice versa. Makes passports that get 'lost,' as in 'stolen,' all that much more valuable. They look real because they *are* real, even the stamps. Lots of money in that business. Lots of people these days want to come into the country on the sly. Or leave in a hurry. If you give me a minute, I'll find Flash's number. It's unlisted. You want me to call him?"

"Yes. Tell him to come by and show him the picture. Don't let him have it, though."

"A keepsake?"

"It's the only one we have. Ask him to ask around. He might be more inclined to do a favor for you than for me."

"That way we won't have to pay him."

"Right. I've got to go over to City Hall."

Chapter Nine

The local FBI office was on the third floor. There was one door, and it was marked only by a number. The Feds were not advertising their presence. I went in and was greeted by a receptionist.

"My name is Riley Fitzhugh." I assumed Bunny had given this name. "I'd like to see Agent Patterson."

"Is he expecting you?"

"Possibly."

She looked at me as if to say this was unusual. People were supposed to know whether or not they were expected. This was the FBI, not an employment agency, after all.

"I'll call him." She did and apparently got a positive answer. "Third door on the left."

I knocked on Patterson's door and went in.

His room was even more like a dreary post office than mine. And smelled like one, too. Dust and paper. Patterson was seated behind a metal desk surrounded by piles of books, files, and magazines and an empty carton of Chinese food. He looked like a graduate student studying the potato crop in Silesia. His jacket was off and his sparse hair was sticking in all directions. He wore wire-rim glasses, a white shirt, and plain tie and suspenders. He looked too young to be a G-man. I couldn't imagine him blasting a Most

What Hamlet Said

Wanted criminal with a Tommy gun. But he had a very pleasant smile and seemed glad to see me. He stood up and I could see his baggy suit pants, the victims of hours spent at a desk. He was about five and a half feet tall, rosy-cheeked and healthy looking, despite his air of frustration and muddle. I noticed that his pistol and shoulder holster were shoved into a very full bookcase.

"Mr. Fitzhugh? Bill Patterson. Glad to meet you. Have a seat."

"Thanks. Call me Riley."

"Okay. Excuse the mess. I'm trying to make some sense out of the Balkans."

"Not easy," I said.

"No. If I do, I'll be the first one in history. Do you know what Bismarck said about Schleswig-Holstein?"

"Not offhand."

"It was a famously complicated international problem. He said there were only three people who ever understood it—one of them was dead, one of them went insane thinking about it, and he was the third, and he forgot. And Schleswig-Holstein is nothing compared to the Balkans."

"I know the politics are confusing. That's about all I know."

"Not just the politics. Do you know there's a place called Slovenia and another called Slavonia, and they're virtually next door. You'd think they could come up with some different names. It's impossible to keep it all straight."

"I suppose the question is—can *they*? Keep it straight, I mean."

"Yes, that is the question. And the answer is—yes, they can. That's part of the problem. All the Slavs know only too well what region they're from and where their ancestors were from, going all the way back to the Flood. They are hostages to myth and memory, as someone might have said. History there doesn't proceed on a straight line, or even a zigzag. It goes in circles. Things keep coming around again and again, ad infinitum, most of them terrible." He paused. "I don't mean to lecture. You get started on this subject and get sucked into a whirlwind of confusion."

"Not at all. As a matter of fact, I'm interested. My, ah, girlfriend comes from that part of the world."

He brightened up at that. "Yes! Bunny told me. Yvonne Adore! I love her! I saw her in that desert movie about the White Russian princess. What was it called? *Desert Rhapsody*? What's she doing now?"

"She's in Yuma, working on another desert movie. She plays another White Russian princess."

"You are a lucky man, in case you haven't noticed. What on earth did you do in this or any previous life to...?"

"Deserve her? Sometimes I wonder. Most times, I try not to think about it."

"It makes us mere mortals despair. Or maybe hope. The yin and yang of human existence."

"I often say that."

"Yes, of course. But what's your interest in all this Balkan political stuff? Bunny said you were a private detective."

"Yes. I'm working on a couple of cases that may be related somehow, but I'm not sure how. The common thread seems to be some kind of murky European connection. It may turn out to be nothing, but somehow I think I need to understand what's going on over there, because it might have a bearing on what's going on here."

"Yes. You never know. I'm not puzzling over this insanity because it's interesting; it just might have some impact on national security. If only very slight."

"Maybe we can help each other out."

"Could be. I'll give you just the barest outlines of the situation. Take it for what it's worth. The key thing to understand is that most of the people in each of these Balkan regions want to be independent. Croatia most of all. But they aren't, because, after the war, when the Balkans were finally free of the Hapsburg Austrians, some of the regional politicians got together and dreamed up a new country called Yugoslavia. The word means 'southern Slavs.' They thought it was a good idea, since most everyone in the area is Slavic. But lots of others didn't like the idea at all."

"Like the Croatians."

"Most of them, yes. They felt they'd finally gotten rid of the Austrians and now there was a new bunch of political meddlers trying to absorb them into a country that had never existed before— a cobbled-together piece of abstract art that consists of a half dozen regions and three separate religions—Roman Catholics, like the Croats; Greek Orthodox, like the Serbs; and Muslims, like the Bosnians. Ever hear of them?"

"No."

"Neither had I, until I donned this yoke of sorrows. Now the difficult part of this new arrangement is that these three religions all hate each other. Why, you ask? Who knows? So you have a brand-new country with no democratic traditions made up of squabbling regions and religions. It's a jigsaw puzzle with pieces that don't fit. The only thing everyone seems to agree on is that the Jews should be run out of town. Or worse."

"Convenient scapegoats?"

"Eternal scapegoats. As a matter of fact, the very idea of a scapegoat is Jewish. Old Testament. How's that for irony? Anyway, even when cooler heads prevail and they try to put aside their differences and work together, they can't. The center holds only through coercion. State police. That sort of thing."

"Like the Gestapo in Germany."

"Yes. But at least all Germans can agree that they're Germans. No Croat believes he's a Yugoslav. And a Croat has known for a thousand years that he's not a Serb; that's the last thing he'd want to be. Other than a Turk. Well, you can't blame people for wanting independence, especially since there's always been someone interfering with them. Sometimes they came from the outside, like the Austrians or the Turks or the Russians or the Italians. But just as bad are fellow Slavs *within* the region who want to run things."

"The ones who came up with the idea for the new country."

"Yes. Which, by the way, was originally called the Kingdom of Serbs, Croats, and Slovenes. It was changed to 'Yugoslavia' after a few years. It was pasted together as a constitutional monarchy, and the King of Serbia was appointed king of the whole shootin' match. Serbia had managed to get out from under the Turks in the nineteenth century, so they at least had experience with self-government. Anyway, the new kingdom does have a parliament, but now and then there's a fatal shooting during working hours, and now and then the King suspends it and sends them all home. Not exactly the House of Commons. The capital is Belgrade, which is in Serbia. With a Serb king and a Serbian capital, you can guess who became the first among equals. The Croats don't like the Serbs, and... wait for it... the Serbs don't like the Croats!"

"Yes, I know that for a fact."

"Yvonne has told you? Of course. So, the dissident Croats decided to form an independence movement. Only the latest in a series. There was plenty of support for it, because, as I said, the Croats have always wanted to be left alone. The Serbs didn't like it, so they outlawed the group. To no one's surprise, the extremists decided to go underground. They formed a militant group called the

Ustache. The word means 'uprising,' more or less. Heard of it, by any chance?"

"No. I don't think so."

"Well, one of their boys assassinated the Yugoslav King Alexander while he was visiting France. Shot him dead in Marseilles. That was a couple of years ago. That didn't go over well with the Serbs, because Alexander was one of theirs. Anyway, after assassinating Alexander, a lot of outlawed Ustache members fled the country. Some went to Italy because Il Duce was sympathetic, politically. So was the Vatican. Others scattered to other places where they would get friendly receptions and bide their time. And maybe do a little fundraising."

"Among family and countrymen."

"Yes. And when I say fundraising, I don't mean sending out mailings with return envelopes. Money is the lifeblood of any secret organization, and the members are never squeamish about where it comes from or how they get it."

"Robberies? Extortion?"

"Why not? If you wanted money and could turn off your conscience by telling yourself you were a righteous freedom fighter, a hero of the revolution, where would you look? Personally, I'd start by looking at a bank or a Brinks truck."

"Has there been any activity here? In the U.S.?"

"Pittsburgh seems to have attracted quite a few. Lots of peaceful Slavs emigrated there because of jobs in the steel mills. That makes a handy community to get lost in and a pretty safe haven, where they can carry on the fight or whatever you call it."

I knew that story pretty well. Youngstown, Ohio, where I'd found Myrtle originally, was a mini-Pittsburgh, complete with steel mills and ethnics of all persuasions. Norman Rockwell never painted scenes from that town.

"How about here? In LA?"

"Wouldn't be surprised. We haven't been able to connect the dots on any particular crime, but that doesn't mean anything, necessarily. Ever go out to San Pedro? Lots of interesting things going on out there, we hear."

"As a matter of fact, I know a good place for strudel."

"Then you also know a good place for gossip. The fact that you know some people there could be useful. If I went there, or someplace like it, I might as well wear a sign saying 'Ask Me About Careers in the FBI.' But if you should happen to hear something while you're having strudel, we'd be interested."

"Of course. I'll keep my ears open. You mentioned the Italians meddling. What about the Germans?"

"So far, they seem to be taking the sensible approach and leaving things alone. Bismarck said the whole of the Balkans wasn't worth the blood of one Pomeranian grenadier. But Adolf might have other ideas down the road. The Ustache are Roman Catholics and fierce anti-Semites, so it would surprise no one if they threw in with Hitler —if they were forced to choose. And if there's a war, *everyone* will be forced to choose—except the Swiss, I suppose. They'll be everyone's friendly banker. As for Italy, Il Duce has had his eyes across the Adriatic for years. You'd think trying to govern the Italians would be enough of a headache. But what can you expect from somebody who invaded Ethiopia, for God's sake? What would he want with it? He seems capable of anything."

"I guess the question is, why does the FBI care about any of this?"

"That is the question. I care personally, because my boss told me to care. But *we* care, because some of these centuries-old squabbles might very well spill over into this country, especially given tensions with Germany and Italy and especially given our large immigrant population. If war breaks out in Europe, who knows what will happen in Yugoslavia? The Balkans would be one hell of a place to fight. 'Balkans' is a Turkish word for mountains. Tanks don't do well going straight up the side of a cliff."

"How about the Japanese?"

"They might very well be dipping a toe in these waters. There are lots of them in California trying to look invisible. Frankly, we have no idea what they're up to. But we're watching. So, in short, we've got to be alert to all sorts of grim possibilities, including Fifth Columns—if we should get dragged into a war. You probably know that the FBI is responsible for domestic counterintelligence."

"Yes, I did know that."

"Otherwise, we wouldn't give a damn about all this stuff. At least, I wouldn't. Oh, how I miss Prohibition," he said with mock melodrama. "Everything was so simple then. An idyllic world of right versus wrong. Arrest the bootleggers, confiscate the booze, have a party. The good old days! Gone with the wind, to coin a phrase. Speaking of that, I read that they're casting a wide net for the girl to play Scarlett. I heard Katharine Hepburn is a good possibility. Please say it isn't so." He made a sour face.

"I don't know. No one has said anything to me about it."

"Oh, well. I don't suppose your good lady is in the running."

"No. With her accent, it might be hard to portray her as a Southern belle."

"Yes, I suppose you're right. Not even Garbo could have done it. Well, let's hope *they* get it right. Have you read the book?"

"I've started it."

"Do you know what Dr. Johnson said about *Paradise Lost*?"

"No. But I'm always interested in what he has to say about anything."

"He said 'None wished it longer.' Ha! Applies in this case too, I think. Now, then, Bunny told me you might have something of interest."

"It's possible. First of all, I think there's been a kidnapping. That's a federal crime now, isn't it?"

"Yes. Ever since the Lindbergh baby. But there has to be a crossing of state lines before we jump in. Why?"

I filled him in on Lulu's murder and Jimmy Hicks's disappearance, and my encounter with Alphonse and *his* disappearance.

"You think Hicks may have been kidnapped? And possibly murdered?"

"It seems like a strong possibility."

"Two things," he said. "First, with regard to Jimmy Hicks, right now it's a missing-persons case, not a kidnapping. That's the cops' business, even if it turns out to be murder. When you get a ransom note postmarked Nevada or some place across the line, or a body in Mexico, let me know and we'll talk."

"Okay." If necessary, I could figure out a cross-border angle to the case. After all, Tijuana wasn't that far away.

"But... what does interest me is the business about Acme Management and Lulu. If it's a simple murder, that's one thing. But if it's something else, then maybe we'd want to get involved. The thing that makes my antennae quiver is that you thought you recognized Alphonse's accent."

"Yes. Croatian."

He smiled, tolerantly.

"They all sound the same, Riley. They all speak the same language back in the old country, so when they come here and learn English, you can't tell one from another. But it *could be* Croatian.

And that *could be* interesting, because there *could be* a connection to the Ustache. And if so, we *would be* interested."

"Pretty thin, I suppose."

"Yes. But 'thin' only means thin, not chimerical. And a daisy chain may be made of daisies, but it's still a chain of things, one leading to the next."

Chimerical? I liked that word. I'd look it up later.

"One last thing—a headless, handless corpse floated into the marina this morning. Does that suggest anything to you?"

"As in a secret society? A signature or ritual execution? No. Doesn't ring a bell. It does suggest someone who might have seen something he shouldn't, been in the wrong place at the wrong time."

"Yes. I was thinking the same thing. Well, thanks very much for your time. I hope we can help each other out."

"There is one thing...." He seemed suddenly shy or embarrassed. He may have even blushed. "I was wondering..."

I recognized the signs.

"Why, of course." I said. "I'm sure she'd be happy to meet an FBI agent, especially one so interested in her country. Maybe the three of us could have lunch, when she finishes shooting."

"Really? Wonderful! I was only going to ask for an autographed picture."

Chapter Ten

I went back to my place at the Garden of Allah. It was just about sunset and the starlets were sitting around the pool, waiting for someone famous to appear. They were a new bunch. They didn't know yet that they'd only get tired writers who almost didn't have the energy to lie to them. Almost.

In fact, there was already a tired writer there. Hobey was sitting by himself, staring into a gin and tonic. He seemed to think there were answers in there, and although there never were, he was an optimist by nature and kept looking.

"Greetings, friend," he said, somewhat dispiritedly. "Join me in a drink to celebrate my first story conference with the producers."

"Go well?" I asked, although the answer was obvious from the look of him.

"No. It was disappointing. But I should have known better. I've been out here long enough to know that they've never learned that writing is not a team sport."

I knew what he meant. All these writers from the east who cut their teeth on novels and short stories and plays never got over the fact that the money men put movies together the way Ford assembled cars. They boast about moviemaking being a collaborative art, but if that's the case so is working on an assembly line. Almost invariably they'd hire a team of writers to work on the same project and then take bits and pieces that they liked from each and paste it all together and call it a script, after which they'd give it to a director who'd make his own changes and then fight with the producers to keep them. Then the producers would review what was shot every day and decide on more changes. Someone once said a camel was a horse put together by a committee; so too the movies. But the funny thing was, nine times out of ten these camels made money. And sometimes were even good-looking, by camel standards. But that was small consolation to a writer who thought he had written *Cyrano de Bergerac*, only to see the final product turn out as *The Three Stooges in Paris*.

Hobey continued: "I explained to them my idea about Rhett being the key to the story. And how I wanted to show him aboard his ship running the gauntlet of the Union blockade. See, the blockade symbolizes the obstacles the romantic hero has to overcome in order to win the Dream Girl, in this case Scarlett."

"They didn't buy it?" I wasn't the least bit surprised.

"Not really. They said the budget was already too big to start bringing in ships, and shooting at sea is always much more expensive than any other kind. You can't depend on the weather, and so on. Plus, real ships are terribly expensive, but scale models in a tank look too cheesy for a major picture like this."

"Some sense in that."

"I suppose. Then they told me that Scarlett was definitely the focal point of the movie, not Rhett. You should have heard them —'*You know who wrote this schmaltz of a book? A woman. You know who buys this schmaltz of a book? Women. You know who goes to the movies? Women. You know who drag their schlimazel husbands to the movies? Women. You think women give a damn about a schmuck with a complex? No. In this picture Rhett Butler doesn't think! He doesn't have doubts. He doesn't recite meshugenah poems. All Rhett Butler does is stand around and look good!'* So they told me to try again and come back next week."

"At least you got invited back."

"That is something. But it's depressing. I don't think of Rhett Butler as a schmuck with a complex. They're missing the whole point of the Romantic Egoist. But these are the kind of people who say things like 'If nobody wants to come, nothing can stop them.' I once had a conversation with Thalberg, and he told me his theory of creative production. When you come to a decision point, he said, it doesn't matter what you decide, as long as you decide *something*. And then stick with it. Can you believe it? My problem is, I keep expecting them to get it one day."

"I heard they're thinking of Katharine Hepburn for Scarlett."

"Yes. Can you imagine? Have you ever heard her say 'beautifully'? She pronounces each letter. In that awful voice. Speaking of which, they're also thinking about Bette Davis. What a choice—a skinny schoolmarm or an evil stepsister. If either of them showed up at the Fair Oaks barbecue, the men would scatter like quail. Southern belles, my ass. And believe me, I know Southern belles. Dream Girl? Not hardly, as they say out West, which, by the way, is east of here, which tells you something about this business." He took a long pull on his drink and sighed and sat back to let the setting sun reflect off his face. He sighed again and then, typically, smiled. "Still, there are worse places to be in the world and worse things to be doing right now," he said. "And they're still paying me. For the time being. It won't last, but what does?" He had remarkable resilience and immunity to disappointment. It was one of his more likable qualities.

"Did Hedda get the Miss Lonelyhearts job?"

"Yes, indeed she did. Don't ask me how, and I do mean how. Not why. The 'why' question cannot be answered. But if you have any problems regarding matters of the heart, feel free to write to her. If they print your letter, you'll receive a five-dollar gift certificate for Fanny Farmer Chocolates. So make it a good sob story. I wouldn't follow her advice, though."

"The last piece of advice I ever took was not to take any advice."

"Good. Free advice is worth every penny."

"Sounds familiar."

"I suppose. Somebody probably said it sometime. Well, I'm ready for a refill. You?"

"Why not."

He filled our glasses from the bottles on the table, the ice from the bucket, and the limes he had already cut and arranged in a circle on the plate. He was obviously in a mood to commune with his alternating disappointment and high hopes, far into the night.

"Speaking of stories," he said. "I have some ideas about that business with the sinister foreigners."

"Good! What have you got?"

"The Japs are involved in some way."

I wasn't expecting that. "Really? How?"

"Before we get into that, let's review the facts. Sort of set the scene. First of all, there's the lovely Lulu, strangled and left on a beach."

"Actually, she was shot. With a forty-five pistol of the kind used and owned by the chief suspect. Both of which are missing."

"Details. Shot, strangled—whatever. The point is, there's nothing unusual about the way she was killed. Apparently, it was a run-of-the-mill murder. Happens all the time. And as you mentioned, there's even an obvious suspect—Jimmy Hicks. But there's no apparent motive. From what you told me about Jimmy Hicks, he doesn't seem like the kind who'd be a sociopath or psychopath. Or even a hothead."

"No. I didn't get that impression. Of course, you can never tell about people."

"True enough. And if he did it, it stands to reason he'd disappear, which he has. But if he didn't do it, why did he disappear? He was her last known contact."

"And by running, he looks even guiltier."

"Yes. If he ran. But all we know for sure is that he disappeared. That's not necessarily the same as running. Suppose somebody wanted to frame him for the murder? What better way to do that than to spirit him away, either for good, or until he was no longer necessary, for whatever reason?"

"That has occurred to me. They may have snatched him, or he may have gone back to see her the next day—after he talked to me—and they got them both. And did I tell you about the headless, handless body floating in the Marina?"

"No! Really? Even better. Unidentifiable. Could be Jimmy, could be a John Doe. It was a John, not a Jane, right?"

"Correct. They could at least tell that much."

"And there's another complicating factor—the mysterious stranger from Acme Management, who talks funny and is obviously a foreigner. Lulu's agent. And most likely a European, yes? And *he* disappears."

"Yes. He's a white man, not Japanese. So where do they come in?"

"I'm coming to them. But let's assume that Jimmy is innocent of the murder. Okay?"

"Yes. I think that's more likely than not. And if he's not innocent, it's not our concern. Strictly a police matter."

"Right. And if he's not guilty, that leaves the sinister foreigners."

"But they're not Japs. We've established that."

"That's why it makes sense. If the Japs are anything, they are subtle. Their whole theory of war, and even martial arts, is to do the opposite of what your opponent thinks you're going to do. What's more, the tensions between Japan and the U.S. are getting worse. They might very well be preparing for war. Even if they want to avoid it, they'll still prepare for the possibility. Of course, *we* don't think it's likely; *we* never do. They are different from us, because they actually think ahead and examine all possible scenarios and plan for each one, whereas we never believe anything dreadful will ever happen; then when it does, we wonder why it happened—and only then do we start thinking about what to do about it."

"All right. So we're idiots. So what?"

"So part of preparation for war involves spying on your potential enemy. Espionage. You can bet the Nips are knee-deep in it. But..."

"But?"

"But they have a problem: they are easy to spot. Put one in the lobby of the Princeton Club and he'll stand out. There's not one American in a hundred who can tell the difference between a Jap and a Chinese. But one hundred out of one hundred can tell the difference between a Jap and a white man. That may not be a problem in certain settings—midnight creeping and lurking, and so on. But in others, it would be—any place where the spy might be noticed. They therefore need white people to do certain kinds of spying, people who would not be conspicuous. And who better to recruit than agents of a potential ally? And who are these potential allies?"

"Germany and Italy."

"Yes. *But...* they have their own agendas and their own professional intelligence networks. They may not be all that anxious to share anything, even with a potential ally. As far as we know, the

Germans and the Japanese haven't made any formal deals yet. And all these intelligence services are naturally highly secretive. It's the nature of the business, and they don't share information willingly. Even our amateur organizations are parochial. Do you think the FBI talks to Army Intelligence?"

"They should."

"Right. They should. But they're too worried about their own turf. So they don't."

"How do you know?"

"Human nature. It's my field. Plus, I read. Besides, both the Italians and the Germans are almost totally concerned about Europe, and if they're interested at all in naval secrets, it will be about our Atlantic fleet. And the Royal Navy, more to the point. Only the Japanese care about the Pacific. So if you're the Japanese, and you need to hire white men as agents, where do you look?"

"You tell me."

"How about a secret organization, one that needs money and is also sympathetic, if not to your cause, then to the politics of your allies? And one that has a legitimate front?"

"Like Acme Talent Management?"

"Why not? You mentioned the Balkans. A pot of seething politics. What better place to recruit agents? Not there, literally. But here, among the expats and immigrants. And if you were a naval power interested in the navy of your potential adversary, meaning us in this case, who better to recruit than dock and shipyard workers? Using them would involve no risks, cost only a few dollars, and potentially provide useful intelligence. If they get caught, who cares? The chain of command is likely to be untraceable—a handler and paymaster who easily disappear—melt back into the scenery like Manny Stairs's houseboy. Or somebody's gardener. This sort of thing is not new, you know. There have always been mercenary soldiers and paid spies."

"Makes a certain amount of sense."

"I know. I'm thinking of turning it into a treatment for a movie. Maybe a novel, if I ever get the one finished that I'm working on now, thanks to the story you and Catherine Moore gave me." He sighed again. "She looked wonderful at the party the other night."

"No arguments there."

"Do you know, thinking back on our night of bliss together, she even smelled good in the morning? How many women do you know who can manage that?"

"Just one other. Of course, I don't claim that my survey is all that comprehensive."

"Don't be modest, my friend. It doesn't become you. Besides, neither of us is finished quite yet." He paused, remembering that night with Catherine. "I wonder what she thought of me."

"I wouldn't ask her. She has a way of being honest."

"Yes. You know what T. S. Eliot said about that sort of thing —'mankind cannot stand too much reality.'"

"Good line. He should write his stuff down, instead of just saying it to you and his other friends. By the way, what does 'chimerical' mean?"

"It means something highly improbable, like a satisfying and fulfilling career as a Hollywood screenwriter."

* * *

The more I thought about Hobey's theory, the more sense it made. As Bill Patterson had said, there were lots of Japanese in the area trying to look invisible, and there was our Pacific battle fleet docked in San Pedro. A Japanese with a camera wouldn't pass security, but a dockworker or civilian maintenance worker could, very easily. And by combining Bill Patterson's information about the Ustache with Hobey's theory, it made some sense to get some more strudel and maybe have another chat with the FBI. Yvonne/Myrtle might not like the idea of my snooping around her countrymen, but she didn't have to know about it. I was fond of the old Spanish expression "What the eyes do not see, the heart does not feel." Over the years, I found it coming in handy in a number of different situations. And maybe it wasn't a Spanish saying, after all; maybe it was one of Doctor Johnson's. I'd have to ask Bunny.

Chapter Eleven

I soon realized that Hobey's theories were all very well, but my immediate business had to do with finding Amanda Billingsgate's blackmailer. She was the only one paying me. All the other stuff was just mystery on the fringes. And even someone with Hobey's expansive imagination would be hard pressed to connect all those dots. I was just doing a favor for Ethel. I hoped Jimmy Hicks would turn up alive at some point, but it really wasn't any of my business, if you define business as something you're getting paid for. And I did.

The next morning, I went to my office. Della was already there, typing and smoking.

"You know, they say those things aren't good for you," I said.

"They said the same thing about Perry, and they were right about that too. But I got both habits, so they can preach on some other corner. Flash Gordini called, by the way. He's coming by the office."

"Good! Did he give you any advance information?"

"None that you'd be interested in. But on Friday I gave him the photo to show around to his fraternity brothers over the weekend, and he's bringing it back. Wants to talk to you in person. Didn't seem to think talking on the phone was a good idea."

I'd told Della not to give Gordini the photo, but she'd gone her own way, as usual. No harm done, apparently.

"If he doesn't want to use the phone, that means he's got something."

"There's no doubt of that. And his friends all hope it'll clear up. Anyway, he'll be here sometime this morning. You can never tell with Flash. In his business, punctuality's not all that important. Sometimes he has to take the long way around to be sure he's not being followed."

"Paranoid?"

"Nope. Just cautious. Also, Ethel Welkin called."

"Did she say what she wanted?"

"Not in so many words. It didn't sound urgent, if you follow me."

I went into my office to call Ethel. I didn't bother closing the door. There was really no use.

"Ethel? It's Riley."

"Hello, darling. Any news about Jimmy?"

"No. Nothing." There was no sense mentioning the body at the marina.

"It's very worrying. There's absolutely no sign of him anywhere. What are you doing tonight?"

"Tonight? I have a meeting. Why?"

"It's the crew's night off on the *Shutter*, and I thought you might like a little evening Champagne and lobster on the fantail. Isadore's in New York, scouting chorus girls. He says it's strictly business; they're planning a big new musical. Ha!"

"Oh. Well, I'm sorry I can't make it, but if things change, I'll call you."

"Don't let it go too long. You know the old saying, time and tide wait for no man. Bye, bye."

What Hamlet Said

Time and tide and *Ethel* wait for no man. Well, it was a nice offer, but it wasn't Wednesday and Ethel had plenty of other gallopers to choose from. I flattered myself that I was the favorite, but I knew I was only the first among equals, if that. I liked it that way. It removed all romantic pressure and possible entanglements. Ethel was probably the fairest-minded woman I ever knew. She only wanted a little occasional fun and didn't expect anything in return. What's more, she didn't expect *you* to expect anything either. Fair's fair. Madame Bovary was at one end of the emotional spectrum, Ethel was at the other. And if you're wondering how I know about Madame Bovary, I read a lot.

Besides, I did have some vague plans for the evening, assuming the Honorable Amanda was available. I planned to call her after I talked with Flash Gordini.

He arrived just as Della was leaving for her Braunschweiger and onion on rye, martinis on the side, up or on the rocks, it didn't matter. She was as broad-minded about martinis as she was about everything else.

"The chief's in his office," she said to Flash. "He's the one behind the desk."

I was expecting a shifty-eyed, furtive weasel of a man dressed in a checked suit and derby hat. I was not disappointed, for so he was. All that was lacking was a toothpick in the side of his mouth.

He sat down in one of the two chairs after checking behind the door to make sure we were alone. He took out a toothpick and placed it in the side of his mouth.

"Pleased to meet you," he said. "Della says you're a good fella. Perry too."

"Good to know. It would also be good to know what you know about that picture she gave you."

95

"I don't suppose you've got a bottle of Bourbon in that desk drawer there?"

"No, unfortunately. My last client drank it all."

"Too bad."

"I'm as unhappy about it as you are."

"Life can be disappointing. My mother used to say that to me."

"To or about?"

"Couldn't say, really. She didn't pay much attention to us kids. She'd rather go bowling."

"Hard to believe. What about the picture?"

"I think I can help you there." He took the folded eight-by-ten out of his pocket and laid it on the desk.

"Some dish," he said.

"I agree."

"I'll bet you wouldn't think it to see her dressed. My experience, that's often the way. Personally, I like it when things ain't so obvious, you know? Some of these dames have headlamps like a Buick and when they take it all off, everything seems out of balance, you know? Too much of a good thing ain't a good thing, the way I see it."

"Symmetry is the essence of beauty, is that it?"

"That's how I see it. More is less. You know who said that? Me."

"Well, I look forward to reading your memoirs, but right now I want to know what you can tell me about this picture. Who took it, and why?"

"Well, I'm a businessman..."

"Five bucks," I said.

"Fair enough. This here photo was taken by one Hobart William Smith. That ain't his real name. Got it off a college somewhere in New York or back East. Nobody knows what his real name is, mostly because nobody cares, and it ain't worth finding out. Goes by Smitty."

"How'd you identify him?"

"I showed it around. Guys talk. The usual."

"Did you make copies?"

"A few. Just for my own use and to give to friends, kind of like a greeting card. Was that wrong?" He smiled innocently.

"Does it matter? Did you talk to Smith about it?"

"Well, I'm a businessman…"

"Another five." Now I understood why he didn't want to discuss things over the phone.

"Yeah. I talked to him."

"Who was he working for?"

"That's where it gets interesting. He's not real sure. The guy called Smitty and told him he had a job for him and to meet him in a diner on Sepulveda."

"Which one?"

"El Greco's. Know it?"

"Yeah." I ate there once in a while. They served good meatloaf and mashed potatoes. And one of the waitresses has headlamps like a Buick.

"So Smitty goes there and meets the guy. He told Smitty where the subjects were going to be and when, and what kind of shot he was looking for. He gave Smitty a hundred bucks cash and told him to meet him at the same place and time after he got the shot and had it developed."

"Did Smith develop it himself?"

"Yeah. He has a walk-in closet that he made into a darkroom. Does all his own work. Just throws his clothes into a pile in the corner. Looks kind of wrinkled all the time, but he don't care. He's a professional and knows you have to give up some things for the sake of business."

"Did he hand over the negative too?"

"Let's just say he gave up *a* negative along with the print. But you know us photographic artists. It ain't usual to take only one shot of anything. You always need at least one safety."

"And Smith kept the second."

"Yeah. And he says it's even better than the first."

"In what way?"

"He didn't say. But I'd guess you saw more, though that's hard to believe. You see plenty in this one."

"What about the guy who hired him? Did he say anything about him?"

"No, not particularly. They met again in the diner, Smitty gave him the picture and a negative and the guy gave him another hundred. Smitty had a good couple of days. But the best part was, Smitty said the guy liked his work and gave him some more jobs. Tailing the same broad. He did it for a couple of days but got nervous 'cause he thinks she may have made him."

"Seen him following, or maybe taking pictures?"

"Right."

"What did the guy look like? The guy in the diner."

"Just a guy. About forty. Dressed nice. Talked kind of funny. But that's all Smitty said about him. He was trying to protect his client. Didn't want the rest of us to horn in. A guy who pays two hundred bucks cash for an afternoon's work don't come along that often. Smitty didn't want the rest of us to know who he was. As if we'd poach on a colleague's business."

"Hard to believe."

"Ain't it?"

"Talked kind of funny: how, exactly?"

"He didn't say. Maybe what they call one of those speech things."

"Impediment?"

"That's it."

"Could it have been a foreign accent?"

"Could be. Like I said, he didn't say for sure."

"Well, that could be important. I need to talk to him. Do you have his address and phone number?"

"Well... I'm a businessman..."

"Another five." After all, it was Amanda's expense money. And I figured all this was worth the fifteen bucks of hers I'd just spent.

Flash gave me the number and address and then got up to leave.

"Remember me if you need anything more," he said. "Della can tell you I do good work, cheap."

"I'll keep it in mind. Do me a favor, though, and only send copies of this picture to your closest friends and relatives. I wouldn't want it to get around to the general public."

"It'll go no farther than my maiden aunts."

Who probably ran a pornography racket. But there was no way to protect The Honorable Amanda's modesty now. She was in what's known as the "public domain."

Chapter Twelve

I called Smith's number, but there was no answer. His apartment building wasn't too far away from my office, so I decided to drive over there and maybe catch him sleeping one off.

His apartment building was a depressing five-story affair just off Santa Monica Boulevard. It had started life as a hotel and was sliding gradually downhill toward its ultimate fate as a flophouse and an insurance fire. The sign above the door said "Valhalla Arms. Deluxe Apartments. Steam Heat."

It was hard to find a place to park because there were four or five cop cars outside along with an ambulance, and I had a funny feeling about why Hobart William Smith hadn't answered his phone. I finally found a place and walked back a couple of blocks and went in the front door. One of the cops recognized me; I had done him a favor once. He waved me through. "Kowalski's on the third floor," he said.

"Who got it?" I asked the cop.

"Some little guy in a wrinkled suit."

It figured.

I went up the dingy staircases toward the third floor. Kowalski was standing in the open door of apartment number three.

"Somehow I ain't surprised to see you," he said.

"I was in the neighborhood. What's with the 'ain't'? You, a college boy."

"Have to keep up appearances." This was nothing less than the truth. Most of the cops on the force could sound out Katzenjammer comics but didn't go much farther than that. They were suspicious of anyone who'd made it through high school, much less San Diego State.

"Who's the victim?" I already pretty much knew the answer but had to ask for form's sake.

"One Hobart William Smith, aka Smitty. Know him?"

"Not personally. He took some hotel-room photos of one of my clients, and I was coming here to find out who'd paid him. And if he had any others."

"Man with woman or woman with man? Or something else?"

"If you mean who's my client, it's a woman."

"Plain vanilla blackmail?"

"Pretty much. They haven't contacted us yet with any demands, but they sent a copy of the picture this guy took."

"Hot stuff?"

"Habanero meets Scotch Bonnet. What happened to him?"

"Forty-five. Third eye. Reminds me of the woman on the beach. Same MO."

"Anything in his pockets?"

"No, nor in his wallet. Just his driver's license. Should there be?"

"He got paid two hundred bucks a couple of days or so ago. Subtract the price of a jug of Four Roses and a couple of blue plate specials, and he should have had most of it left. This isn't any robbery, though. I'll bet your pension that whoever killed him was the same guy who hired and paid him. Getting the money back was a side benefit to the real motive. Or a cover-up."

"Something to do with the photos."

"That's the way it looks. Anybody hear the shot?"

"In this place? Only people who rent these rooms are related to those three Chinese monkeys. Hear No Evil and his cousins."

"I thought they were Japanese."

"Whatever."

"It'll be interesting if the ballistics match Lulu's."

"Won't it."

"How long ago did he get it?"

"Not very. The ME is still in there."

"Mind if I look around? I want to see his darkroom."

"Go ahead. Do I have to tell you not to touch anything?"

"One of these days you're gonna hurt my feelings."

The crime scene boys were still going over the apartment. I couldn't help feeling that it was a lousy place to die, steam heat or not. Everything was brown or dark green. And it's hard to think of anything more depressing than a Murphy bed. You could hardly see through the one window, and it had been painted shut. The only bright color came from a poster saying "Ski Mont Blanc." I was guessing that it came with the room. Smitty didn't seem like the ski-club type. Of course, you never know about people. Just about then, I was in the mood to hope that one time he had gone to France and learned to ski and met some luscious French woman over a few glasses of après-ski wine and spent the weekend in the sack with her, learning to say "Encore, s'il vous plait." Everyone deserves something like that at least once. Still, I had to admit he didn't look the type. Certainly not now.

Smitty was stretched out in the middle of the room, lying flat on his back and staring at the ceiling, his head in a patch of dried blood. There was a bullet hole in his forehead. And, yes, his suit was very wrinkled.

What Hamlet Said

I knew the ME. He was kneeling over the body, doing whatever it was he did. What a way to spend each day, I thought. Who'd want to do that job? And where did he graduate in his med school class? At the bottom would be my guess. Otherwise, he'd be playing golf instead of poking at stiffs.

"Hi, Doc. Any idea how long ago this happened?"

"Couple of hours, I'd guess. Somebody worked him over before they shot him. Poor guy. Whoever did it must have wanted something. What are you doing here?"

"It's my day off."

The door to Smitty's darkroom was open, so I went in, pulled on the light switch, and turned the closet red. The room was empty except for some bottles of solution, some trays, and some blank photo paper. Nothing hanging from the clothesline, nothing tacked to the bulletin board. And certainly there were no cameras on the shelf. The last earthly works of Hobart William Smith were all gone. So, too, his possessions.

It was surprising that none of his photos were tacked on the walls of his room. Granted, things like the picture of Amanda and Joachim might not be appropriate if Smitty's mother came to tea, but you'd think he'd have some of his more artistic landscapes and people portraits displayed. All of these guys take those kinds of pictures when they're not hiding in hotel closets or trying to keep their lenses from fogging up in some steam room. When they're not working, in other words. And they all got into the business because they actually liked the art of taking pictures. They only did the shabby things they did so they could keep doing what they liked. It was their métier. But aside from the patch of blood on the worn-out carpet, there'd never be another trace of Smitty once they removed the body. I'm guessing they would leave the rug. Then again, there were his missing photos. There had to be. So something of him might survive. What the Honorable Amanda would think about that was another story. She didn't strike me as the sympathetic type.

As I left, I said so long to Kowalski.

"Any clues about the headless yachtsman?" I asked.

"Nope. Anything new on Jimmy Hicks?"

"Nope."

"Our progress ain't progressing all that fast."

"Nope."

I went to the drugstore on the corner and called Amanda's number in Bel Air. For someone who claimed to have no money, she and the Honorable Freddie had a very fancy address. Maybe their house was owned by the British consulate, or maybe her idea of being broke was different from mine and most other people's.

She answered on the first ring. Waiting for Joachim to call, I imagined. Beautiful women don't pick up on the first ring unless they've got something going and are really into it.

"Amanda, it's Bruno Feldspar."

"Oh." Pause. "Hello. You did tell me that's not your real name, didn't you? I forget."

"That's what I told you."

"That's a relief."

"That's been said. Are you busy tonight?"

"You don't waste any time, do you?"

"That's also been said."

"As a matter of fact, I am… busy. Why?"

"There have been some developments. We should talk."

"Can it wait?"

"As far as I'm concerned, it can wait till doomsday."

"Because you're getting paid by the day?"

"No. Because fundamentally I don't really care whether that picture of you ever gets recovered or not. And if those pictures start to circulate, you could have the world's second-most famous smile, after the Mona Lisa."

"I thought I was gasping, not smiling."

"Maybe. I haven't studied it." That wasn't precisely true, but it's not good for the client to get too uppity—especially a client like The Honorable Amanda.

"Are you saying there are copies?"

"Not yet, as far as I know." There were, but she didn't need to know Flash Gordini was starting her fan club. "But I do know that the blackmailer has the negative. I don't suppose you've heard from him yet."

"No. Not a word." She paused to think things over. The possibility of multiple copies floating around were worrisome, even to someone with her brass—brass, I might add, that was a little suspect. I was pretty sure it was an act. It usually is. "I'm meeting Joachim tonight. Out on the *Lucky Lady*. Do you know it?"

"Very well."

"He loves to gamble."

"I believe that."

"Maybe you could join us out there. It might help to have you meet him. I can't think why, exactly. But it might. He knows about the blackmail letter and the picture, but doesn't seem too worried."

"That doesn't surprise me."

"No, I don't suppose it would. Anyway, we can find a few minutes to talk while he's losing his money."

"What time?"

"Nine. Maybe you could bring someone, too. Just so he doesn't get the wrong idea."

"About what?"

"Don't be coy. See you tonight."

Chapter Thirteen

The *Lucky Lady* was a gambling ship anchored permanently outside the three-mile limit and therefore beyond the reach of California gambling laws. Della's husband Perry, an ex-navy chief bosun's mate, ran a water taxi out there. He made the runs out and back eight hours a night, and there were other water taxis doing the same thing, twenty-four hours a day. There were three other ships anchored nearby, offering essentially the same service—all forms of gaming, dinner, dance bands complete with crooner and girl singer. But the main attraction were the tables—roulette, craps, blackjack—and slot machines—a couple of hundred of them, hard as that is to believe. And there weren't many standing idle. There was even chuck-a-luck, which was even a faster way to lose—one of those hourglass-shaped cages with three dice in them. It was an easy game to play—pick a combination, get it wrong, and pay up. You could get a turkey dinner for twenty-five cents. It would cost you more if you didn't want turkey, but not much more. And of course there were bars everywhere you looked, and girls in fishnet stockings and skimpy satin cheerleader outfits wandering through the crowd carrying trays of cigarettes and cigars. The girls all had smiles pasted on their faces, and some of them looked almost sincere. They were mostly actresses waiting for the big break. A few were actresses who had learned the big break wasn't coming. They were the ones whose smiles seemed less sincere.

Whenever there was a table that wasn't getting much action, management would send a lightly clad starlet-in-waiting to stand there and look available. Pretty soon the flower would attract the bees.

The *Lucky Lady* was the largest of the four gambling ships and could accommodate as many as three thousand suckers at a time. It would be a long swim back if there was a fire or something, because I was pretty sure they didn't have enough lifeboats. But here again, they were beyond the reach of California laws. From the side, the *Lucky Lady* looked like an aircraft hangar perched on a flat deck the size of a football field. The hull was from an old coastal steamer. The main-deck room was one giant room—the entire hangar—and that's where most of the action was. There was another big hall downstairs for bingo. And although bingo may seem like pretty lame entertainment, they'd pack five hundred people in there just for the chance to win twenty bucks. And I bet the thrill of yelling BINGO! in a crowded hall was worth even more than the money. And they weren't all just little old ladies. Some were little old men.

This whole operation was run by the local mob, of course. And the "manager" of the *Lucky Lady* was a wiseguy named Tony the Snail Scungilli—a scungilli being some sort of salt-water shellfish, hence the name.

I'd never met Tony, but I knew all about him—more than I needed to know, in fact. For one reason, his girlfriend was Catherine Moore, the devoted wife of Manny Stairs. She had known Tony before she married Manny, and she was a loyal friend to anyone she took a liking to. She saw no reason to break things off just because she'd stood through a ten-minute ceremony of some sort, during which she wasn't really paying attention. And Tony was broad-minded too. He liked the fact that Catherine was so tied into the movie business. Like a lot of California mobsters, Tony was a little star-struck. He even suggested to Catherine one time that he wouldn't mind if she got him a screen test, but when she laughed her hundred-decibel laugh, he dropped the idea and pretended that he was only joking. Tony was also the guy who'd been with Manny's first wife in that motor court in Joshua Tree. When she overdosed, he was the one who called it in and then took off—a knight "*sans peur et sans reproche.*"

So Catherine's ongoing relationship with Tony the Snail was all very adult, if that's the right word. If Manny suspected anything, he didn't mention it. He knew her well enough. He also knew California divorce laws. Besides, he loved her. He didn't just turn *a* blind eye to whatever she was doing, he turned both of them.

So, when the Honorable Amanda suggested I bring a date, there was only one good choice, since Myrtle was still in Yuma. And I happened to know that Manny Stairs was on location somewhere trying to keep a director from blowing up the budget on a western. So if she didn't already have another date, Catherine would most likely be available.

"Catherine? It's Riley."

"Hello, Sparky. Guess what I'm wearing."

"Are you alone?"

"Would that matter?"

"I guess not. Let me guess. Nothing."

"Wrong. A mink coat. Manny had it delivered this morning. But you'd be right about what's underneath. It feels so good."

"I'll bet. But I'm surprised you didn't have one already."

"I do. This is a different colored one."

"What are you doing tonight?"

"Nothing. Why? What do you have in mind?"

What Hamlet Said

"The usual."

"Mmm. My place or yours?"

"Neither one, at least not at first. I need to meet someone out at the *Lucky Lady,* and it would help if I had a date, especially a stunner like you." I had the feeling that seeing Catherine might arouse something in Amanda. Maybe a little competitiveness. Why did I care? No reason. Or, rather, the usual reason. "Are you and Tony still friendly?"

"Oh, sure. I'll wear my new mink. Maybe it'll give Tony some ideas the next time he wants to buy me a present. He tries to get by on the cheap every once in a while. He's a slow learner. Like his name."

"Sounds good. Wear something under the mink, though. I've got to keep my mind on business for a while."

"Smooth talker. I'll wear something extra special nice. Just for you. Like Chanel Number Five and my best pearls."

So that was settled. If you wonder why I felt no apprehension squiring a gangster's sometime girlfriend out to said gangster's floating casino, well, Catherine could talk all her men friends into anything, or out of anything. Besides, he'd assume that I was sort of on the fringes of the movie business and for that reason would almost be welcome. Tony knew, or thought he knew, that Catherine went out with a lot of men and that it was strictly business. And that was half true. She did, but it wasn't.

I arranged to meet Catherine at the Santa Monica Pier where Perry kept his water taxi. She'd have Manny's chauffeur, Jesus, drop her off. He would wait for her, no matter how late or early the hour. Like most men who ever met her, he was devoted to her and would keep her secrets. Catherine liked to say that some people were waiting for Jesus to come back, but she didn't have to wait.

Her Jesus was always right there. "Is that bad to say?" she'd ask, all innocence.

I wanted to have a word with Perry before going out to the *Lucky Lady*.

Perry was standing on the dock next to his boat. It was a sleek thirty-footer with an awning to shelter the sports from the spray. He could take twenty or more suckers out to the *Lucky Lady* in under ten minutes, if the sea was calm. As you would expect from an ex-chief bosun's mate, the boat was immaculate and gleaming.

Perry looked the part. Shaved head, suspicious squint, bulldog physique, Popeye forearms well covered with tattoos—anchors, mermaids, and women's names, not including Della's. "I met her later in life," he explained. "I offered to find a place for her name, but she said she didn't want to be lumped in with a bunch of broads. Can't blame her. She's a classy lady." Then he'd laugh.

"I know," I would say. It was a routine we usually went through after not seeing each other for a while. I liked him. And he and Della had done some favors for me and Myrtle that went way above and beyond the call of duty.

"Hello, Chief," I said.

"Hello, Chief," he responded. "Thinking of losing some money?"

"No. Strictly business. You remember Catherine Moore?"

"Tony's playmate? Big shot's wife? Real looker? Sure. Don't tell me you've joined that club."

"I'm a charter member. But she's just a friend. She's sort of a beard tonight."

"That's a new name for it."

Not if you've read Chaucer, I thought. But no sense bringing that up. Nobody likes a prig.

"On another matter, are you still in touch with Blinky Malone?"

"You need to ask?"

"Next time you see him, would you find out if he's done any work for some Europeans lately? Guys with heavy accents. Peter Lorre types. Passports, mainly."

"Like for new arrivals?"

"Yes."

"I know there's been a boom in Mexicans and your various yellow races. I don't know about those other guys, but I can find out."

"Good. Thanks. And ask him if he has any information at all about one Hobart William Smith." I could have asked Flash Gordini the same question, but I trusted Perry.

"Smitty? Word is someone shot him. Damn shame. He was a harmless little guy. He do some work for you?"

"Not directly. But I'm interested in anything Blinky might know about what he was up to. I know Blinky gets around; he might have heard something. Smitty took a picture of a client, and I'm pretty sure whoever killed him is the same guy who hired him. The guy probably had an accent of some kind."

"Accent again?"

"Could all be the same guy or set of guys."

"Okay, Chief. I'll check it out."

Just then, a Rolls limo pulled up and Catherine stepped out wearing her mink, looking like she smelled good all over.

"Here comes your beard," said Perry, grinning.

Chapter Fourteen

The sea was pretty calm that night, and Perry got us out there with his usual efficiency. There were a half dozen or more other couples in the taxi, and the women mostly wore sour expressions because the men they were with couldn't keep their eyes off Catherine. I couldn't blame them, really, and I smiled inwardly with self-satisfaction because I knew in perfect detail what they could only wonder about.

At the gangplank, we were all greeted by a gorilla in an evening jacket. His name was Vinnie. Of course.

"Hiya, Catherine," he said pleasantly.

"Hi, Sparky. You know my friend Riley?"

"No." He looked at me suspiciously, but I merely smiled, again knowing what he could only wish to know. He also knew she was only a dream as far as he was concerned, not only because he had the face of a retired prizefighter and was repulsive even to a sexual democrat like Catherine, but also because she was the boss's girlfriend and therefore out of reach, except in his imagination. It was enough to make you sigh, if you were the sighing type.

I nodded pleasantly to him and followed Catherine into the gigantic main salon.

What Hamlet Said

The huge room was under a cloud of tobacco smoke, and the noise was deafening. The band was playing *I Get a Kick Out of You,* and the slots were playing their own peculiar form of music. The dealers and croupiers were singing their mantras, and the suckers were groaning and occasionally shrieking with glee. People at the crowded bars were shouting drink orders. The crowd was not in any way fashionable, for the managers of the gambling ships knew that all money was green, and you didn't have to wear a tuxedo or a Balenciaga gown to lose it. There were more flat caps than top hats and quite a few sailors who really didn't care if they lost money, as long as they could do it in the company of beautiful waitresses and girl dealers. And if the band was good, so much the better. Besides, drinks were cheap and the Shore Patrol only came when called, which was rare, because Tony the Snail took care of his own security. You could see his goons stationed all throughout the room. They were conspicuous to one and all, and meant to be.

"Who're we looking for, Sparky?"

"A tall Englishwoman, blond, with a sort of damn-your-eyes attitude and a German aristocrat of some kind, also blond. And reportedly very handsome and charming."

"I'll bet that's them, over there talking to Tony."

And so it was. It was hard to tell what they were talking about, but it didn't seem like a friendly social chat—more like a professional conference, as if Tony and Joachim were discussing some kind of business deal.

Tony was dressed in his official "I am a mobster" outfit—dark shiny silk suit, dark shirt with matching tie, gleaming pointed Italian slip-ons. He was short and stout and wore a gigantic diamond ring on his pinky. His dark hair was well oiled and slicked back. In dress, style, stature, and demeanor he was the precise opposite of Bunny Finch-Hayden, although they both wore pinky rings. Joachim, on the other hand, was in a flawless tuxedo. His blond hair was cut short in an approved Prussian manner. He was tall and slim and straight as the proverbial ramrod. I noticed he was not wearing a monocle, but otherwise he might have come from central casting. As Catherine and I walked toward him, I could see the three-inch dueling scar on his left cheek. I had seen these things before. They were considered stylish among German aristocrats who acquired them in dueling societies at their universities. They fought with real swords but wore masks that exposed only the cheeks, so in my mind the scars were slightly bogus badges of honor. I'd have been more impressed if they actually tried to kill each other, instead of just trying to give and receive a signifier of social position. But upper-class Krauts thought they were the ultimate in ornaments. Of course, an African with a bone in his nose thinks he's a fine-looking fellow too. People get funny ideas about style. But if you looked closely at pictures of Hitler and his gang, you'd notice that none of them had these scars. Well, that told you a lot.

Standing next to Joachim, Amanda was wearing a slinky silk number, white and clinging, low-cut front and back. If she was wearing underwear, it was only below the waist. Her chin was elevated slightly, although, given her height, she didn't have to do that to look down on Tony the Snail. She looked as cool as a trout and about as friendly.

"Tony thinks wearing black makes him look thinner," whispered Catherine. "Do you think it does?"

"You'd know better than I."

She giggled.

"I know. Why is it I'm married to one short fat guy and going out with another one? Why can't I find someone tall, dark, and handsome like you, Sparky?"

What Hamlet Said

"You already have."

"I know. It was just one of those whatchamacallit questions."

"Rhetorical?"

"Smooth talker."

Tony the Snail suddenly went off to do whatever he did. He hadn't noticed Catherine or me, and he disappeared through the crowd toward the end of the main salon and the rear of the ship, where he had his offices, the bedrooms for himself and his men—and the strongroom where they kept the cash and various valuables people had turned over when they ran out of cash.

"It's like a high-class pawn shop in there," said Catherine. "Believe me, I know."

We walked up to Amanda and Joachim. If they were delighted to see us, they didn't show it, although Joachim looked at Catherine appreciatively. Well, who could blame him?

We went through the usual introductions, and Joachim was charming, as advertised. He kissed Catherine's hand, and she took it like a duchess, not at all impressed by Teutonic gallantry. I shook hands with Joachim, who quite obviously knew who I was.

"What kind of name is Feldspar?" he said, smiling pleasantly. "It sounds Jewish. But you don't look Jewish."

"I'm not."

"Feldspar is his *nom de guerre*, Joachim," said Amanda.

"Ah. Good. We will get on better that way, I think, although I personally have nothing against them. And I understand that it would be hard to be a Jew these days."

"Less hard here than in other places," I said.

"You mean Germany, of course. I agree. No one likes them there."

"It's been in the news."

"Yes. It's too bad, really. It's not good for anyone. They're like the annoying boy in the playground who's always following you around and pestering you about something until finally you have to beat him up. And the funny thing is, that only makes him want to be friends even more. Which of course makes you want to beat him up again and even harder."

"Of course."

"Anybody else would see that they weren't wanted and find some other place to go. Not them. They come cringing back no matter what you do to them. It brings out the worst in us, I'm afraid. That sort of submissiveness stimulates sadistic responses in some of our people. Why do you think that is?"

"Some of your people are not very nice?"

"You make a joke. But perhaps you are right. On the other hand, perhaps it is not a German characteristic at all, but a universal, human one."

"Could be. Mark Twain said God invented the human race because he was disappointed in the monkey. He could just as easily have said it the other way around."

"Ha, ha! That's a good one. I must remember it. But you know, the Jews are an odd people—always on the outside, always wanting to be in. Who would want to live like that? Even that Jew Groucho Marx said he wouldn't want to be a member of any club that would accept *him*. Ha. Very good. But the Jews *do* want to be a member of a club that does *not* want them. Some of them think they are really in the club, that they are real Germans, because they have lived there and speak a kind of German. But they're not. I feel sorry for them. Things are not going well in Germany for them."

"So I've heard."

"Yes, it is a great shame. Synagogues getting burned down. Shop windows being broken. Such a waste. I'm afraid it's only going to get worse. None of that would happen if they just went away. But they don't." He paused and studied me, smiling pleasantly. "Let's change the subject, shall we? Politics can be so tiresome. Don't you agree?"

"To talk about, yes."

"Good. So... you are a private detective, like the ones in the films."

"Not entirely. For one thing, I don't smoke."

"Good. I approve. Very bad for the health. And you don't seem like a tough guy, if you don't mind my saying so."

"No. I never even beat up an annoying kid in the playground."

"Ha. Ha. That's a good one. Do you carry a gun?"

"Sometimes, but only when I'm planning to shoot someone. Other times, it's uncomfortable and ruins the cut of my jacket." I figured this was as good a time as any to use the line.

"Don't let him fool you, Fritz," said Catherine to Joachim. "He keeps a bottle of Bourbon in his desk drawer, just like in the movies." Catherine had been watching the interplay between Joachim and me. And she knew men; she recognized that Joachim was trying to establish some sort of dominance. It's sometimes called dick-measuring. Some guys just can't help themselves. But she wasn't having it. "And I've seen him blackjack some waterfront guys, until they cried for the mommas they never had. Fact is, he doesn't take anything from anybody. He just doesn't make a big deal out of it."

"Ah," he said, looking at me with more respect, and not at all offended by being called Fritz. Well, coming from Catherine, a man will be happy to be called almost anything.

"Well, I feel better," he said. "It seems you were being modest, Mr. Feldspar. At least we are back on script. And, speaking of blackjack, I think I will give the tables a try. I have the feeling the cards will go my way for a change. And I think Amanda has something to talk to you about." He turned to Catherine. "Would you like to come with me and bring me luck?"

"Why not?"

"Where'd you get her?" said Amanda, when the other two had sauntered off.

"She is the wife of the most powerful film producer in this town. She's also the sometime girlfriend of that short, fat, very dangerous goombah you and Joachim were talking to before we showed up."

"Oh."

"Yes."

"So she's not your girlfriend?"

"We have a history. We're friends."

"I see. Is the fat goombah the one who pushes the buttons?"

"No. He's the guy who flips the switch on the guys who push the buttons."

"He doesn't look so dangerous."

"None of them do. Most of them look like Knights of Columbus. And most of them are." I was pretty sure she didn't know who the Knights of Columbus were, but she got the point.

"Rather a nice mink coat, she had," said Amanda. "Do you think she's very beautiful?"

"I don't have to think about it."

"Rather exaggerated, though."

"That's one word for it."

"Yes, I suppose it is. Well, thank you for bringing her. Joachim will not get any wrong ideas after seeing her. Maybe *about* her, though. That's something else." She sighed a little. "Well, as far as that's concerned, I'm beginning to think it doesn't matter much." Was the sigh a signal? Hard to say. Maybe just the universal expression of aristocratic ennui. But not a pose. It was legitimate.

"Bloom coming off the rose of romance?" I asked. I figured, what could it hurt?

"Doesn't it always?"

"'Aye, in the very temple of delight, veiled melancholy has her sovereign shrine.'"

"Who said that?"

"Keats."

"The poet. I've never really read him. I'm impressed."

"You were meant to be."

"Most girls of our class in England aren't educated. We're only taught what's done and what's not done, and how to do the one and how to avoid the other. We know everything about those two subjects and almost nothing about anything else. For an LA private eye, you are surprisingly well educated."

"Not really. But I read a lot. If I had more business, I'd have less time to memorize lines to use with beautiful women. So I think of it as coming out even. Less money, more lines."

"And more women? Well, of course you won't say, one way or the other. Far better to let me think whatever I like. Much better tactics."

"Tactics?"

"Don't be coy."

"You've already said that."

"Did I? I'm sorry. I'd like to be more original."

She paused and looked at me almost with sincerity. There was something lacking there, something missing in her life, apparently. It wasn't hard to spot. There was a lot of it going around. And I wasn't being melodramatic or romantic. Nor was I seeing something that wasn't really there. She was sad about something. Or rather melancholy, as the poet said. That was as plain as the fact that she wasn't wearing underwear, at least on top.

"I heard from the blackmailer today," she said, finally.

"How much does he want?"

"Fifty thousand."

"Ambitious."

"It might as well be fifty million."

"Did he call, or write?"

She reached in her silver handbag and pulled out a letter. The demand was made from words cut from newspaper headlines and pasted on a sheet of plain typing paper.

"GET FIFTY THOUSAND. SMALL BILLS. WE'LL SEND INSTRUCTIONS."

"Rather theatrical, I think," she said.

"Yes. The 'small bills' suggests he's seen too many movies. Do you have the envelope it came in?"

"No. I threw it away. It was just plain."

"Can I keep this?"

"Of course. I won't have any trouble remembering what it says. You said you had something to talk about."

"Yes. I found the guy who took the picture. Unfortunately, the guy who paid him to do it got to him first. Put a bullet in his brain."

For once, the Honorable Amanda registered completely unprotected emotion. She was scared.

"My God," she said. "This is more serious than I thought."

"I agree. I searched his rooms. All his prints and negatives were stolen, along with the two hundred bucks the blackmailer paid him. So if there were other negatives of you and your boyfriend, he's got them now."

"How likely is that?"

"One hundred percent. Photographers never take just one snap. And more than one snap means more than one negative."

"And what does *that* mean?"

What Hamlet Said

"It means that even if you paid the fifty thousand for the first set, the blackmailer has another, and maybe more than that, in his drawer; and *that* means you'll be getting more mail in the future."

"God. What a mess. What about the police? Do they know?"

"They know about the murder. And they know about the connection to blackmail. I didn't tell them about you. And they won't ask until they decide it's important to their investigation. Which they'll come around to soon enough."

"What shall we do?"

"Decide whether you want to be a second Wellington and tell them to publish and be damned, or keep investigating and hope we get the guy before it all goes to hell in some way we can't predict. Your call."

"No. Keep going. I can't have this all get out. There are reasons..."

There usually were. Well, as I said, it was her call.

Joachim and Catherine were coming back. He was looking very unhappy. He had lost, apparently, and it hadn't taken long.

"Oh, dear," said Amanda. "He's lost again. He'll be in a foul mood."

"Looks pretty unhappy already."

"Yes. Call me tomorrow, will you?"

"Sure."

"I... I'm going to... I'm going to need a friend. Even at twenty-five dollars a day."

"You must not have heard—you can't put a price on friendship." Weak, I know, but somehow appropriate just then.

She smiled sadly and squeezed my hand. And for the first time, her expression showed that the Honorable Amanda was not anything like what she pretended to be. Well, who is?

Chapter Fifteen

The next morning, I was reminded of something Hobey had said.

"Good morning, Sparky," she said, fragrantly. "What time is it?"

"Seven."

"That's good. I should leave in half an hour. How shall we spend it?"

And in half an hour she did leave, smiling. But then she was usually smiling. I didn't take much credit for that. Not much, anyway. Jesus was waiting for her in the Rolls.

"He's such a dear. Very patient, and he doesn't mind sleeping in the car. Well, it's a Rolls. And he's used to it."

"Don't tell me that. I'll get jealous."

"Smooth talker. Best of all, though, Jesus can keep quiet in two languages."

I had heard something like that before—about some German general of the past. Von Moltke, I think it was. He spoke six languages and rarely said anything in any of them. Whether Catherine got the line from reading history or made it up herself, was just a guess. But I had a pretty good idea.

After she left I put on my bathing suit and took my coffee cup down to the pool. Hobey was there alone, reading.

What Hamlet Said

"Good morning," I said.

"For you, yes. I thought I saw Catherine leaving a few minutes ago. At least I think it was her. But as the poet said, 'Was it a vision or a waking dream?'"

"Some of both, I suppose. We met one of my clients out on the *Lucky Lady* last night, and Catherine wanted to bunk over rather than go all the way back to Malibu."

"Yes, it is rather a long way. Would you say twenty miles?"

"Twenty-one. Besides, traffic is bad at one A.M. What are you reading? *Gone With the Wind*?"

"Just the opposite. It's called *Miss Lonelyhearts*. By a guy I know, Nathaniel West. He's a fellow sufferer in the screenwriting trade. Also a failed novelist and so a twice-told confederate. The book came out a couple of years ago and immediately disappeared. Drop an anvil in the ocean and it might make a momentary splash before it's gone—gone with the waves, to coin a phrase. But at least it makes a splash. A book that disappears never leaves a trace. But it's quite an interesting little novel. Seventy pages or so, unlike Mrs. Mitchell's door stop. About a guy who's driven insane by his job as an advice columnist. He can't stand the suffering and misery of the letters he receives. One little girl writes that she'd like to go out with boys, but she was born without a nose and no one will ask her. Stuff like that. I remembered the book after Hedda got her new job. I'm not in the least worried about her sanity, though. She is immune to thought."

"Sounds like a comedy."

"The book? It is, actually. Of a kind. Very dark. Listen to this. The main character is talking about his fiancée—'She was like a kitten whose soft helplessness makes one ache to hurt it.'"

"Hysterical. You should try to work something like that into your script."

"You may scoff, but there's something disturbingly accurate there, about the human psyche."

"Some, maybe. Personally, I have nothing against kittens, soft or otherwise. But I did have a conversation with a German army officer last night, and he said something similar about the Jews in Germany. Basically, it's unfortunate for all concerned, but they are only getting what they deserve. A lot of them feel they have it coming."

"Yes, I understand. Their submissive helplessness makes them contemptible, and contempt turns into murderous rage among the many-headed, as Wodehouse might say. It's not quite the same thing that West was talking about. Slightly more primitive. But it's in the same category of emotion, in some way. Not sure how. But I see it. Empathy's evil dark side. Speaking of our soon-to-be enemies, any news about your sinister foreigners?"

"No. But I'm thinking of going over to San Pedro today to look around a little."

"Good. Please keep me informed."

"So you think there's going to be a war?"

"As sure as the missing nose on that little girl's face."

"I hope not. But you're probably right. How's the script going?"

"Badly. I can't seem to make them see that Rhett Butler is the only possible character who's at all interesting. I think Humphrey Bogart would make an excellent Rhett. What do you think?"

"You know best."

He looked up and made a wry face. Hedda was coming down the steps from Hobey's cabana.

"And speaking of Miss Lonelyhearts, here she comes in the flesh. Didn't I tell you the mornings do not become Electra?"

It would have been ungallant of me to say anything. But watching Hedda coming over to the pool, I had to agree that Hobey had a point. On the other hand, I had seen her at her best, and that was not at all bad. Mysterious, these transformations.

"You wouldn't care to mix me a drink before you go?" he asked. "It would be a kindness."

"Sure. Your soft helplessness makes me ache to pour gin."

"Make it a double, will you? I don't want to face the morning alone."

After making Hobey a tall drink that was gin with only a passing reference to tonic, I got dressed and thought about going to the office. Driving there I came to the conclusion that so far, I had been trying to manage Amanda's case the easy way—find the photographer and, one way or another, find out who had hired him. Now that Smitty was dead, I'd have to do it the official Sherlock way —by figuring things out, starting with motive and opportunity, the classic twins of detective fiction, and real life too. Obviously, the motive for blackmail was money. Wasn't it? Otherwise, why bother? Well, that was as good a working premise as any. So, was the blackmailer someone who just needed cash and saw an opportunity, or was it more professional, a shakedown as part of an ordinary criminal enterprise? It seemed unlikely that it was professional. The whole operation had the feel of amateurs. That business about the newspaper clippings and small bills tipped it off. Fifty one-thousand-dollar bills are a lot easier to carry and conceal than a suitcase full of ones, twos, and fives. And a professional criminal has no trouble fencing large denominations. Hell, any friendly bank will break them for you, no charge, and guys like Tony the Snail had lots of friendly bankers. Besides, to guys like Tony, this was small potatoes, hardly worth the effort and risk. He was running an enterprise bringing in millions, some of it legitimate. He wouldn't be bothered. So it seemed safe to assume that it was one person, or at most a small group, and unrelated to the people who really knew what they were doing.

The questions then became: Who had provided Smitty with the information about where the lovers were trysting? How did they know which hotel to tell Smitty to stake out? And why did Joachim —a man of the world, who surely knew better—why did he reserve a first-floor room that made it child's play for Smitty to get the pictures? That led to the obvious question with an apparently obvious answer: Who was the one person who certainly knew where they would be and also seemed to need money? Joachim.

That would be too simple, though, wouldn't it? Maybe. But there was the Occam's razor theory that said the simplest explanation was usually the best. Amanda said that Joachim was a gambler who regularly lost. Maybe he was in debt to Tony the Snail—not a comfortable place to be. Maybe that's what that serious-looking business discussion was about. But did Joachim need money so badly that he'd resort to blackmail? Wouldn't he think it beneath him, somehow? Maybe not. One of his predominant emotions seemed to be lofty contempt for those beneath him. And all but a handful of people in the world were beneath him, in his view— probably even the Führer and his various henchmen with bad breath. Surely a Prussian aristocrat would look down on that crowd. What had Hitler been in the war? A corporal? Perhaps that attitude would also translate into an equal contempt for the law. Maybe Joachim had the übermensch complex and felt he could do anything he liked. But didn't he know that Amanda had very little, if any, money? Hadn't she said something about that to him? She'd made no secret of it to me, but then I was involved in her case and needed the facts. She might have been pretending to Joachim. She certainly had the style and the attitude to pull off the role of a wealthy diplomat's aristocratic wife. And Smitty had told Flash

What Hamlet Said

Gordini that his "client" had an accent, or rather, talked kind of funny. What could that mean? A lot of things. And why murder Smitty? He was harmless. He was used to getting sleazy assignments and keeping his mouth shut. You didn't risk the gas chamber for blackmail. But murder was another matter. But didn't foreign diplomats have immunity? Did that extend to cultural attachés, and if so would that make someone like Joachim a little less reluctant to do away with someone like Smitty—a nondescript, unimportant loner—a grown-up, annoying kid from the playground? Maybe Joachim, the Prussian soldier, wouldn't think much of shooting a pathetic loser like Smitty, a loss to no one.

Flash said Smitty met his client at El Greco's Diner on Sepulveda. That would be a good place to ask a few questions. Just then, a blue plate special of meatloaf and mashed potatoes sounded pretty good. It makes a good breakfast, and everyone knows breakfast is the most important meal of the day. So I decided to skip going to the office and headed for El Greco's. I also made a mental note to call Kowalski. I was interested in whether the bullet that killed Smitty had come from the same gun that killed Lulu. In other words, was all this stuff tied together somehow? And out of curiosity, what caliber were the German military handguns? Lugers, were they? Yes, I thought so. And lastly, what the hell had happened to Jimmy Hicks?

I don't think it's a law that all diners have to be owned by Greeks, but they all seem to be. And, as its name El Greco suggested, this one was too. His name was Stavros Katavalous. I knew him casually, because we both followed LA's minor league baseball team, the Angels. I'd see him out there during day games. We both liked to sit on the first base side and drink beer. Being a restaurateur of a kind, he wouldn't eat hot dogs, but I knew what they were made of, and I didn't care. I'd always get two, one with mustard and one with ketchup. I liked them both ways. I left the great debate over which was proper to other people to worry about. The Angels were pretty good, but I didn't care about that either. That wasn't the point of going. The point of going was to be there. And the point of being there was to be there, nothing more, nothing less.

I went in, and Stavros greeted me like a Parisian maître d'. He led me to a booth and gave me a menu. We both knew there was nothing different on it, but it was the way things should be done, and Stavros did things that way. It was midmorning, so the breakfast crowd was gone and the lunch people hadn't arrived yet. It was a good time to chat up the waitresses, and one in particular—the one who reminded you of a Buick's headlights. Her name was Jessie. She might have been Della's kid sister. They had the same outlook on life and the same taste in hair color, although the Health Department made Jessie wear a hair net and a kind of nurse's hat. Jessie could still arouse impure thoughts, though. She hadn't let herself go, despite the close proximity of so many pies and cakes. And her uniform dress was past its prime and was limp, so it clung to her and didn't disguise much. She knew it, too.

"Hello, honey," she said. "Where have you been all my life?"

"Looking for you. But every time I come in here, you're too busy to give me the time of day."

She looked at her watch.

"Ten thirty," she said. "*Now* what's your excuse?"

"I've been busy getting divorced. And I'm sorry, but I forgot the diamond necklace I promised you. I'll bring it next time."

"That's nice. Is it real?"

"As real as my devotion. Sit down. I'll buy you a cup of coffee."

"Honey, I'm a waitress in a diner. If you think you can sweet-talk me by buying me coffee, you need some new material."

What Hamlet Said

"Point taken. But I don't suppose you'd do me a favor now, would you?"

"Depends on how long it'll take."

"Just a minute or two."

"You sound like my ex–old man. But things are slow now. What's up?"

"Did you ever see a little guy named Hobart William Smith? Used to go by 'Smitty.' Always looked sort of rumpled and disheveled, like he slept in his clothes. Might have been carrying a camera now and then."

"Bad tipper?"

"Probably."

"Is he the guy who got shot in the flophouse?"

"Yep. Although to be accurate, he got shot in the forehead. It just happened in the flophouse."

"Smart guy, eh?"

"I apologize. But did you ever see him?"

"Yeah. I recognized his picture in the paper. Kind of a shame. He came in here now and then. Like someone else I know. What'd he do to get himself shot?"

"Got in with the wrong people. Speaking of which—did he ever meet anybody here?"

"Most of the time, he was alone. Liver and onions was his usual."

"Good to know. But...?"

"But he did sit with some guy a couple of times. Just last week."

"What'd the other guy look like?"

"Better than Smitty. But that ain't hard. My ex looks better than Smitty, and he's no maiden's dream."

"I heard you were getting back with him."

"I might, when he gets out."

"But you didn't notice anything special about this other guy? Can you describe him at all? Did you hear his voice? I think he may have had a foreign accent. Any scars? On the face, maybe?"

"No. None of that. At least I don't remember anything like that." I figured that Jessie would probably remember someone like Joachim. She would notice a good-looking man, and if she didn't remember the guy Smitty was with, I was pretty sure it wasn't Joachim. "The guy left Smitty to pay the bill. That's how I remember, 'cause, like I said, Smitty was a bad tipper. But Smitty must've come into some money, 'cause he paid with a twenty. Left a quarter."

"But the guy was well dressed? Looked respectable?"

"I'd say so. But that's all I can remember. Is he the guy who shot Smitty?"

"Could be."

"Damn shame. Sorry I can't remember more. This place gets busy, you know."

"Sure."

"So... are you going to just sit there looking ugly, or are you gonna order something?"

"Would you recommend the meatloaf?"

She rolled her eyes. "Smart guy," she said. "Mashed and mixed veggies?"

"Got anything else besides mixed veggies?"

"Nope."

"Then I'll have that. How's the cherry pie?" I looked at her suggestively. It was a game we played.

She just looked back and smiled and batted her eyelashes. She had a sweet smile.

"Nice try," she said.

It was a game we played.

Chapter Sixteen

After breakfast, I drove over to San Pedro. I didn't need dessert, but strudel was in my future. I drove by the house on the side street that used to be Acme Management's office, but the house was obviously still empty. You could tell, because the front windows were being broken by a couple of urchins throwing rocks.

"You boys see anyone hanging around this house lately?" I asked them.

"Who wants to know?"

"You see anyone else?"

"Smart guy, eh?"

"Yep, and a smart guy with a badge."

At that, they took off down an alley. One of them turned around on the way and considered throwing his last rock at me, but thought better of it. But it was safe to assume that Acme's birds had not returned to the coop.

I drove over to Joe's Bakery. Magda was in the front room, waiting on a table full of guys who had just come off the four-to-noon shift at the docks and were having coffee, sliced nut roll, and tumblers of Joe's homemade plum brandy. Magda sometimes made the nut roll with poppy seeds, but I didn't like that quite as much.

"Riley!" she said. "How nice to see you! How is our Mirta?"

"Fine. She's away for a few weeks."

"Ah! Poor Riley. You must be lonely. Come. Sit. Eat. The nut roll is fresh. The pogacha is fresh. The strudel is fresh." These things usually were fresh, since nothing Magda made lasted more than a day. It was either eaten or sold. Each day, she had to start again, and she was happy about that. Then she whispered "The plum brandy is not fresh at all. It's just right. Joe knows what he's doing."

I sat down at an empty table. The four guys looked over and were not friendly, even though Magda had made a fuss over me. Well, this was their club. They naturally resented outsiders, even those who knew the owners. They were a rough-looking bunch, but stevedores generally don't look like characters from an Oscar Wilde play.

"What do you like?" said Magda, looking for all the world like everyone's grandmother. She was stout and had rosy cheeks and blue eyes and snow-white hair, and she smelled of fresh bread. And her teeth were so white and straight, you might have thought they were dentures.

"I would like some strudel, please. And coffee, and maybe a little plum brandy on the side."

"Good. It's good for you. I tell Joe you're here. Have you heard our Nicky is going to join the Navy? I don't like it, but he's a big boy now. Maybe they make him a cook. I get your food. Sit. Think of Mirta and be happy."

Thinking of "Mirta" was easy enough to do. I suppose I should have felt some sort of guilt, because I had not exactly been faithful to her these last few days. And if I was honest with myself, I was planning to call Amanda Billingsgate later today with the idea of being even less faithful. That picture had a way of sticking in your memory. But in all honesty, none of my adventures, if you could call them that, meant anything at all. I know that's the cad's or the guilty husband's usual response. But I felt I was on firm ground, because I knew for a fact that at least in Catherine's and Ethel's cases, our trysts meant even less to them than they did to me, if that was possible. Amanda was something else, maybe, and I would proceed carefully, making sure not to entrap her with my fatal charm. But she had said she'd never been in love with anyone, and I could believe that. Was I going to be the one to break the spell, to melt her aristocratic heart? I hoped not. And what's more, I didn't believe for a second that I would. If she had a heart in the usual sense of the word, she hadn't wasted it on her husband or her lover and on who knew how many others, and she wasn't about to waste it on a twenty-five-dollar-a-day private eye. Was she? Not hardly, as they say out West, that place east of LA. Besides, she had asked me to call her today. She needed a friend. I was just being obliging to a client. No harm in that. Right?

So I could sit there and think of "Mirta" with an almost-clear conscience. We weren't married or engaged and only admitted to being half in love with each other. But it was not a subject I wanted to dwell on too long, and I was glad when Joe emerged, carrying two glasses of plum brandy. He sat down and put a glass in front of me.

"A little of this will solve your problems," he said. "Too much will create them."

"Moderation."

"Yes. The most difficult trick of all," he said.

"Yes." I remembered Bunny quoting Doctor Johnson about moderation, but I didn't recall exactly what he'd said. Something along the same lines, though.

The brandy was smooth and sweet and went down easily. It would not be hard to have too much.

"So," he said. "What brings you? Strudel?"

"Partly. And partly curiosity."

"Ah. I don't have to tell you what happened to the cat."

"No. I know."

"So?"

"I had an interesting meeting the other night... with an official from the German consulate. A colonel. Very Prussian." Joe raised his eyebrows slightly. "And I remembered something you'd said before."

"What was that?"

"That some people back in your old country would be... receptive to the German point of view, if war came."

"That is one way to put it." He said this quietly and glanced toward the other table. "Many Germans are Catholics. Especially in the south. So that is one thing. And sometimes we have similar ideas about how things should be done. That is another thing. So some of our people find them sympathetic. Is that the word?"

"Yes."

"So. That's all there is to it."

"Hitler?"

He shrugged. "Who is perfect?"

"What about the Jews?"

"What about them? You know as well as I do that no one in Europe likes them. That is not news."

"How about here, in this country?"

"How do you mean?"

"Are those same kinds of attitudes prevalent?"

"Prevalent? Meaning?"

"Do many people here feel the same way?"

"Well, that is difficult to say. But what is not difficult to say is that people do not leave their ideas behind when they move to another country, especially to a country where so many of their countrymen are already living. When Magda and I and the children came here, did we open an Italian restaurant? No. A Chinese laundry? No. A Jewish delicatessen? No. We brought our bread and pastry recipes with us from the old country. It is the same with ideas. They travel easily."

"About independence?"

"Is that not an idea?"

"Yes."

"As I said. Ideas travel better than wine. They are not affected by time or the motion of a ship, like some wines."

"Or plum brandy?"

"Plum brandy does not have to travel. We make it here. Like this strudel Magda brings us. Did she tell you Nicky has joined the Navy?"

"Yes. What do you think?"

"I hope they make him a cook and that there is no war."

"I hope so too."

"There," said Magda, laying her heavenly pastries before us both. "Eat. Eat. Good for you."

"Joe, how in the hell do you stay so fit, living amidst all these wonderful foods?" I said.

"Like I said. Moderation."

That was about as much as I was going to get from Joe. But it was enough to figure that if the Germans wanted to sow a little trouble in some as-yet-undefined way, they'd probably find a receptive audience among some of Joe's countrymen. And I wondered again just what a cultural attaché did. I was going to ask Joe about the Ustache. I wondered if Joe had heard anything about them, whether they had been trying to raise money in the community. But Joe seemed only too well aware of the other table.

And I thought they were only too well aware of me. It was a subject for another time.

I went back to the office to make some calls. Della was not working today, so there would be privacy of a kind, if you didn't count Mavis, the telephone exchange girl. She enjoyed staying up to date on everyone's business.

First call, the cops.

"Kowalski, Homicide."

"Ed? Bruno. Any news?"

"The Angels dropped a double-header. That horse Della gave me faded in the backstretch. And Katharine Hepburn ain't getting the part. That's all the news I got. You?"

"I'm not sure I have anything."

"Call your doctor. They can usually tell."

"What did ballistics say about the bullet that got Smitty?"

"They said it was a thirty-eight."

"Not a forty-five."

"Nothing gets past you, does it? No. Not a forty-five. Which is disappointing to us flatfeet who like things to be connected and neat. That suggests either two separate, unrelated murders, or one murderer with two different guns. My money's on the first."

"That's why you're the rising star."

"Exactly. But it does make life more complicated. The only similarity between this and the Lulu babe is the location of the wound. Nothing else. And here's a flash for your memoirs—people who get killed by a gunshot quite often have holes in their foreheads. It's a common wound and it's pretty much always fatal, especially when the bullet comes out the back and keeps on going. That's what we professionals call a dead guy."

"I've got a question for you. What's the caliber of a German army sidearm? A Luger?"

What Hamlet Said

"Or a Walther. Or a few others, I guess. It's called a nine-millimeter parabellum. That's the most common."

"What's that in American?"

"A little over point thirty-five caliber."

"Close to a thirty-eight."

"Pretty close. But maybe not if you have calipers and microscopes. But I'm just a cop, not a ballistics expert. I will say that the bullet was pretty well deformed. Smitty had a pretty hard noggin, apparently, plus it hit the wall behind."

"Oh?"

"Why do you ask?"

"I might have something going on. But I'm not sure."

"That's what the old guy said to the chorus girl. Care to share your theory?"

"It doesn't rise to that level yet, speaking of the old guy. But you might ask the ballistics boys if the bullet could have come from a nine-millimeter, instead of a thirty-eight."

"I can do that. But like I said, the bullet was pretty well deformed. It went through Smitty without passing Go."

"And the killer got the two hundred bucks."

"Ha. Good one. Anyway, the bullet ended up clanging off an I-beam wall joist. They don't build flop houses like this anymore. It's a solid building. That could be why nobody heard the shot—that, and not wanting to. Lots of steel and fireproof asbestos. When the owners decide to burn that place down, they'll have a hell of a job on their hands. A guy with a can of gas and some rags won't fool anyone, much less the insurance investigators."

"We all have our troubles."

"One other thing: I get where you're going with that nine-millimeter question. You're thinking—maybe a foreign connection?"

"It occurred to me."

"Well, bear in mind that a thirty-eight police special is about the easiest handgun to get hold of, legally or otherwise. So why would someone contemplating homicide, some shadowy foreigner in your scenario, risk using his personal army sidearm—a gun that might be traceable—when he could pay a few bucks for a thirty-eight in any pawn shop and throw it away when he was finished with it?"

"You have a point."

"The murder was obviously planned. Not a spur-of-the-moment crime of passion. Smitty wasn't the kind to inspire some Othello-like rage. So the guy had plenty of time to get a cheap pistol."

"Othello! Impressive reference."

"English 101, San Diego State."

"Any news on the headless floater?"

"Nope. Still on ice at the morgue. His condition is not expected to improve. What's more, there's nothing new on Jimmy Hicks, and I'm beginning to think the two might have something in common. Like being the only son of the same mother."

"I'm afraid of that too."

"That's about it. Good news about Katharine Hepburn, eh? Couldn't see her in it. Don't be a stranger."

He hung up.

Next, I called Bill Patterson at the FBI office. He was out, so I left a message.

Then it was Amanda's turn.

She didn't answer on the first ring. What's the song? All alone by the telephone? Not Amanda. Not this time, anyway.

"Amanda? It's Bruno."

"Oh. Hello." She paused. "Is there something else I can call you? That name sounds so... ethnic. It's really quite dreadful."

"Well, it was supposed to sound sort of Semitic. The studio gave it to me when I was an aspiring matinee idol. In this town, being

Jewish can be a help." Actually, the name was Ethel's idea, not the studio's. The studio might have changed "Riley Fitzhugh" to Fitzhugh Riley, thinking it would be more sophisticated. But as the saying goes, it was much of a muchness and a detail that didn't need explaining. And the funny thing was that the actors who actually were Jewish, and had obvious Jewish names, were given All-American names. A Goldfarb became a Smith. But of course everyone in town knew who was who and what was what. But while my *nom de guerre* didn't do much for my acting career, it was something of a help in generating business from the producers and studios. So I kept it.

"Yes, but those days of youthful stardom are over," she said. "What does your girlfriend, what's her name, call you?"

"Sparky. But she calls every man she knows Sparky. It's easier than remembering names, probably. And she's not my girlfriend. Just a beard for that night." That at least brought a laugh. She had told me she was uneducated, so I doubt she got the Chaucer reference. But it was an easy joke without it. "But if you like, you can call me Riley. That's my real name."

"Irish," she sniffed. "Almost as bad."

"How about Rhett?"

"Better. And I'll be your Scarlett."

"The unattainable dream girl?"

"Is that what she is? I thought she and Rhett finally get together. Of course it ends badly. Everything always does, you know."

"I only read the first few chapters. I'm saving the rest for my golden years."

"Take my word for it—everything always ends badly."

Apparently, Amanda was back to being the old Amanda. That scared, needy girl from the night before had recovered her sangfroid, if that's the right word.

"You asked me to call you today," I said.

"I know."

"Well?"

"I think we should talk."

"Okay."

"Not over the phone. I'm not sure it's safe."

"Really?"

"This house belongs to the British government. Who knows what sort of listening systems they've installed."

"All right. What are you doing for dinner?"

"Having it with you."

"Good. What would you say to the Polo Lounge?" I smiled to myself, thinking that if I asked Catherine that question, she'd say "Hello, Polo Lounge." But not Amanda.

"Fine. Dinner at eight. I'll meet you there."

She hung up. And suddenly I was pretty sure I was in no danger of being swept into a maelstrom of guilty passion and more infidelities. It was something of a relief. On the other hand, I was also mildly deflated. It was hard to forget that photograph.

Chapter Seventeen

Next, I called Bunny. He was still in his office at UCLA.

"Hello, my friend. Always good to hear from you. What's on your mind?"

"Just a little information from someone who travels in exalted circles."

"Meaning me? Well, I can't say I don't get around, double negative aside."

"What can you tell me about Joachim Embs?"

"Ah. You are on Amanda's case. Good. Well, let me see. He's from a very old Prussian family. Very grand. Very rich. The family boasts generations in the army, all the way back to Odin's father. Not a blot on their escutcheon of any kind. That sort of thing. They are the kind of people who looked down on Otto von Bismarck as being too common. You can imagine what they think of Hitler and his crowd. An Austrian paperhanger and a former corporal. *Mein Gott!*"

"But Amanda said Joachim was a true believing Nazi."

"That doesn't mean he's likely to ask Adolf to tea. The aristocrats will tolerate Hitler and the party as long as he succeeds in bringing Germany back to prosperity and respect. And, of course, power. So far, he's done a pretty good job, from their point of view. But that won't change the fact that quietly they despise him. You know, Americans sometimes confuse the words 'despise' and 'detest.' They are related of course, but 'despise' really means to look down upon someone with utter contempt and disdain. 'Detest' just means to dislike intensely. A peasant can detest someone, but he's not in a position to despise anyone. Except maybe a beggar. The aristocrats may tolerate Hitler, but they hold him in private contempt. Trust me on that. And don't think Hitler doesn't know it. Another double negative."

"Ego te absolvo."

"So, tell me, why are you interested in Joachim Embs?"

"Just wondering about this whole blackmail problem. I know he gambles and generally loses—enough so that it makes him very... testy, shall we say."

"I see. And you're wondering if he had money troubles and might stoop to sending Amanda anonymous notes? Is that it?"

"It crossed my mind."

"Well, no German aristocrat likes to lose at anything. And, as a matter of interest, he doesn't always lose. I'd be willing to bet that over time, he comes out relatively even, or as near as to make no difference. To him. So I think you can strike money troubles off your list. He is personally as rich as the proverbial Croesus, even apart from his family. I'm quite sure he wouldn't lower himself to such a tactic even if he weren't. But he is. How much did the blackmailer demand?"

"Fifty thousand."

"I've seen Joachim win nearly that much at bridge during a consulate party. You know some of your friends in the movie business are high-rolling gamblers. And not very good card players."

"Ironic, isn't it?"

What Hamlet Said

"What?"

"That Joachim would be happy to play bridge with them and take their money, given what Hitler says about their cousins in Germany—and what Joachim seems to think too."

"Never be surprised by irony, my friend. Or its twin brother hypocrisy. Never. They are as inevitable as death and taxes. Joachim may despise and detest the moguls in his heart, but their money bears no taint. You might more profitably wonder why *they* would choose to play with *him*. That is harder to explain."

"Yes. Isn't it?"

"But the point of the story is, I'd look elsewhere for the blackmailer if I were you. Joachim doesn't need the money—and even if he did, he wouldn't go about it that way. Even if he were broke, it would be beneath him."

"One last thing: What exactly is a cultural attaché?"

"A spy, old man. A spy."

Promptly at eight, I showed up at the Polo Lounge. I knew the people there but was not at all concerned about word of this meeting leaking out to Ethel. The staff would say nothing; and if they did, Ethel wouldn't care. And besides, it was a business meeting. Wasn't it?

Amanda wasn't there yet, but she showed up in just a few minutes, not caring to be fashionably late. I had the feeling that when she was writing her book on what was Done and Not Done, being late would fall under the Not Done category.

"Hello, Rhett," she said as she slid into the booth next to me. "You look dashing tonight."

"And you look ravishing." I liked that word, and it was appropriate. She was wearing a silky gown, low-cut in the front and back, much like the one she wore on the *Lucky Lady,* except this one was black. She wore a string of pearls and earrings to match, very little makeup, but just enough to emphasize the best features of her face, especially her eyes. They were the color of chocolate—good chocolate, Belgian chocolate. In matters of style, she knew precisely what she was doing. That was, no doubt, one of the things they taught the English Honorable girls. And if they never taught them another thing, that was quite all right as far as I was concerned. I was also pleasantly surprised that she seemed friendly and not guarded. Not very, anyway.

"Did you order drinks?" she said.

"No. I just got here. What would you like?"

"Champagne, of course. Let's pretend we're rich tonight and splurge."

Well, she was eventually going to get the bill for all of this, so I was happy to oblige. The truth be told, I might have been anyway. Simple P.I. that I was, I probably had more money in the bank than she and the Honorable Freddie combined. Where it came from was a story for another day. Still, I would keep the receipts tonight. And, as Catherine would say, was that wrong? Then one little part of me whispered: yes, it probably was, a little.

I signaled to the wine steward, a friend of mine named Harvey Olson who went by the professional name Maurice Duvalier. He had a phony French accent, too. If any actual French-speaking person spoke to him, he responded that he was Romanian, not French. No one speaks Romanian. And there weren't many French people in Hollywood, so he was rarely challenged. And never caught out. He played bit parts in movies now and then. Whenever some producer or director wanted a wine steward, they sent for Maurice. He never had to audition: his job at the Polo Lounge was an ongoing audition. He seemed content with his lot in life and apparently had no ambitions to play a Latin lover or a desert sheik or anything other than what he was. At the end of the war, he had stayed in France for three months and worked as a dishwasher in a Lyon restaurant. That gave him enough experience to establish himself as a wine expert in Hollywood. He had never been in action, but wore the Croix de Guerre ribbon in his buttonhole; he'd bought it in an antique shop in Paris.

He came over smiling, as if to congratulate me for something. I knew what it was: he was looking at Amanda with approval.

"Ah, the usual, sir?" he said.

"No, Maurice. We'd like to have Champagne. Any preferences, Scarlett?"

"I'd love it if you have Veuve Cliquot."

"Ah," said Maurice, "I have an excellent '28. Will that suit?"

"Yes. That sounds lovely. Okay, Rhett?"

"Okay, Scarlett."

Maurice did not bat an eye over this silliness, bowed, and floated majestically away to get the wine. He made a very good sommelier, I had to admit. Life imitating art. Or was it art imitating art?

Amanda looked around the room. "I've never been here before. It's quite the hangout for the Hollywood people, isn't it? They seem to know you. The staff, I mean."

"From my former life as a matinee idol." This was not true, but just one more thing that didn't need explaining.

"Seriously? Did you really make movies?"

"Just one. But it won the academy award. I can't take too much credit for that, though."

"I'm impressed. How did you get into the detective business?"

"Reading crime novels. Plus, I realized pretty quickly that acting was not for me."

"I'm surprised. You are very good-looking, you know. And you *do* know it."

"Maybe. But in the movie business, good-looking guys are a dime a dozen. Plus, on the set there's a lot of shouting and tantrums as well as a lot of sitting around waiting for something to happen. It was pretty annoying and boring at the same time. Besides, I like being my own boss, and nobody is his own boss in the movie business. And I kind of liked what Sam Spade did in the novels. It seemed interesting and didn't seem too hard."

"You're teasing me."

"No, I'm not. Not much, anyway."

"So, one day you just announce the fact that you're a detective?"

"Pretty much. You need a license, but that's easy enough to come by." I didn't think it was necessary to go into how Ethel's influence had gotten me started.

"And then you buy a gun and a blackjack and a bottle of Bourbon and go about solving crimes and getting paid?"

"Just like Sam Spade. Only I don't smoke."

"Ah. I remember you said you read a lot. I'm completely ignorant, I'm afraid. Rather a bore."

"I don't think so."

"Thank you. Of course, you would say that."

"You're wrong there, Amanda. I generally mean what I say. I don't always say what I'm thinking, but when I do, it's pretty much the truth. And if I hadn't used the word already so recently, I'd say you were ravishing, and that applies to more than just how you look."

She looked at me almost with "wild surmise." Certainly with mild surprise.

"Really?"

"Really."

"I'm... glad you think so." And she seemed to be. She even appeared to blush. And she blushed in the most charming places.

What Hamlet Said

There was a pause. In a movie, this would have been the time to light a cigarette, maybe two, and hand one to her. But she didn't smoke either.

"Bunny told me you were writing a book," I said finally, after we'd stared at each other for a few seconds, wondering if something was going on.

"Yes, I suppose I am. It's quite fun, really."

"Which do you prefer? Putting the milk in first, or second?"

"Ah. Bunny must have told you about that. It's one of those eternal questions and continuing debates. Like free will and determinism."

"Yes, of course. But which is it? Which is the Done Thing?"

"Do you really want to know? I mean, are you really interested?"

"I'm really interested." And I was, in more ways than one. And she understood that, too.

"Then I'll tell you. The real answer is: it doesn't matter. That's the whole point, you see. The key to it all is that you must know in your bones that whatever *you* do is, by definition, correct. It doesn't matter what it is. It doesn't matter what anybody says. What's more, you don't have to think about it, ever. You never have to ask yourself those kinds of questions. You simply know. Once you have mastered that certainty, you have arrived. Well, not arrived. Because you would not have reached that conclusion unless you were already there to begin with and didn't need to arrive anywhere. And I shouldn't use the word 'master.' There is no need to 'master' it, because you just absorb it from the time you are little. It's simply part of you. The knowledge. Do you see?"

"So your book is worthless as a guide."

"Completely. If you have to ask, you'll never have 'it.' And if you have 'it,' you'll never have to ask, or think of consulting a guide. That's the great joke. Of course, I'll have to write down some rules, but they'll all be for fun. Things like whether you should say 'notepaper' or 'stationery.' That kind of thing. Bunny thinks it will be a best seller. If so, it will be the first absolutely useless guidebook ever to make the top ten."

"Will you say whether it's okay to drink Bourbon out of a Dixie cup?"

"Oh, no. I won't say anything about *that*. Some things must remain secrets. Between us. But we both know that it's perfectly all right to do. Don't we?"

"Yes, indeed. Because we did it."

"Exactly."

"I suggest they put your picture on the back cover. It will help sales."

"Oh, dear. You can't be serious. Have you found that line effective with other women?"

"I've never gone out with an author before, so that was the line's maiden voyage. But actually, I am serious. And I'd suggest wearing that dress."

"Not a tweed suit and a trilby?"

"Not if you want to sell a lot of books. The décolletage is worth a Book of the Month Club selection alone. So is your smile. Even more so, I would say." I said this with complete sincerity which, for me, is pretty close to the real thing. I didn't want it to sound like some cheesy line, because it wasn't. The truth was, she had gotten to me a little bit, and a little faster than I'd expected. It was surprising, even to me. And I'm well aware of my susceptibilities.

"That is very kind of you," she said, softly. And I started to wonder what kind of men had she been going out with all these years. Were they blind *and* inarticulate? Were they incapable of anything other than irony and joking? Maybe her manner put them off, but maybe the way they treated her, and each other, caused her manner. Maybe it was a group ethic: the Bright Young Things posing as sophisticates who cared about nothing—and, least of all, each other. It was all a game. Everything was fancy dress, the name they used for dressing up in costumes and masks. But wasn't it about time that somebody treated her right? Like a woman? Wasn't it about time for some Lochinvar to come out of the west and rescue her from the likes of the Honorable Freddy? And I was pretty sure that Joachim Embs was not her Lochinvar. He probably was immune to gentle humor and also devoid of much tenderness, both of which I told myself Amanda needed in equal measures. At least that's how it appeared to me. Of course, in all honesty, I was prepared to dislike Joachim for a number of reasons. Amanda was only one of the reasons. But she *was* one of them.

"You are surprisingly nice," she said. "Not at all the tough guy."

"Don't tell anyone."

"I won't. But you also seem very sure... of yourself," she said after a moment.

"I am. I have an inherent belief that whatever I say or do must be correct, by definition."

"A natural aristocrat?"

"An Ohio Presbyterian, which is even rarer in LA. We have lots of English aristocrats here. Perhaps you've noticed."

"Yes, they're all playing butlers. Except the ones playing diplomats."

She favored me with another smile. It was genuine and rather sweet. But there was something in her eyes and manner that suggested nervousness, something I hadn't noticed before, and I wondered if her earlier and very understandable fear had returned sometime between when I'd phoned her and her arrival here. If it had, I could hardly blame her; after all, there was at least one dead body associated with her case, and maybe more. I hoped there wouldn't be, but I had a funny feeling there might be. And I remembered that she wanted to talk, privately. I had forgotten about that part of it, when she came walking in here in that dress.

Maurice arrived with the Champagne. "Would you like to taste it, madame?"

"No, thank you. I've never, ever sent a bottle of wine back. Frankly, I know nothing about quality. Don't know the difference between good and bad. I can tell the difference in tastes, of course, but I quite like them all. And for some reason, Veuve Cliquot is the only Champagne I can remember. Are you shocked?"

"No, madame."

"Nothing shocks Maurice," I said after he poured the Champagne, put the bottle in the silver ice bucket, and left, with a Gallic bow.

"Good. I'm beginning to like this place more and more. Is he really French?"

"This is Hollywood. What do you think?"

"I'm glad. It's so good to be in a place where everyone is someone else and takes great pleasure and pride in it. Where I come from, everyone is too much themselves and all the same, always the same. Very dull. Is there anything duller than predictability? Even predictable gaiety?"

"I suppose not. If you feel that way, you've come to the right place. Self-invention and reinvention are American specialties. There's a book called *The Great Gatsby* about that very thing. You might like it. The guy who wrote it works out here now."

"I've never heard of it."

"Not many have."

"Does it end badly?"

"As a matter of fact, it does."

"Then it's true to life. Will you lend it to me?"

What Hamlet Said

I looked at her for a minute. Blond hair and brown eyes really do make a fine combination. And in the warmth of the room, her scent had become slightly more noticeable. Or maybe it wasn't just the warmth of the room.

"Right now, lady, I'd do just about anything in the world for you."

Well, it just popped out. It surprised me as much as it surprised her. Maybe more.

"Goodness," she whispered.

"I'm sorry, sort of."

"Don't be. No one... has said that kind of thing to me in quite a while. If ever. Should I believe you?"

"Yes, you should."

"That's lovely. I hope you didn't get it from some book."

"I didn't."

"I'm glad."

Then she more or less tried to change the subject. At least, that's what it seemed like to me.

"What are the rooms like in the hotel?"

"Very elegant."

"You would know, I suppose."

I merely shrugged and smiled and tried not to look knowing, and to look knowing, at the same time.

"I assume they have room service."

"Of course."

She looked at me for a moment, and I tried to decipher whatever message she was sending, if any. But then I didn't have to. She took my hand the way she'd taken it on the *Lucky Lady*.

"Did you bring a toothbrush, Rhett?"

Chapter Eighteen

As a matter of fact, I had tucked one in my jacket pocket. A toothbrush, I mean. After all, you never know. But when I'd left my rooms at the Garden, I really hadn't expected anything romantic to happen that night. And experience tells you that even if you're prepared for anything all of the time, most of the time you won't need whatever it is you brought. Ask any teenage boy about that Trojan in his wallet. But as an old cowboy actor I knew once told me, it's better to have it and not need it than to need it and not have it. He was referring to his six-shooter, but the same reasoning applies to a toothbrush.

I thought our dinner meeting was going to be all business. But it didn't turn out that way. I had guessed right about some things, though. Having spent some considerable time looking at her photograph, I had imagined that she had reserves of passion that she kept tucked away, or hidden, for reasons that only she could understand. And I was right. They were there. I didn't need to understand why she kept them hidden. I could guess, but it didn't matter. I was just grateful that she was not hiding them that night, not hiding them from me.

I was right about something else too. You know the song "Try A Little Tenderness"? It's often good advice. It was with Amanda.

Once again, I wondered what kind of men she'd been with all her life. Maybe they had unlocked her secrets too. Maybe. But I somehow doubted it. Of course, you will think that I am making myself a hero of romance. But not really. I just think that she hadn't been treated with tenderness very often, and she liked how it felt. And showed it. And responded. For myself, I liked the way her silky legs felt and how she smelled and tasted and how she was lithe and athletic and without an ounce of unnecessary flesh. I liked all that very much. I had imagined her sighs and gasps when I looked at her photo. Tonight, I heard them in the flesh. Much better that way. Much.

After about a half hour or so, and after we had both regained our breath, she whispered "I think I'm beginning to like you."

"Does that mean you'll eat barbecue with me at the Twelve Oaks picnic?"

"Why, of course, Rhett darling."

"In that case we should have more Champagne."

"We should probably order some dinner, too. I'm starting to get hungry."

"Okay. What would you say to a little cold lobster?"

I was feeding her a line but didn't expect anything.

"I'd say—'Hello, little cold lobster'."

Ah! And she said it with a giggle. I wouldn't have thought she was capable of a giggle. Well, it just goes to show you. You never really know about most people.

"I think I'm beginning to like you too," I said. And I was.

"How lovely."

She was lying on the bed without any covering. She was stretched out languidly like Modigliani's Odalisque. Or somebody's Odalisque. She was smiling with undisguised affection and warmth.

She looked like a woman on the threshold of something, or maybe a woman who had just crossed one.

"Speaking of appetites, you remind me of a line," I said.

"Another one? One of yours, or borrowed?"

"Borrowed. From one of your people."

"What is it?"

"'Other women cloy the appetites they feed, she makes hungry where she most satisfies.'"

"My God. How beautiful. What's it from?"

"*Antony and Cleopatra.*"

"Yes, I remember now. I saw it not long ago. But it was very sweet of you to say it."

"Nothing but the truth."

"Liar. But...."

"But?"

"But a very lovely liar. Can you... postpone ordering dinner for a while? I want to make you hungry again."

Room service arrived eventually, and we had cold lobster with mayonnaise and more Champagne. We had put hotel robes on while the waiter was serving but took them off when he left.

"Isn't it wicked to be eating while absolutely starkers? I love it."

"Something for your book."

"No. That's another thing for us."

At first, I felt a little glimmer of doubt about whether there had come to be an "us" and whether that was such a good idea. But then I remembered something: she was married. The future of an "us" appeared unlikely. And suddenly that seemed a shame. Which of course was in some way ironic and inconsistent. One moment I was mildly alarmed about maybe getting into something complicated, the next mildly disappointed because I wasn't, and couldn't be.

There's no pleasing anybody, I guess. But, if there was irony there, I followed Bunny's advice and was not surprised.

When we finished dinner, we went back to bed.

"You taste of lobster and mayonnaise and Champagne," she said.

"So do you."

"Mmmm. Aren't we lucky? Do you think lobster and Champagne are aphrodisiacs?"

"They seem to be."

"Or maybe it's the mayonnaise."

"That could be. There's a small dab on the corner of your mouth." I kissed her and then said "Here will I dwell, for Heaven is in these lips with their little dab of mayonnaise on them, and all is dross that is not... Amanda."

"Oh, dear. I am quite close to being swept away. What's that from?"

"Marlowe's *Faustus*. Part of it, anyway. I added the bit about the mayonnaise."

"And is he really saying that to someone named Amanda?"

"No. Helen of Troy. But as they say, it's much of a muchness."

"You're very literary, darling."

"I read a lot. Speaking of that, would you like to try something new? I just read about it in some book on Indian lovemaking."

"The Kama something?"

"Yes. Want to try it?"

"Yes, please. Do I have to turn over or sit up or stand on my head or something?"

"I'll show you."

It goes to show you, you can never tell when one sort of experience will come in handy somewhere else. Ironically, I had acquired that very experience, position sixty-four I think it was, in this very hotel not more than a couple of days ago. And once again, I was not surprised by the irony. If that's what it was.

It was about two in the morning when she finally told me what she wanted to talk about.

"I got another letter today," she said. "Or rather yesterday." She was lying with her head on my shoulder, and we were both well and truly spent and languorous.

"Newspaper cutouts again?"

"Yes. Like before. It said 'Get the money. You have twenty-four hours. After that—kaput!' And there was an advertisement for Forest Lawn Cemetery, pasted just below."

"'Kaput?' That's odd."

"I thought so too. For a minute, I thought it might be Joachim playing a joke, but why would he? He's not the kind to play jokes, anyway."

"No. I think we can rule him out as a joker or a blackmailer. Bunny told me he's filthy rich and not as bad a card player as I'd assumed. How did getting that letter make you feel?"

"A little creepy at first. And frightened, a little. But then I got over it. Do you think they're serious? About the threat, I mean?"

"I don't know. But I do know we have to assume they are. Have you mentioned any of this to the Honorable Freddie, by any chance?"

"No, of course not."

"Where is he, by the way?"

"Out of town, doing something or other."

"When will he be back?"

"I don't really know. Sometime."

"What does he actually do at the consulate?"

"He's a cultural attaché. Goes to parties."

What Hamlet Said

"Hmm. Do you think it's at all possible that Freddie is something more than he seems?"

"No. But it's very possible he's something less than he seems. Hard as that may be to believe. Why?"

"It's just that Bunny told me that Joachim, who's also a cultural attaché, is really a spy of some sort. And he implied that cultural attaché is a common cover story."

"Joachim? Yes, I can believe that. He's the type. But Freddie? You've got to be joking. His specialty is doing card tricks. He makes Bertie Wooster look like *un homme serieux*."

I liked the P. G. Wodehouse reference. She wasn't as illiterate as she pretended.

"An aristocratic nincompoop? What could be a better cover?"

"In theory. But I can't believe it."

"How long have you known him? How long have you been married?"

"Long enough in both cases to know he's no secret agent."

"Do wives always know all there is to know about their husbands?"

"Unfortunately, yes. It would be better for all concerned if they didn't."

"Really?"

"Yes, because it would mean the husband was interesting enough to have secrets."

"And what about you and Joachim? Now, I mean?"

"Jealous?"

"Familiar with Othello?"

"Was he jealous?"

"Probably he overdid it. But understandably."

"That's sweet. Actually, I did know that. As for Joachim, he's very charming, but it was never more than a fling. Out of boredom, really. You know that old line: he's just a friend. If I told him you and I were planning to run away to Tahiti, he'd send a bon voyage basket of wine and cheese. And it would be good wine, too, not that I'd know the difference."

In the morning, I drove her home. She did not seem at all disturbed about arriving in the morning wearing a slinky evening gown and being dropped off by a guy in evening clothes driving a Packard convertible. I therefore assumed that the Honorable Freddy was not expected and that the staff were discreet and only gossiped among themselves.

I pulled up in front of her very swanky house. The British foreign office apparently did not care how it spent its money on cultural attachés.

"Does your staff live in the house, or do they commute to work?"

"They must commute from somewhere. I never asked."

"So you're alone at night when Freddie's not there."

"I'm alone at night even when Freddie is there."

"What a waste."

"Him or me?"

"Both, in a different sense."

"You're pretty sweet, you know? Has anyone ever told you that?"

"Not lately. There's a spare thirty-eight in the glove compartment. Put it in your purse. And be careful: it's loaded."

She looked at me, questioning.

"Like the old cowboys say, it's better to have it and not need it than to need it and not have it," I said.

"Like a diaphragm?" she said, with a look of innocence.

"Yes. Like that. Do you know how to use one of those things?"

"The diaphragm, or the pistol?"

"You know... until I met you I never realized Honorable women were so..."

What Hamlet Said

"'Naughty' is the word you're looking for. And aren't you pleasantly surprised?"

"Pleasantly is the word I was looking for, yes."

"As for the pistol, no need to explain," she said. "I know how to use one."

"Really? Another surprise."

"Is this the point in the scene where I say 'You don't know the half of it'? Or does that come later?"

"Later, I think."

But it did make me wonder. I'd read enough English novels to know that the upper classes were pretty much all involved in blood sports. But you don't chase foxes or shoot pheasants with a .38-caliber snub-nosed police special. In fact, you really can't shoot *anything* with one of them, unless you get very close and hope the target is pretty much standing still. Then I remembered the hole in Smitty's head. Somebody had gotten pretty close to him. Close enough not to miss.

Chapter Nineteen

"Morning, Chief," said Della. "You know it's not considered proper to wear a dinner jacket this time of day."

"It was a long dinner. Any calls?"

"Nope."

"Where's Perry this time of day?"

"I often wonder. But if I had to guess, I'd say he was getting his boat squared away for this evening's festivities. Then he'll probably go to his favorite bar for breakfast. O'Malley's. Know it?"

"Yeah. I may join him."

"He might have something for you."

"Good."

I went into the office and called Kowalski.

"Ed? Any more info on the bullet that killed Smitty?"

"Nothing new. They tried to run more tests, but it was too deformed. They're sticking with a thirty-eight. And before you ask, there's nothing new on the floater or the missing actor."

"Swell."

"Ain't it the truth?"

I went back to the Garden of Allah and changed my clothes. There was no need to shower: Amanda and I had taken care of that together. Then I drove over to the Santa Monica Pier. As Della had figured, Perry was there making sure the brightwork on his boat was up to his standard. He was just finishing up.

"Hello, Chief," he said.

"Hello, Chief. Glad I caught you. Interested in a little breakfast?"

"No, but I'm interested in a big one. It was a long night. O'Malley's suit you?"

"Let's go."

It was only a couple of blocks to O'Malley's.

"Della said you might have something for me."

"It may not be anything. But you asked about Smitty. Well, it turns out he did some work now and then for Blinky. Photos for passports. That kind of thing."

"I'm kind of surprised Blinky doesn't do that work himself."

"It's just as easy to farm it out. Guys like Smitty and Flash Gordini have their own darkrooms and so on, so they deliver a finished product fast and easy. Leaves Blinky to do what he does best."

"So, did Blinky hear anything from or about Smitty? What he was doing? Blackmail stuff?"

"A little. Smitty played it pretty close to the vest. But he did tell Blinky that he was working on a peeper for a foreign gent."

"Peeper? Gent?"

"A peeper. You know—a peeping Tom shot. 'Gent' was the word he used for his client. That's all Blinky got from him."

"That confirms what we pretty much already knew. No idea who this gent was, I suppose?"

"Nope. But it sort of suggests that he was a white guy, you know? I mean if the guy was a Nip or something, most likely Smitty would have said that. I don't think he'd use the word 'gent.' And the same goes for a skid road bum or a dockworker. Know what I mean? Suggests somebody who's high-class—or does a good imitation."

"That makes sense. Narrows it down a little, I guess. You've gotta think that Smitty got shot by this gent who hired him."

"Who else would want to kill him? Who else even knew he existed? He didn't have any enemies, like an ex-wife or a wife of any kind. And he for damn sure wasn't playing around with some other guy's wife. He was no Clark Gable. Speaking of which, I hear they're thinking of him for Rhett Butler."

"I can see that. Anything else from Blinky?"

"Yeah. And that's where it gets interesting. Seems he's been doing big business with some recent arrivals right there in Pedro. Passports, work visas, that sort of stuff. Blinky said they were a real hard-looking crew. Not a choirboy among them."

"How many?"

"Half a dozen."

"Where'd they come from, did he say?"

"He said not one of them would say a word. Just the leader. He arranged everything and did all the talking."

"That guy wasn't wearing a hand-painted Hawaiian tie, by any chance?"

"Blinky didn't say what he was wearing. Who wears that kind of thing, anyway?"

"You'd be surprised."

"I guess. Ever since my subscription to *Vogue* ran out, I ain't up on the latest fashions. Anyway, these guys just showed up, and Flash took their pictures for the documents right there in Blinky's shop. Brought the developed photos back that afternoon. And that was it. Nobody said a thing. A silent movie. And Blinky didn't ask any questions. They paid in cash, and they didn't try to haggle. Paid full price. But Blinky said they made him nervous, especially so soon after Smitty got it and especially since he was overcharging them."

"How can you overcharge when you're the one setting the market?"

"Huh? You think Blinky don't have competition?"

"Never gave it a thought. I don't suppose the names on the new passports will tell us anything about where these guys came from."

"Not unless you can get anything from names like Smith, Jones, Johnson, and what have you."

"No Skis or Viches?"

"No, nor Svens or Adolfs."

"I wonder if Flash kept the negatives."

"Negative, Chief. That was part of the deal. These guys didn't want there to be any copies. They took the documents and the negatives. The whole shootin' match. Then the guy who talked took a match and burned the negatives right there."

"Sounds like they have plans that are not strictly legal."

"Ya think?"

"Do you think there might be a connection between the two jobs? The peeper and the passports?"

"Hard to say. These guys ain't what you'd call gents, even the one who talked. Not from the way Blinky described them."

"But they all are foreigners—the gent and the hard cases."

"Yep."

"I suppose it's possible the hard guys might be working for the gent."

"I guess it's possible. Seems like a stretch, though."

"I guess. Well, thanks for the info. Let's get something to eat."

We went into O'Malley's, and O'Malley himself greeted us like brothers.

"I'm surprised a tavern like this sells breakfast," I said, as O'Malley stood there with his order book.

"We don't," said O'Malley. "'Cause we don't have a license. What'll you have, Perry?"

"I'll have four eggs over easy," said Perry, "bacon, sausage, toast, coffee, a double shot of Jameson's, and a pint of beer."

"How about you?" said O'Malley.

"I'll have the same, but without the Jameson's." Amanda made me hungry where she most satisfied, and just plain hungry in the normal way. Cold lobster in the wee hours doesn't go very far.

O'Malley waddled off to the back room.

"I thought he said they don't sell food here."

"They don't sell it. They *provide* it free for special customers. Also known as friends of the family or guests."

"I see. What do you have to do to become a special customer?"

"Walk through the door. O'Malley ain't prejudiced. 'Course, he expects you to make a donation to his favorite charity in exchange, but that's only fair. The suggested amount is written just opposite the various things he can give his guests."

"Sounds like a menu."

"To you it sounds like a menu. To O'Malley it's just a helpful list of suggestions for people who can't decide how much to donate. But this way he don't have to deal with the Health Department, which, as you probably know, is filled with corrupt characters who take bribes in exchange for clean bills of health and licenses. For twenty bucks a month, an inspector won't notice a ten-pound cockroach or the remains of a recent alley cat."

"Taste like chicken?"

"Cats? Not any chicken I ever ate, but use enough garlic and onions and who's to say?"

"It's a wicked world."

What Hamlet Said

"Ain't it? The thing is, those payoffs eat into the profit something cruel, and O'Malley's second wife has what you could call expensive taste."

"What happened to the first wife?" I felt once again like I was feeding straight lines.

"Went back to Ireland. It saved the cost of a divorce, so O'Malley figures, so far, he's ahead; but the way the new one spends, he won't be for long. Ain't a surprise, though. That's what happens when a fat old man marries a young, sort of good-looking woman who likes to shop. You could make book on it."

"Or write one. Did I mention it's a wicked world?"

"You did, and it is."

Chapter Twenty

"So, the Japanese don't seem to be involved," said Hobey.

"The Japanese?" I asked. "No. There's no sign of them so far. There're plenty of other foreigners running around in the shadows, though."

We were sitting around the Garden of Allah pool at cocktail hour. Hobey's current girlfriend, Hedda Gabler, was sitting there with us, though she was busy reading through her mail. Her job as Miss Lonelyhearts meant quite a bit of reading, something Hedda was not very good at. But she was diligent. She was wearing a skimpy bathing suit and a look of intense concentration. It was not hard to see what Hobey saw in her, although her expression wasn't part of it.

"I'm surprised," he said. "I was sure my theory was a good one."

"It *was* a good one. It just doesn't seem to be true."

"Speaking of a good one," said Hedda, "listen to this. 'My wife says she's never satisfied. She says it has to do with my physical size. What should I do? Sincerely, Puzzled.' Do you think I should print this one in the paper?"

"I wouldn't," said Hobey. "You'll get mail from the League of Decency." Then, turning back to me, he said: "So tell me about

Amanda Billingsgate. Word is, you were seen together at the Polo Lounge."

"Strictly professional."

"Really?"

"No. But the truth is, she's being blackmailed over an affair with a certain German diplomat, and she doesn't want it to get out."

"Ah. That's interesting. Who's the German?"

"A guy named Joachim Embs. Works at the consulate. Bunny says he's a spy. And a very rich aristocrat, to boot."

"Good! That adds a little spice to the story. How much are they asking for?"

"The blackmailers? Fifty thousand. She doesn't have it. Says it might as well be fifty million."

"Hmm. Doesn't have it. Even so, it's not all that much money."

"Seems like it is to me."

"Yes: to you. And to an impoverished scribbler like myself, it is a lot. But not to the great and good of English society."

"So what does that suggest?"

"It suggests that the blackmailer is nothing more than what he seems: a petty crook with no imagination."

"Meaning there're no hidden layers involved. Just a straightforward shakedown. No nefarious politics or international intrigue."

"That's the way it looks."

"That's pretty much the way I see it too."

"Yes. It's too simple a conception to be anything else. German spymasters, for instance, would have come up with something far more elaborate and sinister, if they were involved. They probably wouldn't even have asked for money—just information. Maybe not even that. Maybe just willingness on her part to pass information that seems innocuous but is somehow important to the Krauts. The

Japanese would have been even more baroque. Ever read Mr. Moto? Pretty good stuff."

"They might try to recruit her as a secret agent, or something?"

"Right. Foreign intelligence services often resort to blackmail to recruit agents. But they most certainly would never ask for money. It would complicate things unnecessarily, and they obviously don't need the money. If anything, they would *offer* money, along with the blackmail threats. Carrot and stick."

"How do you know all this stuff about espionage?"

"Common knowledge, old sport. Bottom line, it looks like just a cheap scam."

"Here's another one," said Hedda, who was paying no attention to me or Hobey. "'Dear Miss Lonelyhearts, I am so afraid of my husband that comes home drunk every night and slaps me around like James Cagney in that movie. What should I do? Signed, Worried.' That seems like a good one. What do you think I should tell her?"

"Tell her not to buy grapefruit," said Hobey.

"Huh? I don't get it."

"Never mind. She's the one who mentioned Cagney. She'll get it. If not, does it matter?"

"No. I guess not."

"People don't read that column for your advice. They read it for the misery; it makes them feel better."

"Really? Gosh. People are funny."

"So," he said to me, "how are you going to catch this two-bit blackmailer?"

"I don't know. He's made some threats if she doesn't pay up. I guess we have to wait for him to make the next move."

"She's the cheese in the trap? Does she know it?"

What Hamlet Said

"If she thinks about it at all, she'll know it. And she's pretty sharp. I can't believe there's any real danger. What would anyone gain? They might try to frighten her, but I can't believe it'll go beyond that."

"No. I wouldn't think so either."

"I lent her a thirty-eight, just in case. But aside from getting round-the-clock protection, which she won't agree to for obvious reasons, I can't think of anything else to do until we hear from him again. If he really is just a cheap crook, he might get cold feet and disappear. The same when he realizes there's no money coming."

"Is the gun registered to you?"

"Of course. Why?"

"Just wondering. What about the husband?"

"Clueless, and going to stay that way if she can help it."

"Afraid of divorce, is she?"

"Not really. It's more a matter of being afraid of scandal and especially of being linked with a German and a high-ranking Nazi aristocrat to boot. The timing is very bad."

"Yes, I can see that. Why don't you seduce her and woo her away from the charming Siegfried. I'm sure you can manage it. Or have you already?"

"Just between us, I don't think the charming Siegfried will be in the picture going forward."

"Bravo! Aren't you worried that he might challenge you to a duel?"

"Not at all. Amanda says he won't care. It was just a fling for both of them. But that still leaves the mystery blackmailer lurking somewhere with what we have to assume are bad intentions of some sort. The problem is a very graphic photograph of the two of them—Embs and Amanda."

"Locked in a steamy embrace?"

"The steamiest."

"So the end of the affair does not put an end to the problem."

"No."

"Here's another one," said Hedda. "'Dear Miss Lonelyhearts, I was born without a nose and the boys make fun of me. What shall I do? Signed, Funny Looking.'"

"I thought you had that one last week," said Hobey.

"No. That was from that book by that guy," said Hedda.

"Once again, life imitates art. It's enough to make you weep," said Hobey.

"Ain't it the truth," I said. "Speaking of which, how's the screenplay coming?"

"Slow. Slower. And slowest. I can't seem to get my ideas across to the powers-that-be. And now they're talking about getting Clark Gable to play Rhett Butler."

"I heard that."

"Can you imagine? Does he seem like a Romantic Egoist to you?"

"Maybe. In one sense."

"Okay. Maybe. But Humphrey Bogart would be much better—he has that air of existential sadness, which is exactly what I'm looking for—and yet they laughed when I suggested him."

"Hard to believe. But maybe they think existential sadness won't sell tickets."

"Could be. As one of my favorite producers put it, 'When people don't want to come, nothing can stop them.' I don't know. Sometimes I think I may have gotten the wrong end of the stick. It wouldn't be the first time. How about a drink?"

"Good idea. My treat."

"Here's another one," said Hedda. "Listen to this! Talk about creepy..."

What Hamlet Said

I didn't wait. I walked over to the poolside bar to get a couple of stiff gin-and-tonics. I was pretty sure Hobey really did have the wrong end of the stick, as far as his script was concerned. Nobody would want to see Humphrey Bogart moping around over some woman. I just hoped Hobey would get hold of the other end of the stick before they fired him from the picture. But one thing was sure: right now he'd want to start with a double.

I brought the drink to Hobey, who grasped at it like the proverbial drowning man reaching for a raft. Hedda was giggling over another letter. I went to my bungalow and called Amanda. The maid was just about to leave for the day but said Amanda had gone to a party at the consulate. The Honorable Freddie had come back from wherever he'd been. I figured that was a positive development. At least she wouldn't be alone in the house. I really wasn't all that worried about her security, but I did think about it.

Chapter Twenty-One

The next morning, I called Bunny. I wanted some information on the Billingsgate family.

"Very old," he said. "They can trace their roots back to the Conquest, or near enough. Their name is a corruption of some Norman French phrase of some sort. I forget what it is."

"How's their financial situation?"

"I couldn't say, really. I do know Freddie a little. We see each other at parties and so on. And of course he's always moaning about money and expenses, but you have to take that with a grain of salt. These people are always doing that. They claim not to have the proverbial chamber pot, but what they are really saying is that they're chronically short of cash, because all their wealth is tied up in land and stately houses and stables and horses and grouse moors and what have you. They have legions of tenants, veritable moujiks by the hundreds, who pay rent regularly. But a lot of that cash—if not most of it—goes for upkeep on the estates."

"The difference between cash flow and net worth."

"That's it. Imagine if you had a box of diamonds worth a million dollars in a safe-deposit box, but you were working as a waiter in a diner to pay your monthly bills. Could you say you were poor? Not at all. Would you moan about tips? Probably."

What Hamlet Said

"Why not sell off a diamond or two?"

"Well, you might want to, but you might not be able to. The estate may be entailed, which means it's in a sort of trust and can't be touched, so that it can be passed intact to the heir. And from him to the next heir, and so on. The reason they have such arrangements is to prevent some wastrel from selling off the family castle to pay off gambling debts or support a courtesan, which would beggar subsequent generations and toss them into the gutter—or, worse, suburban housing and regular jobs. I don't know that the Billingsgates' properties are entailed. But the family certainly share the traditional view that the land and stately houses must be kept intact for future generations. I'm quite sure of that."

"They could borrow against the property, I suppose."

"Yes. But that's a short-term solution that makes the long-term problem worse. Bankers have a nasty habit of wanting their money back, with interest."

"Is Freddie the heir?"

"No. He's the second son—the classic formula for genteel poverty. The oldest son, the heir, gets everything—once again, the idea is to keep the ancient property intact. The second son gets an invitation for Christmas and a week or two of grouse shooting. He may get an allowance of some sort. And he can call himself The Honorable. Also, his tailors will still give him credit. Up to a point. But odds are he'll be as poor as a vicar, but without the troubles of parishioners to console him."

"Do you know the heir?"

"Algernon? Yes. Typical squire-in-waiting. Beefy. Huntin', shootin', fishin' sort of man. Hates London. Stays in the country. Thinks all things foreign are bloody. That sort of thing."

"Healthy?"

"As a horse."

"Married?"

"Yes. To a woman as beefy as he is. Prudence is her name. Hockey goalkeeper-type."

"Hockey?"

"Field hockey. Traditional girl's game at school. They always take the widest girl and put her in goal. No children as yet, which I assume was your next question. So if Algernon breaks his neck while hunting, Freddie becomes the heir. So Freddie has prospects of a kind. Of course, his brother has to die first, which puts Freddie in a ticklish moral position."

"Do they get along? The brothers?"

"Couldn't say. Probably not. But why all the interest?"

"No reason. Just trying to get some background."

"I think I see where your suspicious mind is trending. Casting around for motives and alternative plots?"

"Maybe. But it looks very much as if the trend stops here. One final question, if you don't mind: Is the Honorable Freddie as big a twit as Amanda says?"

"Well, of course I know Amanda's opinion of her lord and master. Perhaps you do, as well. But you must remember that marriage can be fertile soil for acrimony and disappointment. Especially at the beginning, after which things often get worse. Imagine a new bride waking on the morning after the wedding. What do you think her first thought is likely to be? 'Oh, how blissful is this life!' or 'My God! What have I done?'"

"Let me guess: 'What have I done?'"

"More often than not, yes. Closely followed by 'I hope he won't want to do *that* again.'"

"I know you've made a study of the subject of wives."

"In my own modest way, yes. You know the expression 'no man is a hero to his valet.' Well, no husband is a hero to his wife, once she's heard him snore. And worse. Mistresses are far more forgiving about such things. Even—and especially—when they are other men's wives."

"They know the arrangement is only temporary."

"Yes, bless them. Which is why I prefer them. Much more civilized. Besides, they can forgive a lover for the same transgressions they detest in a husband. Perhaps because spending the night together is neither necessary nor even advisable. The French 'cinq a sept' is the perfect arrangement, of course. It gives you a full working day, but at five o'clock you have two hours of uncommitted passion and Champagne. Then at seven there's a tender 'a bientot' and off you go in separate directions—she to her home, you to a dinner party, followed by a night of solitary sleep uninterrupted by conversation or demands. C'est parfait!"

"I look forward to your memoirs."

"As well you should."

"But regarding Amanda's opinion of Freddie...?"

"Yes. So—even allowing for the animosity that is common in any marriage, I have to say that Amanda is not far wrong. If the Grand National were a race of fools, Freddie would clear all the jumps with ease."

"I see. No chance he's a spy, then, like his German counterpart?"

"Good God. I hope not, for all our sakes. But I'll tell you this in all sincerity: if it comes to war, Freddie will make an excellent junior officer of infantry. Give him a pistol and a whistle and tell him to lead his men over the top, and he'll do it and not think twice. Or even once. Thinking's not his strong suit. But he's a gentleman and will do his duty. If war comes, the Huns will underestimate men like Freddie at their peril. A man with no imagination and complete self-assurance makes a dangerous enemy."

"There'll always be an England."

"Yes. There will."

"Well, thanks for your time."

"Quite all right, old man. Any time. Give my love to Pansy. Not that she needs it. She's the perfect mistress, you know."

"You may be right."

Chapter Twenty-Two

After I hung up with Bunny, I grabbed my hat and drove over to City Hall. I wanted to check in with Bill Patterson. None of the pieces in the puzzles I was working on seemed to fit, but at the same time they all seemed to have something in common. The only problem was that I didn't know what it was. So I figured an in-person visit to the FBI was better than a phone call, since I really didn't know what I was looking for. Maybe a face-to-face would help me out. And it was just possible that I had something to offer him too.

As before, Patterson was in his office, surrounded by files and papers and books. And as before, he had the look of a harried graduate student with a paper coming due.

"Have a seat," he said, genially. "If I were a real detective instead of a government swot, I'd offer you a drink. But Mr. Hoover frowns on such things."

"That's all right. I wouldn't want to upset Mr. Hoover."

"No. Believe me, you wouldn't. What's up?"

"I've been investigating a disappearance—an actor named Jimmy Hicks."

"I know. You mentioned that the last time."

"He was last seen with a woman who went by the stage name Lulu Marquessa. A would-be actress. She was found on the beach in Santa Monica with a bullet in her head. But the local cops identified her as Irena Steponovich. And Jimmy Hicks hasn't been seen since. She was shot with a forty-five, and Jimmy owns a forty-five, which has since gone missing too."

"Yes? And?"

"Lulu's management company, if you can call it that, was based in San Pedro, in a crummy part of town. I talked with her manager. Some kind of foreigner. I'm pretty sure a central European of some kind or other. He claimed to know nothing about her disappearance, and he has since disappeared, too."

He nodded, as if to say, "Yes? And?"

"I'm also working on another case involving blackmail and murder, and as a result of that I've run across a guy, also in San Pedro, who specializes in passports and work papers and that sort of thing, and he told me he'd just done a job for a bunch of hard cases who looked like they'd just arrived from the Land of Hard Knocks and Misery."

"Blinky Malone?"

"Oh. You know about him."

"He keeps us informed."

"I didn't want to mention his name."

"Understandable. But we're all friends here. Blinky's been on the team for a while now. He tells us what he's up to, and we tell the cops to leave him alone. It works out well for all concerned. Of course, what he's doing is a federal crime, but so is tax evasion, and if we rounded up all those people we'd have to sublet Russia's prisons. So Blinky's information makes it worth looking the other way. But how do you think the disappearance of your Jimmy Hicks is related to Blinky's customers?"

"I don't. But my nose seems to tell me the questions are worth asking."

"Well, your nose has not led you astray, at least in the case of the former Lulu. The truth is that Irena Steponovich was an agent of the Yugoslav government. She was a Serb, and you will remember our talk about the Serbs and Croats. She was sent here to infiltrate the local branch of the Ustache. Apparently she did. And apparently they discovered who she was."

"So you knew who she was?"

"Yes. She was a legitimate agent of a legitimate foreign government that is more or less friendly with the U.S., and if war comes and the Germans go south or the Italians go east, the Serbs are likely to oppose them—for their own reasons, foreign and domestic. That makes them our friends, more or less."

"While the Croats are likely to support them. The Germans, I mean."

"Yes. So when Irena let us know what she was up to and why, we agreed to give her a hand here and there, if we could. We helped her establish her cover as a would-be actress. And we would have done more, but they uncovered her before she could call for help. Acme Management was obviously just a cover operation—a way to explain the comings and goings of all sorts of dodgy-looking people. So when they killed her, they closed up shop and went underground."

"Do the local cops know all this?"

"Well, I have to say the communications channels are not what they should be. Especially with all this war talk. We need to tighten up those channels, but that's above my pay grade. You wouldn't believe the turf wars back in Washington, and LA is what they call a microcosm of all that."

"What about Jimmy?"

"Wrong place at the wrong time would be my guess."

"The headless floater?" It looked more and more likely.

"I wouldn't be surprised. Two dead bodies in that short a time frame seem a little too coincidental. Then again, this is LA. So, it could be a movie critic. Lots of people hate them."

"But if it is Jimmy, and they dismembered him to prevent identification, why wouldn't they give Lulu the same treatment?"

"Sending a message, maybe. Telling their government they're on to their tricks. If they'd chopped her up and scattered her around town, she'd just be a missing person. This way they're telling the folks back home—and their operatives here—that they know the score. That's just a theory, though. Who knows for sure? Well, they do. But we don't."

"What about Blinky's mysterious strangers?"

"Hard to say. But it wouldn't surprise me if they were some new recruits on the run from the old country."

"Ustache?"

"As I said, it wouldn't surprise me. When we find out where they are, we'll have them in for a talk. But as of now, they've disappeared too. Seems like that's going around. And no one in Pedro is talking."

"I can believe that. One more thing. Is it true that the cultural attachés of the various consulates are spies?"

"Yep. Almost every one of them."

"Even the Brits?"

"You mean our good friends and allies? I'll tell you one thing— when it comes to the intelligence business, the Brits can teach everyone what to do and how to do it. Been at it for centuries, literally. The Germans and the Japanese are not far behind, but the Brits are the masters of the trade."

"How about us?"

"Babes in the woods. Well, that's not exactly true. The truth is, we're not up to even that level yet. But don't let it keep you awake worrying. We're learning."

"Well, thanks for the information."

"You're welcome. Keep in touch."

I was scheduled to have lunch with Ethel. I wasn't looking forward to it. I'd have some bad news for her, which would take the edge off things more than a little. Not that I was all that interested in learning number sixty-six.

Chapter Twenty-Three

"Are you sure it was him?" said Ethel.

"No. Not sure. But if I had to guess..." I had told her the cops and I both thought the body they'd found was Jimmy's. I didn't go into the whole background on Lulu and whatnot. I just let Ethel think it had been a random murder and the body couldn't be identified. I had to tell her why.

"Oh, I hope it wasn't Jimmy," she said. "He was—is—such a sweet kid."

"Can I ask you something?"

"What?"

"Were you ever intimate with him?"

"Why?"

"Well, he's still in... storage... in the morgue. If you were intimate, you might be able to recognize..."

"I get it. The answer is no, I wasn't. Not that I didn't think about it. Besides, that's a lousy idea."

"I understand that it's not very nice, but it would help if we knew who the dead guy was."

"Well, I can't help you. Besides, I'd rather keep thinking he's just missing."

"It's not impossible. We'll keep looking. The cops and I."

"Please do." She gathered her composure. "How was your omelet?" She didn't really care. She just wanted to change the subject.

"Same as always." For our lunches I usually had a mushroom omelet with French fries. They reminded me of a French girl I'd met a while back. She was beautiful and charming and engaged, though not sure she wanted to be. Engaged, I mean. In the end she went back to France and married the guy, I guess. I didn't get an invitation, so who knows. She was a fond memory. Her name was Dany.

When we finished lunch, Ethel made ready to leave.

"If you don't mind, I'm not in the mood for anything today," she said. "This business with Jimmy…"

"I understand." I was not surprised. In fact, I had made an appointment with Amanda for just after lunch. If I'd been wrong about Ethel, I would have pleaded a business meeting, but I didn't think I would be. Wrong, I mean. You go to bed with a woman and you're bound to learn something about her. Not much, but something.

Ethel left, and as I sat finishing my coffee, the maître d', Alphonse Gilberto, came over with the telephone. Alphonse's real name was Sol. I forget his real last name. He'd come to Hollywood to be a stunt man but broke his leg getting thrown off a horse and was never right again. Then he got into house painting and fell off a roof and broke the same leg again. So he became a maître d' with a limp. He told everyone it was a war wound that he'd gotten serving with the Italian Arditi, which was an elite infantry unit. He told a good story about the retreat from Caporetto. He got it from a book, but a lot of people believed him.

Alphonse didn't bother paging me. He knew where I was sitting. This business of getting paged at the Polo Lounge was a big deal to

Terry Mort

some people. It sort of announced that you were important enough for someone to need to talk to you urgently. Some of the small-timers in the picture business paid Alphonse to pretend there was a call and to page them. That was all right with Alphonse.

The call was from Kowalski.

"How'd you know I was here?" I said.

"Called your office. Della said it was Wednesday."

"What's up?"

"Word is you know a dame named Amanda Billingsgate," he said. I didn't like the sound of that.

"Yeah?"

"Well, she's down here at headquarters. Took a shot at an intruder this morning."

"She all right?"

"Little shook up, but not harmed. And when I say she's a little shook up, I mean just a little. She seems like sort of a tough lady, you know?"

"Did she kill the guy?"

"No. She's not even sure she hit him. She thinks she heard him yell. If she did get him, it was not serious. He took off and left only a vapor trail. No sign of him except the ladder he left against the second-floor window."

"Any prints?"

"We're checking, but I'd be surprised."

"Is her husband with her?"

"No. They went to a party last night. He brought her home and then went on his merry way. Never came back. She has no idea where he is. They're a very close couple, it seems. She said you're working for her. True?"

"Yes. On a confidential matter."

184

What Hamlet Said

"Of course. Well, we're finished taking her statement. If you want to collect her, come on down. Otherwise, we can take her home."

"No. I'll be right there."

I drove over to pick her up. It was another perfect California day. There was a breeze off the ocean and not a cloud in the sky. The San Gabriels looked close enough to touch and the palm trees swayed like they were listening to Glenn Miller. And it occurred to me the way it always did on days like this, that this paradise would be one hell of a lot better without so many of the human element. Headless corpses and foreign spies and criminal gangs and gambling ships run by mobsters and all manner of human flotsam or moral jetsam—all conspiring to turn a perfect place into a lousy black-and-white B movie. You name it and we had it, the worst of mankind, all surrounded by this perfection. It was disorienting in one way and depressing in another. It almost made me think about moving back to Ohio. Almost. Of course, I wasn't fool enough to think it was any better there. People lived there, too. No better, no worse. Just without suntans. And I knew the weather was a damned sight worse.

But then I thought—on the other hand, it really was a beautiful day, and I was in a beautiful car and I had some money in the bank and I remembered the way Amanda looked when she was modeling an Odalisque, while we were taking a break between making love and drinking Champagne, and I had to admit I didn't have anything to complain about, really. Philosophy's not my game. And I remembered that old saying by Voltaire: "The perfect is the enemy of the good." Actually, he said the "best," not "perfect," but I think he meant to say perfect. If he didn't, he should have. I'd write him a letter, except he'd been dead for two hundred years, and all things considered I'd rather be where I was just now.

185

Amanda was waiting for me on the steps of City Hall and came skipping down the walk and jumped into the passenger seat. She was wearing a big smile as though I were picking her up for the high school sock hop.

"I love your car," she said. Well, there was no need to ask if she was psychologically damaged by having to fight off an intruder with a police special. "How are you, darling?"

"I'm okay. But more to the point, how are you?"

"I'm fine. Really."

She slid over and sat next to me and put her hand on my leg.

"What the hell happened?" I asked.

"Well, I was asleep. It must have been around five in the morning. It was still dark out. And I heard this knocking outside my window. It sounded like someone was banging on the wall. So I turned on the light, and there in the window was this hideous face. He had a shaved head and no neck and he looked half human. You know Shakespeare. Who's the disgusting character in that play called something or other?"

"Caliban. The Tempest."

"Yes. That's it. Caliban. I swear I've never seen an uglier man, ever. He was sliding the window open."

"Obviously not just a peeping tom."

"No. He was trying to get in. I yelled, but there was no one in the house, and he must have known it, because he kept on coming. I had the gun you gave me on the nightstand, and I grabbed it and pointed it at him, thinking it would scare him away, but he kept pushing the window open, so I pulled the trigger. The glass shattered and he dropped out of sight. I heard him yell. I'm pretty sure I hit him. I wouldn't be surprised if he's missing an ear. You know the trigger pull's a little stiff, so it shoots to the right."

"Try cocking it next time."

"I know. But I was in a hurry and a little flustered. And then I called the police. They came pretty quickly. And you know the rest."

I'll say this for the Honorable Amanda, she didn't frighten easily. You had to like her for that, if nothing else. And there was more there than nothing else. I knew that already, and I learned more about it later.

"I suppose there's not much doubt that this is related to the blackmail letter," I said.

"No. None at all. It's too much of a coincidence otherwise. That's why it didn't really bother me too much. I think they were just trying to scare me into paying."

"Did you tell Kowalski about the blackmail letters?"

"No. I thought I'd better talk to you about that first."

"Yes. Let's think about that. What if he had gotten into your bedroom? I doubt he expected you to have a gun."

"I don't know. But if he was only trying to frighten me, he probably wouldn't even have come all the way in. After all, if it was related to the blackmail, and if they really did want to get paid, they wouldn't gain anything by harming me. What would be the point?"

"I think you're right." I didn't mention a thought that had been fluttering around in the back of my mind—that maybe the blackmail letters were a red herring designed to cover for something more sinister, more deadly.

"Do you think you could recognize the guy if you saw him again? Or maybe a photo?"

"Yes, I'm sorry to say. It's going to be a while before I can forget his awful face. Kowalski had me look through a lot of mug shots, but none of them were remotely ugly enough."

"And where the hell was the Honorable Freddie while this was going on?"

"He wasn't home. I didn't know it at the time. We have separate bedrooms. Very civilized. I never know what time he comes in when he's out late. And he was still out doing whatever he does all night. Some woman, obviously. So I was there alone. It's a very good thing I had your gun, or who knows what might have happened?"

"Are you sure you hit him? If he's going around looking like van Gogh, it'll make it a little easier to identify him."

"I told you, I didn't miss. I heard him yell. I just didn't get him square. If there's a second time, there won't be a third time. Then it'll be just like when Scarlett shot the deserter."

"I never got that far in the book."

"Well, she did. Let him have it in the kisser, as you Yanks would say. And served him right, too."

"Okay, Scarlett. Do you want me to take you home?"

"No, darling. The police are there looking for clues or something. Besides, I'm starved. What would you say to a little lunch?" She grinned at me.

"A straight line? Really?" I said.

"And what would you say to the Beverly Hills Hotel? I like their room service."

Well, I did too. I did a U-turn and headed back where I had come from.

I read something by an English politician who wrote that nothing was so exhilarating as being shot at and missed. Well, Amanda took the opposite view, because she had done the shooting and, whether she missed or not, she was plenty exhilarated. We spent the next hour in our room without even bothering to order room service; and when we finally did, we put on our hotel robes and then took them off again as soon as the waiter had left.

"Don't you just love eating starkers?" she said.

"Starkers? Which ones are those? The things next to the salmon?"

"Very lame. I like you much better when you're quoting literature."

"How about Kipling? Do you like Kipling?"

"I hope you're not expecting me to say 'I don't know, I've never kippled.' I'll have some Shakespeare, please, darling. Or Marlowe."

"'Shall I compare thee to a summer's day?'"

"Yes. That's much better. And what was that line about making you hungry?"

"'Other women cloy the appetites they feed; she makes hungry where she most satisfies.'"

"Mmm. Lovely. And look, there's some butter left."

Chapter Twenty-Four

The people at the British consulate were naturally disturbed by the incident at Amanda's, and they hired a couple of private cops to stand watch round the clock. I was glad about that. Otherwise, I might have had to move her to a safer place. One cop had just come on duty when I finally took her home around five. I knew the guy. He worked security for one of the studios and had his evening hours free, because his wife had thrown him out and he needed the extra cash. He was a friend of Perry's, so I was pretty sure he was a solid guy who could handle himself. His name was DiMaggio, like the Yankee centerfielder. He told everyone they were cousins, but they weren't.

I walked Amanda to the door and checked the house before kissing her and telling her I'd call later.

"Thank you, Rhett," she said, softly. "It was a lovely afternoon." And I really believed she meant it.

On the way back to my car I stopped to say hello to the rental cop.

"Hiya, DiMaggio."

"Howdy, Chief."

"What's the rumpus?"

What Hamlet Said

"Same old thing. Had to rescue one of the studio's new heartthrobs out of a bathhouse. He didn't want to come along peaceably, but he came. What is it with these pretty boys? Girls too easy?"

"Beats me. Any word around town about what happened to that cowboy—Rex Lockhart?"

"You mean Jimmy Hicks? Nope. Not a word. It's kinda funny. Usually you hear things, you know?"

"Yeah, I do. Well, look after the lady."

"She something special to you?"

"Yeah. She's paying me."

"Gotcha. Is there a husband in the picture?"

"What do you think?"

I wanted to call Patterson at the FBI office, but it was after hours. I had used up the afternoon in bed with Amanda. Well, there are worse ways to look after a client's welfare. But I had a hunch Patterson just might have some interesting photos. I did believe that Blinky turned over the passport pictures and their negatives to the hard cases and their manager. But I didn't believe that Flash made only one print from each negative. That seemed a little too honest. And, besides, if Patterson had Blinky on the FBI payroll, it stood to reason that he might also know and appreciate Flash Gordini's talents. And if either Flash or Patterson had an entire set of duplicate passport shots, maybe Amanda could recognize the ugly guy in the window. Caliban might be missing an ear now, but I figured he'd still be recognizable.

I thought about driving over to San Pedro, but Joe's bakery would be closed at this hour. Magda's stuff sold out by early afternoon every day. Besides, Joe hadn't seemed all that interested in giving me much in the way of local gossip. So I decided against it and went back to the Garden of Allah. Once again, I didn't need a shower because Amanda and I had taken care of that just before we checked out. But a swim and a drink or two would be welcome. And maybe Hobey would have some news.

Which he did.

"I've been fired off the picture," he said.

I'd found him in his usual spot beside the pool. Hedda was there too. She was concentrating on a batch of handwritten letters, some of which looked like they'd been printed by a third-grader on lined yellow paper.

"What happened?" I said. I made an effort to look surprised, but I wasn't, and he knew it.

"Well, it came down to the fact that they wanted to follow the book as closely as possible, and I saw the project as an opportunity to use the silly thing as a way to make something of real value. The way I saw it, the book was a departure. Or should be. But they said they weren't going to invest millions in a departure when the audience was expecting an arrival. Or words to that effect. You know, I had come up with what I considered a perfect concept. A classic love triangle. Rhett loved Scarlett, Scarlett loved Ashley, and Ashley had a weakness for Rhett. Well, isn't it obvious? An equilateral triangle. I wonder if Mrs. Mitchell even saw it. Writers don't always understand their own stuff. But it was a perfect structure, potentially."

"And they didn't go for it?" Hard to believe.

"No. I hesitate to repeat what they said about that."

"I'm sorry," I said.

"Thank you. But I'm not surprised. At least I got a check out of it. So, have a drink and let's celebrate my liberation. You know when God closes a door, He usually opens a window."

"Do you believe that?"

"Actually I do, although God doesn't seem all that interested in my career lately. But things do have a way of working out for the best. Now I'll have time to finish my novel."

I'll say this for him—no one I ever knew suffered disappointment better than he did. Unfortunately, he'd had a lot of practice. I guess he was used to it.

"Hey, listen to this, you guys," said Hedda. "'My boyfriend says he was kidnapped by aliens from outer space and they gave him a nasty disease which he gave to me unbeknownst. Should I believe him? PS It burns and itches something awful. Signed Wondering.' Ha! What a line! Do you believe these dopes? What should I tell her?"

"Tell her that aliens don't carry human diseases. Not that kind, anyway. So he must have picked it up somewhere else. Maybe a mosquito bite."

"That's a good one," said Hedda.

"How about another drink?" asked Hobey. He poured out a couple of tumblers of straight gin. Over ice. "Anything new in the espionage business?"

"Yeah, it looks like some of our European friends are using LA as a training ground for their gangs. I told you about Jimmy. The cops still don't know where he is or even *if* he is, and they haven't been able to identify that headless body, but the boys at the FBI figure it is Jimmy because he was last seen with Lulu Marquessa, who turns out to be a foreign agent infiltrating a gang of Croatian separatists. They figured out who she was and killed her. Jimmy just happened to be there, so they got rid of him too."

"Poor kid."

"Any theories?"

"No. But if one comes to me before I finish this bottle and half of the next one, you'll be the first to know. I'm still surprised the Japs aren't involved somehow."

"Here's another one. Listen to this..."

But I figured I might get some use out of the rest of the evening by stopping at the pier and having a few words with Perry, so I left Hobey and Hedda to their miseries, the one personal, the other vicarious.

Perry was getting ready to start his evening shift.

"Hiya, Chief," he said.

"Hiya, Chief. What's the rumpus?"

"Could be something," he said. "I had a little talk with Blinky. He's the kind who hears things, you know."

"So I've heard."

"So what he's been hearing is that something big is in the works. A bunch of hard cases are planning to knock over somebody's shipment of money. Word is it's gonna be a big score. Could get messy."

"Where'd he hear that?"

"The usual."

"That's it?"

"That's it. But that ain't nothing, seems to me."

"No. You're right. No idea about the target?"

"Nope. But if I was in the business of figuring this stuff out, I'd pay attention to the word 'shipment.'"

"Meaning the money's going to be on the move."

"That's the way I read it. Sounds like the great train robbery kind of thing. Ever see that movie?"

"Before my time, wasn't it?"

"I guess it was. Silent job. Saw it when I was a kid. Bronco Billy Anderson was in it. Ever hear of him?"

What Hamlet Said

"No."

"He was sort of famous in his day. Jewish guy from St. Louis. Made a lot of westerns. Goes to show you, I guess. What exactly, I don't know. Anyway, that's the word: shipment."

"You're right. That's a good place to start. Any word on who these guys might be?"

"Nope. And that's something else that should start you thinking. If it was any of the usual boys, somebody would have a clue. One of the boys would tell his girlfriend and she'd tell her pimp and he'd drop a hint just to show he's in the know. But there's nothing on the street. Not yet, anyway. That's not to say there won't be something later."

"I see what you mean. I'd appreciate it if you kept your ears open."

"Always. Well, here comes my first load of suckers. Wanna go for a boat ride?"

"No, thanks. I've got some phone calls to make."

"Tell her I said hello."

"Who?"

"Whoever she is. I ain't particular. Just ask Della."

I went back to the Garden. Hobey and Hedda had called it a night by then, so I went to my room and called Amanda. A maid answered and said Amanda had gone to bed. Apparently the Brits had decided to beef up the domestic staff, too, so now there would be round-the-clock people inside as well as out. That was all to the good.

So I fixed myself a drink and went down to the pool again to think things over. Specifically, what was this business about a "shipment"?

Chapter Twenty-Five

In the morning, I went to the office. Della was there, typing her blackmail letters or something. I never did know what she was working on, but I knew it was rarely something for me. I think she thought of the office as hers and that I was just an occasional visitor to be tolerated. But she did answer my phone and look after me in ways that were helpful. Between her and Perry, I had insights into worlds that otherwise might have been closed to me. And they did the kind of favors I needed doing from time to time. Also, she added the proper tone to a private dick's office. How many minutes do you boil an egg before it explodes? She was just a minute short of that. So it was a good arrangement for both of us. Besides, I liked her, and she liked me too. In her fashion.

"Morning, Chief," she said through a cloud of Pall Mall smoke. She had recently had her hair freshly henna-ed. Vivid.

"Morning, faithful employee. Any calls?"

"Nope."

"How can I get hold of Flash Gordini?"

"With rubber gloves on, if you're smart. But if you just want to talk to him, I have his private number. You want me to call?"

"If you please."

What Hamlet Said

"Hello, Boss," said Flash, once Della had tracked him down. "What's up?"

"I've been wondering. Word is that a certain photographer took some passport pictures of a crew of plug-uglies for a citizen named Blinky and turned over the developed photos *and* the negatives. Ring a bell?"

"No. No bells."

"Would the bells start ringing if there was some cash involved?"

"Ding-dong. But I don't hear so good over the phone."

"What's a good time for you to come by the office?"

"No time like the present. Thirty minutes." He hung up.

Flash showed up an hour later, which for him was punctual. He was wearing the same checked suit and derby hat, and he had his toothpick already at work. He was in a jaunty mood.

"I remember you said you were a businessman," I said after he had sat down in one of the visitor's chairs.

"That's right." He smiled at the prospect of cash and shot his cuffs.

"And I also heard you were tight with the FBI."

The smile disappeared. Flash opened his eyes at that and began to squirm and make noises of denial. But it wasn't working. I hadn't been sure before this that he was a Bureau informant, but I was sure now.

"Don't worry," I said. "We're all on the same team."

"You too?" he said. He seemed to relax, a little.

"Sure. Just ask Bill Patterson, next time you see him. But what I want to know doesn't have much to do with the Feds." This was not strictly true, but there was no sense complicating things. "A client of mine had a nighttime break-in. She saw the guy and put a bullet through his ear lobe."

"Really? Tough broad."

"Yes. She went through all the mug shots downtown, but no dice."

"Funny. They have what you might call a complete collection of the bad boys, especially the ones who like B&E. I'm surprised he wasn't in there."

"Me too. So I was thinking that one of these new boys in town might have been involved. I was told they were a rough-looking bunch. And she said this guy gave ugly a bad name. It's a long shot, but worth checking out. So I was wondering if you by any chance kept some copies of those photos you took."

"Me?"

"Yeah."

He thought about it for a while.

"Some people would say that ain't what you'd call ethical, seeing as how the deal was to turn over the works, and a deal's a deal, you know?"

"I've heard that too. But some other people would say that ethics are a matter of opinion. Some people would say snitching to the Feds is unethical, while others would say it's doing a civic duty."

"What sort of people are you?"

"The sort that appreciates people who do their civic duty."

He thought about it some more. "I'm a businessman," he said finally.

"So you've said."

"So let's say I did have some copies, though I ain't saying I do. But let's say I did. What then?"

"Well, then, I would only ask you to let me borrow them for an afternoon so my client can look at them. Then I'd give them back."

"When people borrow, they pay rent."

"You pay rent for an apartment. When you borrow, you pay interest."

"Semitics."

"But I take your point. We'd be happy to offer something in return."

"How much?"

"Well, 'much' is the wrong word, speaking of semantics. In return for the loan, I'd be willing not to spread it around town that one Flash Gordini not only kept duplicate photos when he wasn't supposed to, but also that he's a stooge for the Feds."

He turned a little white and thought about that for a minute. He was expecting a different kind of interest.

"That ain't fair," he said, finally.

"I know. And some would say it's not ethical either. How soon can you bring the pictures over?"

"Who says I got 'em?"

"No one. But if you did have them, how soon could you get them here? I only need them for a couple of hours. That's not much in exchange for you being able to sleep at night."

"Who says I sleep at night?"

"Or during the day, then. How long?"

He shuffled his feet under the chair. To me it was a simple proposition, but I knew he had considerations that I'd never hear of and that made what seemed simple to me very complicated to him.

"Are we clear that mum's the word on the friends I talk to now and then?" he said finally.

"You mean those same friends I have? Yeah, we're clear."

"If I had cab fare, I could be back in an hour."

"Then what would you do with your car?"

"Leave it here so's I could drive home afterwards."

"Here's twenty bucks."

"Cabs are expensive. It's a long way to Pedro and back, what with the traffic."

"If it costs more than that, make up the difference. See you in an hour."

I knew he'd take his own car and pocket the twenty. It would make him feel better about being leaned on. He could tell himself that he took me for some cash. Well, that was all right. A man's got a right to protect his dignity.

Next, I called Catherine. I figured she was home because it was still morning and she didn't get started with her day till later.

"Hello, gorgeous," I said when she picked up.

"Hello, Sparky," she said in her morning sultry voice. "Which Sparky am I talking to?"

"Sparky the detective."

She giggled. "I know. I'm just pulling something."

"Sounds good to me."

"Smooth talker. What can I do for you at this hour of the day?"

"The usual."

"Mmm. Sounds good to me! I haven't had my bath yet. Do you care?"

"You know what Napoleon said in a letter to Josephine."

"No, but I'll bet you do."

"He said I'll be home in two days, don't wash."

"He must have been some kind of nasty pervert. So what do you really want?"

"I want you to introduce me to your boyfriend Tony."

"Okay. Do I care why?"

"Not really. Would tonight suit you?"

"Sure. Manny's still in Utah or someplace, trying to save money on a western, so I'm as free as air. I'll meet you at the pier like always. Eight o'clock?"

"I'll be the one wearing a smile."

"I'll be the one wearing a mink!"

Chapter Twenty-Six

Flash Gordini was back in under an hour. He came into the office furtively, looking behind the door before he sat down. He dropped a strip of passport photos on my desk. I took a quick look through them. They all looked like mug shots from the San Quentin death row.

"Quite a crew," I said.

"High society they ain't. I'll be back for them at five."

Flash took another look around, as if there were hidden microphones and one-way mirrors in my office. Then he disappeared, avoiding the California sunlight and seeking the shadows. Metaphorically speaking.

I was pretty sure these weren't his only copies and thought about keeping them, but I remembered that Flash had told me a deal's a deal. I called Amanda and said I'd be right over.

"Good," she said. "I'm just about to have my bath."

What was it with these beautiful women, I wondered? It was kind of like the old days when the French king had his leisurely morning levee. No sense rushing into the business of the kingdom. No sense rushing into the morning.

On the way out, I said to Della, "What hour of the day do you take your bath?"

"Who wants to know?"

"Just curious."

"Who says I take a bath?"

"Maybe your hubby."

"You mean Perry? How would he know?"

Della liked to answer questions with questions. It was her way of saying "What's it to ya?"

Amanda's maid let me in and said madam was upstairs in her boudoir and I was to go right up. By this, I assumed that the Honorable Freddie had left for the day or hadn't returned yet from the night. Either way, it didn't matter.

Amanda was wearing next to nothing, just a filmy idea the size of a handkerchief, and she came gliding seductively up to me and folded herself in my arms. She was long and willowy, and she fit against me really well.

"Hello, darling," she whispered, through a delicate mist of perfume. "You said you had something to show me. What a coincidence."

There was plenty of time between now and five, and if I was a little late, Flash could wait.

After a while, though, I got back to what I'd come for. Or, rather, the other thing. We were sitting up in her bed, starkers, as she liked to call it, and looking through the mug shots. The six men were profoundly ugly, and Amanda wrinkled her brow as she studied them, as much from revulsion as concentration. She paused at one in particular—a broken-nosed thug with a shaved head and no neck —which matched her description of the intruder.

"It *might* be him," she said.

"If it is, losing an ear won't matter much to his social life."

"But I can't be sure. Who *are* these Calibans?"

"Recent arrivals on our shores."

"Illegal?"

"Very."

"Where'd these pictures come from?"

"From a guy who takes pictures of illegals for illegal purposes."

"A member of your club?"

"They wouldn't have me. But an occasional resource to us Jack Armstrongs."

"Who's that?"

"Jack Armstrong? The All-American boy? Radio hero? Sponsored by Wheaties, Breakfast of Champions? You've never heard of him? I'm surprised."

"I told you, I'm almost completely ignorant of anything not having to do with the Manners of the Toffs or sex."

"Well, that's more than enough. You know what Voltaire said about perfection."

"No, and I don't care. What are you doing tonight?"

"I have a meeting. Out on the *Lucky Lady*."

"Business?"

"Of course."

"Going alone?"

"No. I'm going with the woman who's going to introduce me to Tony Scungilli. You remember him, I think."

"Yes. Short, fat, and too much cologne. I'm surprised you haven't met him before, in your line of work."

"There hasn't been a need until now."

"Who's the woman? The one I saw you with the other night on the boat? Miss Pneumatic of 1937?"

"Yes. Just a friend. Tony's sometime girlfriend. And what are you doing tonight?"

"Another consulate party. Fancy dress. What you Yanks call a costume party. Everybody dresses up and pretends to be someone else. Rather a good joke in this town. Pretenders pretending."

"What will you be?"

"I'm thinking of a nun. I don't know what Freddie's going to be. Maybe the Queen of the May. We haven't discussed it. Just one of many things we don't talk about. I'm going to meet him there. Hardly the behavior of a happy couple, but there you are. Funnily enough, we actually are happier doing things that way."

"And just where is the Honorable Freddie today?"

"Who knows? Off doing Freddie things."

"Didn't it worry you that he might have come bursting in this afternoon?"

"No. It's not done. He would call first. And do you know why? Certainly not because he cares. It's because he wouldn't want to be embarrassed or be put in a position where he'd be expected to make a scene. He'd have to play the outraged husband. Too 'shame-making,' as my friends used to say—not catching the erring wife, but having to play the role. And he'd have no idea of what to say to you, beyond 'I say! What's all this?' So discovering us in the act is the last thing he'd want."

"Another rule for your book."

"Yes. 'Always call home first.' That rule will actually be useful. But I suppose that's why the blackmailer's photos are so annoying. They can't be ignored or unseen, once seen. They require some sort of unpleasant action, when you'd really rather not."

"Well, speaking of really rather not, I'm sorry to say it's time for me to go."

She made a pouty face.

"Really? It's only four and I don't want any tea. Come, let me make you hungry one more time before you have to go. You should always leave on an empty stomach. And speaking of stomachs, let me roll over."

A half hour or so later, I was just leaving when she said "I forgot to tell you. I got another of those letters this morning. It said 'Next time you won't be so lucky,' 'you' meaning me, of course."

"What? Why didn't you mention it before this?"

"I don't know. Goes to show how little I cared, I guess."

"Was that the only message?"

"Yes. But I'm not at all worried. We've round-the-clock help, inside and out. These amateurs are just trying to frighten me into paying. Little do they know, you can't get blood out of a stone. I'm starting to think that if they threaten to publish the photo, I'll tell them to go ahead and be damned, like the Old Duke. I'm slowly getting tired of the charade with Freddie. Besides, I still have your gun, and this time I won't forget to cock it."

"Yes, that makes the trigger easier."

"I know, darling. I know. And if I pot one of them, maybe it'll teach the others to mind their own business."

I had to smile at that. And I was pretty sure that her security was more than adequate. But more than that, I had to smile at her sangfroid. She didn't seem the least bit frightened. And in point of fact, I was quite sure she wasn't.

"There'll always be an England," I said.

"Damned right. Call me tomorrow, please, darling. You can tell me about your adventures, and I'll tell you about mine."

"You show me yours and I'll show you mine?"

"Don't be vulgar, darling."

After the afternoon we'd just spent, I had to smile at that one. But there was no doubt about it: she really did make me hungry where most others satisfied. *Most* others, but not all, I remembered. A few had her same talent. But I had to wonder again, what the hell was wrong with the Honorable Freddie? And what was the crack about the Queen of the May? Might that have something to do with it?

Promptly at eight I was at the pier chatting with Perry when Catherine's Rolls pulled up and she stepped out, looking like an artist's conception of a mink-coated producer's wife and a gangster's girlfriend all rolled into one.

"Don't you just love it when reality and imagination merge?" I said to Perry as we watched her sashay toward us.

"I love it all to hell," he said, with a grin. "I ain't all that sure what you mean, but I get the gist."

"Hello, Perry," she said and kissed him on top of his shaved head. "And hello, Sparky the detective. How do I look?"

"Good enough to eat," I said.

"Mmmm. I told Jesus to find a place to park and just wait. How long will we be, do you think?"

"Not much more than an hour. That's all I'll need, I mean. You may want to stay longer."

"I doubt it. You know they call Tony 'Tony the Snail,' but that's just because of his last name. When it comes to other things he's just the opposite. He should learn to slow down, but I think it's too late. You know what they say about old dogs. Plus, he hasn't seen me in a while. You know what that means."

"I can guess."

"Well, let's go, boys. Anchors aweigh!"

Fifteen minutes later, we were climbing up the staircase to the main salon of the *Lucky Lady*. As usual, the room was alive with noise. There was music from the dance band and the girl singer warbling "I Get a Kick Out of You." It was almost but not quite drowned out by the collective murmuring and occasional groans and shouts of glee as the suckers lost and now and then won, and the choir of slot machines sang out their cheerful-sounding messages of failure. Smoke hung over the crowd, which was a couple of thousand strong, as usual, and downstairs you could hear an occasional joyous shout of *Bingo!* All together it was bedlam, but a happy bedlam, even for the losers who, I suspect, expected to lose and so were not disappointed. They were having fun doing it. Most were not degenerate gamblers throwing away the baby's Pablum; most were there to be taken advantage of and to enjoy it while it was happening. They were playing a mugs' game and were happy enough to be the mugs.

"Tony's expecting us," Catherine said. "I called him on the ship-to-shore."

"If you ever want a new career, you can be my secretary."

"What about Della?"

"She won't sit on my lap."

"I will."

"I know."

"And I won't even wear anything under my dress."

"I know."

"Smooth talker. We're supposed to go to Tony's office. It's back there." She pointed to the back of the ship—what had been the stern before it was converted to a floating hangar.

There was a muscle-bound goombah standing outside the door.

"Hi, Vito," said Catherine.

"Hello, Miss," he said deferentially. "The Boss is waiting on you."

"He means he's expecting us," she whispered to me.

We went inside. I was surprised at the office. It was actually pretty tasteful. I guess I'd expected zebra-skin couches and velvet landscapes of Genoa or Venice or someplace. But it looked like a normal businessman's working place—a normal *tycoon's* working place, I should say. There were bookshelves mostly containing pictures of Tony with various dignitaries and star entertainers. One shelf had a complete set of the Collier's Encyclopedia to add a touch of literacy and class, I suppose. Tony was sitting behind a huge mahogany desk that was neatly covered with adding machine tapes and ledgers supplied from his counting rooms on a regular basis.

He stood up, grinned at Catherine, and came around the desk and held out his arms. She obliged happily and swept into his embrace.

"Seems like a long time," he said. "You look gorgeous."

"I know," she said. "And it's only been two weeks."

"To me, that's long."

He looked over at me and, to my surprise, smiled as though he was genuinely glad to see me.

"This is the guy?" he said.

"Yep. Let me introduce my best buddy who once saved me from drowning in the Garden of Allah pool, Riley Fitzhugh, who goes professionally by Bruno Feldspar."

"Pleased to meet you," he said, shaking my hand in the proverbial vise-like grip. He wasn't trying to make a point. That's just the way he shook hands.

"Tony Scungilli," he said, as if I didn't know. That was polite, I thought, because he knew it was unnecessary. "Which do you like? Riley or Bruno?"

"Riley. Bruno was a name the studio gave me, and later it stuck around town."

"I get it. I'm surprised you didn't stick in the movie business. You got the look."

"Too many phonies."

He nodded. "I hear you. I thought about it myself but decided against it for the same reason. Besides, who needs another Clark Gable, right? Want a drink?"

Well, he was far from another Clark Gable and he was well aware of it. He was about five feet five in his custom lifts. He was also stocky. That is, he looked fat at first, but on second look you realized there was no flab there. He was as solid as an aluminum beer barrel. His hair was black and slicked back in the approved gangster fashion, and he wore a dark silk suit, dark shirt and matching tie, and, yes, too much cologne. He had a well-maintained suntan.

"So, Catherine tells me you want to talk a little business."

"Yes. Well, sort of."

"Honey, why don't you tell Louie to get you some chips so's you can go win some of my money while Riley and I talk?"

"Okay," she said. "Call me when you're finished."

She left, and we both watched her go, appreciatively.

"She tells me you did a job for her husband. Found her for him."

"Yes. That's how we met."

"She's a dead ringer for Minnie David, the actress."

"I know." Minnie was Manny Stairs's first wife. That's why he wanted Catherine found.

"Yeah, I heard all about it," said Tony. "I knew Minnie. Real looker."

And I knew that too. It was this same affable gangster who had been with Minnie when she overdosed; he took off, leaving her dead in a motor court. But at least he called the cops before he left.

"So, what's on your mind?" he asked. "Any friend of Catherine's is a friend of mine, unless you're banging her. It's bad enough I have to share her with her squirt of a husband."

I was prepared for this. After all, it was entirely predictable.

"No. Hard as it may be to believe, we're just friends. I've got enough on my plate."

"Yeah? Is there ever enough?"

"For me, there is. I can't speak for anyone else."

"Okay. I wouldn't like to find out you're conning me. But if not, we're friends. You're a private dick, am I right?"

"That's right."

"So, like I said, what's on your mind?"

Chapter Twenty-Seven

What was on my mind was the daily boat trip of the *Lucky Lady*'s cash.

"I've been working on a case," I said, "sort of in cooperation with the Feds."

"Which Feds?"

"The FBI."

He nodded as if to say That's okay, I guess, as long as it's not the IRS.

"And it's a pretty murky situation involving possible foreign agents, people we might find ourselves fighting not too long from now."

"Krauts or Nips?"

"Krauts, I think. But maybe not them, directly. Maybe some of their clients, so to speak, people the Germans could be supporting on the sly. Or maybe people acting on their own but who are sympathetic to our potential enemies. People trying to overthrow their governments back home and install a regime that's favorable to the Nazis. That sort of thing. It's hard to tell."

"Revolutionaries."

"Yes. Back home. Or they could become Fifth Columnists or saboteurs here, when the war does break out."

"And it will, sure as three of a kind beats a pair. For a first-generation Italian, it's a goddam shame, 'cause that dick-faced Mussolini will drag Italy into it as sure as he likes to dress up like some opera queen. The old country will end up in a heap of rubble, and all us Italian boys over here will have to help make it happen. But we will, you know. We're Americans through and through. We believe in the American dream, 'cause we know it works. So who are these bastards, and what are they planning?"

"I think they're Yugoslav fascists, and I think they're planning to knock over your daily cash shipment."

"Huh?"

"I could be wrong, but, more importantly, I could be right. The boys at the FBI have been telling me the obvious, which is that money is the lifeblood of all these dissident movements. They have to have it to recruit new members and buy weapons and false papers and just to live on, day to day. And they figure robbery is the easiest way to get it. Well, all that's just common sense. Their problem is finding a target that is both rich and relatively easy to knock over. Gas stations and liquor stores are easy but just chicken feed, and sooner or later they'd get caught. A bank—maybe. A Brink's truck—maybe. But they both have well-organized security. That's their business. Pretty risky. But a lone boat a couple of miles out to sea travelling with just a few guards who make the same run every morning and are not in the least suspicious, or maybe even all that alert—that might be the easiest, fattest target of all."

"How do you know we make a delivery every morning?"

"I hear things."

"Okay. You got my attention."

"So the word from my sources is that there's a new gang in town and they're planning to knock over a shipment—that's the word.

Shipment. Of what, no one seems to know. But it's got to be money. Otherwise why bother?"

"Agreed. Fencing stolen goods takes a network. Mink coats. Cigarettes. You name it. Those networks ain't something you can put together overnight. And I'd know if someone was trying. I hear things too."

"I believe it. So, when I figured they were after a large shipment of cash, I thought I should have a talk with you."

"What about the Feds?"

"I haven't said anything to them yet."

"Do me a favor and don't, while I think about this."

"Okay."

"You have any idea how much cash goes ashore every day?"

"I see the crowds. I can make a good guess. Hundreds of thousands."

"That's right. You know, it's funny we anchored this tub outside the three-mile limit and figured we're safe from the California state boys. And naturally with all the cash going ashore, we think about security. But we figured the only risk was once we landed, so we cover that by having a Brink's truck at the landing every day. The bags of cash get transferred quickly and off to the bank, no sweat. Our boys go along in the truck just to be on the safe side. And two other guys follow in a car. We've never had a problem. But we never gave much—or even any—thought to the idea of a high-seas heist." He nodded his head as if in appreciation of the idea. "I'm embarrassed I never thought of it," he said.

"Do all four gambling ships make the run at the same time?"

"No. The others don't do near the business we do. In fact, we do more than the three of them combined. There's no set schedule for when they make their runs. It's unpredictable. Not like ours."

"Which makes yours the only shipment they can plan for, which is kind of too bad. I was thinking you could join up and make the run together every day. They probably wouldn't try to hit all four boats together."

"I could talk to the others, I guess; but, to be honest with you, we ain't all that friendly. We're competitors. The fact is, it wouldn't break their hearts if we did get knocked off. They'd give us the horselaugh. We have what you might call a little history between us." He considered the situation for a few minutes. "You know anything about these guys? The ones thinking of this? Are they pros?"

"If they're who we think they are, they look like refugees from the mountains of misery. They're Nazis, criminals, and thugs who are used to being on the run. Nothing to take lightly."

"Even so, don't these dipshits know who they're dealing with?"

"They're foreigners. In all probability, they don't even speak much, if any, English. Just arrived. So, no, they don't know who they're dealing with. Somebody'll tell them what to do and how and when to do it."

"How do you think they'd go about it?"

"The same way you would, I imagine."

"Yeah. Pretty obvious. Get a speedboat. Wait for our boat about halfway between the ship and shore. Run right up alongside and open fire and kill everybody on board, grab the money, and take off for some rendezvous, maybe with a trawler or even a U-boat off-shore. Movie stuff."

"That's the way I'd do it. Even without the trawler or the U-boat, it's a perfect setup. In a fast boat, they can disappear in a hurry."

"The sound of gunfire wouldn't bother anybody."

"Not with the Navy always having gunnery practice. No one would think anything of it."

"Pretty smart."

"It could work. Combine the element of surprise with half a dozen thugs with Tommy guns, and you have an almost foolproof plan. They won't bother with 'Hands up and hand over the cash' stuff. Just open fire, grab the cash bags, drop a grenade in the boat, and take off. Thirty seconds."

"If they're all foreigners, who gave them the idea, and who told them about the regular cash boat?"

"I don't know for sure."

"You find out, you let me know."

"You'll be the first."

"What about the Feds? The FBI?"

"Well, to be honest, this is their baby, or should be. They're responsible for domestic counterintelligence. They'd see this as something more than simple robbery."

"Maybe we should talk."

"That might be a good idea. I can set it up, if you want."

"Yeah. Let's do that. In the meantime, we won't send any money boats ashore. Not until we figure out if this is real and, if it is, what to do about it."

"Makes sense. But maybe you should send the boat every day— without any money—just in case they're watching."

"Yeah. Don't let them sniff the fact that we're wise. 'Course, we ain't in the business of setting traps for thieves. We're in the business of making and keeping our money."

"Sure. But it can't hurt to have friends in the FBI. You never know when they'll come in handy."

He studied me for a moment. "I like you, kid. You got a head on your shoulders. You sure you ain't banging Catherine?"

"I'm sure."

I didn't consider what Catherine and I did to be "banging." Tony probably wouldn't agree with such fine distinctions, but I knew Catherine was the soul of discretion, when she wanted to be. I wasn't worried about that.

"So..." Tony thought about things and watched me through narrowed eyes. "Bottom line. What's in it for you? Why bring me this?"

"It's part of a case I'm working on. To tell you the truth, I don't know how this all fits together with some other stuff, but I think it does, somehow. But even if it isn't connected some way, I figure doing you a favor is a good idea."

"You heard we do favors for our friends? In return for favors they do for us? Is that it?"

"That's it. The same goes with the FBI. It doesn't hurt to help them out. They're helping me, too."

"All friends together."

"Just like summer campers singing around the fire."

"Kum by fucking ya? I never went to summer camp. Summer in Brooklyn meant open fire hydrants, stickball in the streets, and stealing cars for joyrides. And trying to get Marie Vanzetti to put out. Good times."

"Did she?"

"Marie Vanzetti? Like a mink. So the bottom line is you don't want nothing for this information—except my friendship?"

"That's right. If it ends up that I save you money, maybe you'll remember that. But that's up to you."

"I got a good memory, kid. Don't worry about that. You got a phone number?"

I gave him a card with my number at the office and also at the Garden of Allah.

What Hamlet Said

"Bruno Feldspar," he said. "Quite a handle. Sounds like a Yid. Don't get me wrong. A lot of our friends are Yids. Ben. Mickey. You probably know who I'm talking about. But we can always use a Mick. So we'll stay with Riley. Okay?"

"Suits me." I wasn't really a Mick, but it wasn't worth mentioning.

Just then, Catherine came back.

"And speaking of mink..." said Tony. "You win anything, honey?"

"What do you think? I always win. The dealers know what's up. Are you boys through yet? I'm hungry."

"You wanna stay and have some dinner?" said Tony to me.

"No, thanks. I need to get back."

"Tell Jesus to take a nap, Sparky," said Catherine. "I'll be along later."

Chapter Twenty-Eight

The first thing next morning, I called Bill Patterson at the FBI.

"How would you like to have a meeting with one of LA's most well-respected gangsters?"

"Love it! Which one?"

"Tony the Snail Scungilli."

"Wow! Sure thing. What about?"

"Mutual interests. As in Balkan thugs."

"Sounds good. Where and when?"

"I'll set it up. I wanted to check first to make sure you were interested."

"Are you kidding? Any time. You know me: always buried under research. Even a mole likes a glimpse of sunshine now and then."

"I don't suppose this would be a conflict with some of your field agents—the guys who actually carry guns instead of using them for bookends?"

"What? Not at all. It's just more research. Right? Besides, I won't bother them unless I have to. Later. Besides, the Balkans are my pigeon, as the Brits would say."

"Right. I'll get back to you."

I was sitting in my office with my feet on the desk, wondering how to put together all these pieces that just would not fit but somehow seemed like they should, when the phone rang. It was Kowalski.

"Kowalski! How'd you know where to find me?"

"I knew it wasn't Wednesday."

"What's up?"

"I got a woman down here that looks an awful lot like one of your girlfriends, except she's dressed like a nun. Frankly, I don't think she's a real nun."

Uh-oh. "What happened?"

"This time, she didn't miss."

"Another intruder?"

"In a manner of speaking."

"Any idea who it was?"

"Yep. A very good idea, because he was carrying his ID. Name, Frederick Billingsgate."

The Honorable Freddie.

"Is he dead?"

"As it gets. Got him just below the widow's-peak hairline. Right through his mask. 'Course a Lone Ranger mask won't stop a bullet."

"Was he really dressed as the Lone Ranger?"

"Hi-ho, Silver."

"And she was a nun?"

"Bless you, my son. But I gotta tell you, she ain't anything like the nuns at Cardinal Mooney High. She doesn't even carry a ruler. Of course, she does have a gun. Or did, anyway."

"Are we sure she shot him?"

"Pretty sure, since she admitted it. If admitted is the right word. There's no mystery about it. The guy came staggering into her bedroom in the middle of the night while she was just getting ready to take off her habit and get into bed. She'd turned out the lights and this guy came bursting through the door, which apparently was locked. Splintered the whatchamacallit. And when he came lurching for her, she let out a yell to wake the house and then grabbed the gun on the nightstand and screamed at him to stop, and when he didn't, she plugged him. Thought he was another of those guys who'd tried to break in before. The only light came from outside the window, and that was weak, so she couldn't see anything but sinister shapes. Her word—sinister. She says she had no idea who it was or what he was up to. But she was terrified. Said she could smell the liquor on him. He reeked of it. Preliminary tests verify that he was very drunk. Maybe he just wanted to cuddle but had forgotten to take off his mask and cowboy hat."

"Or forgot to call first."

"Eh? Well, they are foreigners, after all, so I suppose it's possible they make cuddling appointments. But it's funny. Some people like the mask-and-costume routine. That's what I hear, anyway."

"How is she?"

"I've seen hysterical women before. She ain't one of them. But she could be in a little shock. That's understandable."

"Any charges likely?"

"Well, there'll be an investigation, of course. But it seems pretty open-and-shut. An accident. The servants all verify her story. They heard the whole thing. Plus, they're diplomats."

"The servants?"

"Anyone ever tell you no one likes a smart ass? The question is: does the great county of Los Angeles really care when one foreign diplomat shoots another in their own country's consulate? I don't know for sure, but I kind of doubt it."

"Is she an official diplomat too?"

"She's listed as a cultural attaché, but that could just be window-dressing,"

"That's news to me."

What Hamlet Said

"Well, here's a scoop, Bruno: it's just possible that your various girlfriends don't tell you everything. I only have one wife, and she hardly tells me anything. Which is the way I like it. But I kind of doubt there'll be any charges. It has all the earmarks of an accident. Or self-defense, take your pick. But the D.A. will let us know. For now, she can be released. You want to come collect her?"

"I'll be right over."

"By the way, we're keeping your gun as evidence."

"I have another."

"I know."

As I collected my hat, I wondered: Why did she turn the lights off before she started getting undressed? Then I thought: she'd already had two very unpleasant encounters with peeping toms and break-in artists. Maybe she was just being careful. I guess. But I made a mental note to check on that.

She was standing outside, like the last time I picked her up. But she wasn't so jaunty this time. She walked slowly to the car and got in, looking exactly like she'd had the very rough night that in fact she had had. Her nun's costume made things that much worse. Somebody said incongruity was the essence of comedy, but there wasn't anything funny about her in a nun's outfit, not on the morning that she'd just killed her husband.

"Hello, honey," I said.

"Oh, Rhett, this is so dreadful." She was very pale.

"Yeah."

She didn't slide over. She leaned her head back on the seat rest and closed her eyes. She looked a lot older than a few days ago, when she'd been playing Odalisque. Still beautiful, though, in her way.

"It's been a nightmare," she said. "Poor Freddie. I feel so..."

"Kowalski told me about it. No need to go over it again. Unless there's something you didn't tell him."

"No, I told him everything that happened. I even told him about the threatening blackmail letters."

"Probably wise."

"I didn't tell him you knew about the letters. I wasn't sure about that."

"Also probably wise. If he gives me any trouble about that, I'll just claim client privilege. Absolutely legitimate."

"It was all so awful. Please just take me back to the house, darling. I hate the thought of going there... to that room again, but I have to change and pack a few things. I can't stay there. Besides, I'm sure the police are all over the place looking for things."

"Where do you want to go?"

"If you'll take me to our hotel, that would be best, I suppose. I don't know where else to go."

"No friends? From the consulate?"

"I told you before, no one likes me. But even if they did, they're all English and this business is too..."

"Embarrassing?"

"Something like that, only worse. They'll want to pretend I don't exist. 'Giving everyone a bad name' and 'letting down the side,' and that sort of rot. Anyway, I don't want to see any of them. I want to hide out like a sick animal until this gets cleared up."

The cops were still at the house, dusting for prints and collecting samples of everything from carpet fibers to dust from under the bed. There didn't seem to be much use in any of it, but that was what they were paid to do, and they were glad for the chance to do it.

I went upstairs with Amanda. There was a crime-scene investigator there, scraping bits of the Honorable Freddie's blood and gray matter off the bedroom wall and putting them in an evidence bag. The cops were being thorough.

Amanda tried not to pay any attention to him and went into her closet and threw some things in an overnight bag.

"I need to use the bathroom," she said.

"Are you finished in there? In the bathroom?" I asked the cop.

"Yeah. Go ahead."

She went into the bathroom and closed the door. I heard her turn on the shower.

"You know," said the cop, "it always amazes me the damage a thirty-eight bullet can do."

"Did you find it?"

"The bullet? Oh, yeah. In the door jamb."

"Not much doubt about where it came from, I suppose."

"None at all. The ballistics boys will do the usual tests, but strictly routine."

I looked around the room. Aside from the broken door and the blood stains, there was nothing out of the ordinary, nothing to suggest anything other than what seemed to have happened. Of possible interest were the drapes. They were very sheer. That could explain why Amanda had turned off the light before starting to undress: the drapes were useless for privacy. I noticed a small, three-by-five framed photo of Freddie on Amanda's dressing table. He was smiling into the camera. When the cop wasn't looking, I slipped it into my pocket.

Amanda came out of the bathroom a few minutes later. Her hair was wet and she had merely run a comb through it. She wore no makeup. Style was not important just then. She had put on a modest gray suit and matching scarf.

I drove her to the Beverly Hills Hotel and checked her in.

"Do you mind not coming up, darling?" she said, her voice thick with fatigue.

"No. Of course not. Get some sleep. I'll call Kowalski and let him know where you are."

"Thank you. Call me later. Or I'll call you." She got in the elevator, and I called Kowalski from the lobby phone booth and left him a message. I had meant to ask her about turning off the lights before undressing, but I forgot. No matter. It would keep. Besides, the see-through drapes more or less explained things.

I looked at my watch. Ten-thirty. The way I figured, it was just about time for some meatloaf and mashed potatoes.

Chapter Twenty-Nine

With the dignity of an English butler, Stavros led me to a booth and handed me a laminated menu. The El Greco was almost empty. It was between breakfast and lunch, my favorite time.

Jessie came over and stood there, looking Junoesque and amused.

"Did you bring the diamond bracelet you promised?" she asked.

"I thought it was a necklace."

"Was it? I get so many offers, it's hard to keep track."

"I understand. But in either case, the answer is the same. I've got to work on my forgetfulness."

"Uh-huh. More tears on my pillow."

"See a doctor. They can fix that. Or get a different boyfriend. How's the meatloaf?"

"Same as always."

"I'll have it anyway."

"Mashed and mixed veggies?"

"Got anything but mixed veggies?"

"Nope."

"Then I'll have mixed veggies. And when you've put in the order, come back for a second. I want to ask you a question."

"Okay. But you'll get the same answer: No tickee, no laundlee."

"That's not the question."

She was back in a minute with a cup of coffee and glass of water. She sat down opposite me in the booth.

"So?"

"You remember the last time I was in here, I asked you about Smitty, the photographer."

"Yeah. Got himself shot in the flophouse."

"Actually, he got shot in—"

"I know, I know. So?"

"There was another guy in here with him on at least two occasions." I showed her the picture of Freddie I had taken from the bedroom. "Could this be the guy?"

She studied it for a few seconds.

"Could be. His face is familiar."

"It's about to get a lot more familiar. You'll see it on the evening paper's front page. His wife put a bullet in him."

"Hurt bad?"

"The worst."

She looked at the picture again. "You know, I think this just might be the guy. He was a classy sort. Nice-looking. Not handsome or anything, but put together. Well dressed. That's why I noticed. Seemed odd for someone like that to be with Smitty."

For some reason, I was not surprised. "Thank you. I promise next time..."

"Save it. I suppose you'll want some strawberry pie after the meatloaf," she said, smiling her most lascivious smile.

"Always."

"Ha! Too bad. We're out."

After breakfast, I drove over to Pedro. I had a question for Joe that I thought he might be willing to answer.

What Hamlet Said

I got there just before the early-morning shift got off work, so the bakery was empty. Joe greeted me with a wave, and Magda came out and gave me a floury hug.

"How is our Mirta?" she said.

"Still in the desert, making movies."

"We are so proud of her. You want strudel?"

"Yes, ma'am. If you please."

"Good. I get for you. Sit. Joe will tell you some lies about the old country where he was a famous musician."

Joe shrugged and grinned. "You want coffee?" he said. "Or plum brandy?

"Yes."

He brought over two steaming coffees, two glasses, and a clear unlabeled bottle.

"Thank you," I said, when he had poured the brandy. "I have a question for you."

He wasn't all that happy to hear that. But he was expecting it, I think.

"Yes? What?"

"I hear there are some new people in town."

"People come, people go. It's normal."

"Of course. And I don't really care much about who they are or what they're up to."

"That is always the best way."

"I understand. But you notice things in your community, I imagine."

"Not if I can help it."

"Well, all I want to know is if you've seen anyone who's had a recent accident to his face. Specifically, to an ear. Maybe he's missing one."

"Accidents are common on the docks."

"I understand."

"But that's all you want to know?"

"That's all. I don't even need to know who it is. Just whether you've seen something like that. Maybe a guy going around with a bandage on his head."

He thought about it for a moment. Magda came in and sat down. She brought a tray with three plates of strudel.

"I join you," she said. "Eat."

Joe surprised me by repeating my question to Magda. I knew then that he hadn't seen anyone or heard of anyone who might be missing an ear or any part of one. If he had, he would not have involved his wife. He also knew I'd be more likely to believe Magda than him.

"Ear? No," she said. "Nor any part of face. Everyone has everything God gave them. Some luckier than others. Some not so handsome. Some with too much. Some not enough. Nose. Ears. Too big. Too small. But all with everything as supposed to be. Nobody missing nothing. Yes?"

"That's right," said Joe, with a smile. He had relaxed.

Well, that wasn't by any stretch conclusive. But it was a pretty good indication of something. Joe and Magda were active in their church, and they saw a lot of their people in their bakery, and they lived right there in the Croatian neighborhood. The chances were good that they'd have seen something, if there was anything to see, if only on the street or driving by.

Just then, the same four rough-looking dockworkers came in for their pastry and plum brandy. They looked at me suspiciously, but everyone had his full complement of ears. Some were flattened and some were puffy, but they were there.

I thought about asking Joe if he'd seen any new desperate-looking strangers or heard any rumors about anything, but I didn't.

What Hamlet Said

I had told him I wasn't really interested, and I didn't want to push it. He wasn't going to tell me anyway, especially not with that table full of plug-uglies glowering in the corner.

We finished the strudel, which was heavenly as usual, and I got up to leave.

"Did we tell you that our Nicky has joined the Navy?" asked Magda.

"Yes. I hope they make him a cook."

"Me too," said Magda. "Cooks don't fight."

Joe just shrugged. He knew better.

Chapter Thirty

Driving back to the Garden, I added up what I'd learned: not much. But something, maybe. Let's assume, I said to myself, that Joe and Magda were right and that the recent arrivals were not connected to Amanda's first break-in. For some reason, I had been trying to put those pieces together, even though they refused to fit. And now that fit looked even less likely. Of course, there still might be some guy with a bandaged ear hiding out in a Ustache safe house somewhere, maybe in Pedro, maybe somewhere else. But the odds of that had been reduced somewhat. It looked less and less like the gang that was planning to knock over some "shipment" had anything to do with Amanda's break-in or blackmail. And I guess the only reason I was trying to fit them together was because I was working on both cases and it would have been nice if they were all one big unhappy gang of criminals.

And now that it seemed certain that Freddie had hired Smitty to take the photos of Amanda and Joachim, the whole blackmail thing seemed reduced to an absurd domestic squabble. Maybe Freddie was strapped for cash too, and thought Amanda could extract the fifty grand from Joachim's bottomless pockets and also give him, Freddie, grounds for divorce once he'd gotten hold of the cash. One stone, two birds. Maybe Freddie had hired some nameless and now earless thug to climb up a ladder and grin hideously at Amanda through the draperies, not expecting her to have a gun handy. What Freddie was doing in her bedroom last night was another question, but the simplest answer was that he'd gotten drunk and decided to beat the Honorable tar out of her just for being Amanda. As she told me, no one liked her, and that included her husband. Well, not no one. *I* liked her. But I was apparently in a small minority. Joachim didn't seem to care one way or the other.

So, what was it that kept tugging at me, saying these things were all somehow related? I didn't even know what all the "things" were. But there was one common denominator that I for some reason kept forgetting: Joachim, the apparently indifferent lover and German cultural attaché, also known as "spy." Indifferent, in the sense that his attachment to Amanda was as light as air and he'd watched it float away without a second thought or regretful sigh. But he was very German. And an army officer. And that tied him in at least theoretically with potential allies in the Ustache. Didn't it? Maybe? Wasn't it logical that he would have had some contact with these guys? After all, what else is a German spy going to do in LA? How many times could you count the ships in the Navy base? Now, when things were on the surface at least friendly with the U.S., now would be a perfect time to establish a domestic spy ring or even a fifth-column cell that could sabotage and cause mayhem, if it came to war between the U.S. and Germany. Or, as some people had it, *when* it came to war with Germany. And what better gang to recruit than committed separatists who were sympathetic fascists and who were relying on Germany to swoop down into the Balkans and free them from the Serbian yoke? And Joachim most likely knew about the *Lucky Lady*'s operations. He went out there frequently. Just to gamble? Or did he have other reasons? He would have almost certainly known about the daily cash shipments.

All of *those* pieces seemed to fit, and Joachim was at the center.

Then another random piece presented itself: Who had killed Smitty? And why? Freddie? Maybe. But the why remained. What purpose did that serve? Even if Freddie was blackmailing his own wife, killing Smitty was not necessary and raised the crime to an entirely different degree of seriousness. No cop or D.A. that I knew would bother with a husband sending cutout headlines to his wife, notes that were mildly threatening. Most cops I knew would laugh. But shooting a harmless photographer was something else again, entirely. It didn't make sense.

And what the hell had happened to Jimmy Hicks?

I didn't bother going to the office. I went to my bungalow at The Garden. I would make the calls I needed to make from there.

First was to Catherine.

"Hello?" she said in a sleepy voice.

"It's me," I said.

"Hello, Sparky. I was sleeping. I was up late."

"No need to explain. But could you do me a favor and call Tony? I don't have his ship-to-shore number."

"Sure. He doesn't give it out to many people. What do you want me to say?"

"Tell him the deal with the Feds is a go and that he can name whatever time and place he wants. He can let me know."

"By Feds, you mean the FBI guy?"

"I guess he told you."

"Pillow talk, Sparky. You remember that, don't you?"

"Yeah, but don't mention that to Tony. I told him we were like brother and sister."

"Our secret is safe with me. I'm just about to get up and have my bath. Want to come over and wash my back? Or come in? It's a big tub. We could get all soapy and slick. Jesus won't tell, and my new maid is a Jap and only knows two words of American."

"I would, honey. In fact, I'd like nothing better. But something's come up. Maybe next time."

"Next time will come pretty soon. I take a bath every day."

"That's why you smell so good all over."

"I know."

Next, I called Bunny. He'd probably heard the news about Freddie by now. I had the feeling he might be able to fill in a few details that were bothering me. His secretary said he would not be in until about four, but she was sure he didn't have anything else scheduled and that he'd be available if I wanted to stop by.

I grabbed a beer from my tiny fridge and went down to the pool. Hobey and Hedda were sitting there, as usual. His bathing suit covered more than hers did. She had a stack of letters in her lap.

"What ho, shamus," said Hobey. He seemed a little dispirited. "How's the detective business?"

"Picking up. There's a new dead body."

"Ah! Anyone we know? A *Gone With the Wind* producer, perhaps? Or is that too much to hope for?"

"A diplomat. Or at least a cultural attaché."

"The butler did it. Clear as day."

"No. But the other obvious suspect did."

"The wife? Even better. Jealous rage? Illicit love affair? Insurance money? Inheritance? Self-defense? General disgust? Flatulence? That about covers the standard motives, I think."

"Accident. That's what it looks like."

"Oh, sure. That's what they all say."

"Hey, listen to this," said Hedda. "'Dear Miss Lonelyhearts, My husband is a rat. What should I do?'"

"Succinct. To the point," said Hobey. "Hemingway would approve."

"Should I print that?" she asked.

"Of course. Remember, your job is comic relief for the universally miserable. That should raise a few smiles and probably nods of agreement."

"What should I tell her?"

"Quote Ambrose Bierce: marriage is 'a community consisting of a master, a mistress, and two slaves, making, in all, two.' Or, if you don't like that one, how about the ever-popular Montaigne: 'Marriage is like a cage: the birds outside despair to get in, the birds inside despair to get out.' That's a loose translation."

"I don't get it," she said.

"I know you don't. But I do, and that's the important thing." He turned to me. "Speaking of marriage, I got a letter from my wife today. She wants money for dancing lessons. Incredible. I would have thought she'd have her fill of it after what we did in the Twenties. So... who's the new stiff?"

"Fellow named Freddie Billingsgate. He's with the British consulate."

"Really? I think I've met him. Married to a slender blonde with brown eyes. Reminded me very much of butterscotch, except for the 'what are you looking at, bub?' expression. Beautiful, but haughty. Made you think she was practicing to be an aristocrat."

"She *is* an aristocrat."

"Is that so? Well, then, she does it very well."

"Yes, she does."

Did I actually blush? No. But I confess to a certain annoying and obvious embarrassment.

"Aha! I understand. The handsome Yankee melts the icy heart of the Lady. Bravo. And now that she has freed herself from her encumbrance, be careful she doesn't lure you into places you don't want to go."

"She hasn't yet."

"That's good. And I assume the places you did want to go were satisfactory."

"Very. But it's nothing serious. Mostly work-related."

"Of course. Well, then, how about a drink? My lunchtime cocktails have worn off."

"No, thanks. I've got a meeting. I'll catch up with you later."

"Hey, listen to this one..." Hedda was saying, as I headed for my car.

Bunny was in his office. I knocked and went in.

"Ah. Good," he said. Uncharacteristically, he wasn't smiling. "I've been wanting to talk to you. Dreadful business, isn't it?"

"Yes. It is."

"Coffee?"

"I'd like that, yes."

He rang the bell and his secretary appeared, as usual, with the tray, coffeepot, creamer, sugar bowl, and macaroons. And cups and saucers of translucent china.

"Help yourself," he said.

"I forget: should the cream or milk go in first or second?"

"Please. Mockery is *our* business. Yanks aren't much good at it, I'm sorry to tell you. How is Pansy? Or, I should say, Amanda."

"Upset, of course. I picked her up at the police station and took her to the Beverly Hills Hotel. She didn't want to see anyone or call anyone. She said everyone disliked her and would shun her anyway. Besides, she wanted to be alone."

"Yes. She would feel that way. Poor girl. She's right, you know. Almost no one likes her."

"*I* like her."

"I know. I like her too. But she can be... difficult. Or perhaps imperious is a better word. Even to people in her own class. You know about the book she's writing."

"Yes."

"Well, it's as much a satire of her own people as anything. The English can be such terrible snobs. That's no news to anyone, of course. But Amanda isn't that way at all. And the little snobberies and attitudes make her laugh or make her impatient, depending on the situation and her mood. And she's never shy about showing it. She can be very cutting in some of her remarks. It's too bad she's in this mess."

"Too bad for Freddie, too."

"Yes, well, of course. In more ways than one. Now that he's safely dead, I'll tell you a secret. He wasn't half the twit he made himself out to be—or allowed other people to think."

"Really?"

"Yes. I won't go into any details, except to ask if you've ever heard of Sir Percy Blakeney."

"Sounds familiar. But I can't place him."

"Well, it may come to you sooner or later. Now, do you think I should give Amanda a call? See how she's doing? Just to show that all her old friends don't hate her?"

"I think that would be a very good idea."

"And I'll send her a basket of Godiva truffles and a bottle of Perrier-Jouet. They can take care of that at the hotel, so that the wine will be properly chilled and the chocolates perfect. There never was a woman who could resist that combination. At least I haven't ever run into one."

"For some reason I've been wondering about her family. Her background."

"Why so?"

"I'm not sure. Just a private eye's curiosity, I guess."

"Why don't you ask her yourself? There's nothing like lovemaking to stimulate the desire to tell secrets afterwards. That's one of its few drawbacks."

"I thought you might have a different perspective."

"Well, I suppose I do. Her family, you say? Well, where to start? Her father Lord Readington—Gussie to his friends and enemies—is mad as a hatter. He was deeply scarred—emotionally—by the war. Not that he can't function. He comes off as the stereotypical English eccentric. Gives parties and spends his money locally and all his tenants and villagers rather like him despite, or maybe because of, his oddities. During the war he personally killed seventeen Germans with his service revolver. Not all at once, mind you. But strangely enough, he has always been rather fond of the Huns. Went there to study before the war. He's one of those who cannot abide the thought of another war with Germany, for all sorts of reasons, some of them very good. I suppose it could have something to do with blood, in the sense of a long family history. Like a lot of upper-class English, there's an ancient German connection. The royals, of course, foremost among them. And you know there's a faction in Britain that's actively and openly sympathetic to the fascists. This fellow Oswald Mosley heads it up. Heard of him?"

"No."

"Well, he's making a lot of noise. The point is, there's no unanimity of opinion in England about what's going on in Europe. Lots of disagreement. Lots of people think Hitler and his crowd have got the right ideas about a lot of things. Gussie Readington may be eccentric, but he's not unusual when it comes to politics."

"How about others in the family?"

"Well, Lady Readington is very accommodating to her husband's occasional flights of fancy. He's rather like Mr. Toad in *The Wind in the Willows*. Do you know it?"

"No."

"You should read it. Very good stuff. People think it's a children's book. It isn't, really. Anyway, the wife has little choice but to look the other way, when Gussie occasionally goes off the rails. And there are two daughters. You know one. The other is very political. A communist, in fact. Marches in rallies. Thinks Stalin is misunderstood. She's not alone in that, I must say. But no one thinks very much about her politics. Just another of the Readington girls' madcap ideas. Amanda, on the other hand, takes after her father."

"Pro-German?"

"I wouldn't say that, exactly. I don't know that she's pro-anything. I've always thought she was uninterested in politics. Before she met you, she was having a bit of a fling with Joachim Embs."

"I know."

"Nothing serious."

"So it would seem. Is the family wealthy?"

"Like most of the country aristocrats, their wealth is tied up in the land, but they are perfectly comfortable. They have plenty of money for doing the things that country families like to do. Hunting. Shooting. Fishing. Giving parties now and then, although most of their friends hate going to stay for very long, because they never know what Lord Readington is going to do next. They know he's perfectly capable of burning the house down with them in it. Then there's Lady Readington always sitting in a corner wondering what to say about almost anything, and Amanda's sister, Ophelia, handing out pamphlets about the proletariat and never changing the subject. She's called Dizzy, because she likes to give speeches to anyone who'll listen, like Disraeli. She's considered harmless, but tiresome. Finally, there's Amanda with her occasional waspishness. When she's home and when she wants to, she can sour a party with just a few glances and a nasty remark. Houseguests are always relieved when they hear she's not going to be there. But the Readingtons do put on a very good pheasant shoot the first week in October. No grouse, unfortunately. Too far south, I suppose. Of course, that opens on August 12."

"Of course. Is Amanda handy with a gun?"

"She's a very good shot with a shotgun. But I gather Freddie was killed with a pistol."

"Mine, in fact. A thirty-eight."

"Well, it's safe to say she's comfortable with firearms, if that's what you're asking. You lent her the gun?"

"Yes, after there was an attempted break-in. I'm sorry now that I did."

"Yes, of course. But we can never know how these things will work out. Not your fault. Are you going to see her tonight?"

"I thought about it. I'll call first. She might be sleeping."

"If you do, please give her my regards and sympathy. I may not be able to reach her before then."

"Why do you think she married Freddie?"

"Why does anyone marry anyone? Who knows? He was there, I suppose, at a time when she was ready to get out from under her family. I can't think of any other reason. Certainly, there was no grand passion. I remember *The Times*'s photos of the wedding. They all showed her looking grim and Freddie looking bewildered. Hardly a portrait of 'Good morrow to our waking souls.'"

"She said she thought he had money."

"Well, that's probably true, as far as it goes, but it's also just a convenient and plausible answer to an unanswerable question that she keeps asking herself."

"The old 'What have I done?'"

"Yes, I would think so."

"One last thing: the police said that Amanda was officially a cultural attaché. Did you know that?"

"I heard something about it. I don't think it means anything. Probably just an accommodation of some kind. Maybe it gets her a small stipend. I'm sure she doesn't actually do anything."

"But you said all cultural attachés were spies."

"Perhaps I misspoke. I can't see Amanda doing that sort of thing. She's much too transparent. And indifferent. If she tried, I imagine she'd be very bad at it. Whoever heard of a plain-spoken spy?"

"I wonder if her position will give her diplomatic immunity. I was talking to the cop investigating it, and he seemed to think it would."

"Well, then your friend the cop needs to double-check his notes from police school. There's a difference between a diplomat and a consul. Only the diplomats have extensive immunity. Consuls and their attachés don't have immunity in the case of felonies. Amanda could be in trouble. Technically. But between you and me, I think something like this will get worked out behind the scenes. It wasn't an accident, of course, because she did mean to shoot him. She just didn't know it was Freddie. But in her mind, it was self-defense. No question about that. The previous break-in will substantiate that. What's more, she's a British subject who killed a British subject on British territory, so to speak, so I'd be surprised if it went any further. At most, she might be expelled as undesirable." He smiled knowingly at me. "A good joke, that."

"Well, let's hope you're right and that everything works out."

"The odds are good, I'd say."

Not for the first time, I had the feeling that Bunny knew a lot more than he ever let on and that he was connected to some inner circle of people who made things go around. Now and then, he would drop a few breadcrumbs for me to follow. So I felt fairly confident that Amanda was on pretty safe ground.

"Well, thanks," I said. "I don't know what I was looking for, so I don't know if I got it."

"That's often the way, old chap. Be of good cheer."

And I left, wondering: Just who the hell was Sir Percy Blakeney?

Chapter Thirty-One

I went back to the hotel and tried to call Amanda. The switchboard operator said she'd left a message: she didn't want to be disturbed. So I assumed that included me. Part of me was relieved.

I fixed a drink and started down to the pool, where the usual afternoon drinking-and-complaining party was under way. The small crowd of writers and bit players were all getting slowly plastered, and Hobey was in the middle of the group, reading some of the letters Hedda had received. All the letters got good laughs, and the consensus was that although it was a hideous fate to be a writer for the movies, there were far worse fates out there where the real people lived. Well, that was true enough.

But just as I was leaving, the phone rang.

"Hello, Sparky. Guess who."

"Queen of my heart?"

"Smooth talker. I talked to Tony. He said 'Tell Riley tomorrow at noon on the *Lucky Lady*. Call if that don't work.' Does it? Work, I mean."

"That's just fine. The sooner, the better."

"That's not always true."

"No. With you, the longer and slower, the better."

"Just so you understand," she cooed. "And just so you remember it for next time."

"Don't I always?"

"You have your points. Anyway, Tony said that if that works for you, I don't have to call him back and he'll see you then."

"You're a peach."

"I know."

"Thank you, honey."

"You're welcome, I'm sure."

I called Bill Patterson. Amazingly, he was still in his office, although it was after six.

"Feel like meeting a gangster tomorrow?"

"Tomorrow? Perfect! Where?"

"Meet me at the Pier in Santa Monica at 11:30. We'll take a water taxi out to the *Lucky Lady*."

"I'll be there, hair combed and shoes shined. And thanks. I joined the Bureau for the excitement, and now I'm finally about to get some. Shall I wear my gun?"

"Bad idea."

"Okay. See you tomorrow."

I tried to call Amanda again, but the message was the same. I thought about joining the poolside party, but decided against it. Instead, I went across the street to Schwab's Drug Store, sat at the counter, and had a BLT. There was the usual collection of starlets sitting there, waiting to be discovered. They checked me over for a second but soon decided that I wasn't somebody. I didn't mind. Maybe they had it right.

Promptly at 11:30 the next morning, Patterson showed up at the pier. He was grinning with anticipation and looked like a brand-new teacher about to face his class for the first time: excited, nervous, eager, and young. In a new suit.

"This'll be fun," he said. "I didn't bring my gun."

"You won't need it. No place in town is safer than the *Lucky Lady*. They would have taken it away from you anyway. Just temporarily."

Perry was off that hour of the day, probably at O'Malley's having an extended breakfast. Nor did it turn out that we'd have to take another taxi. Tony had sent his personal speedboat for us. A no-nonsense goombah was waiting at the wheel and waved us over. I recognized him. Name of Salvatore.

"You're Riley," he said. It was not a question. "I seen you a couple of times."

"That's right. This is Bill Patterson."

Salvatore nodded, gestured to us to get in, and we got under way.

As we were speeding out to the ship, Salvatore glanced at Bill a few times, as though not quite believing the story he'd been told.

"So you're a Fed, huh?" he said, finally.

"Yes," Bill said, with a friendly grin.

"I feel a lot safer now," he said.

I had to smile. Salvatore had a hoodlum's gift for double meanings.

"Is he kidding?" Bill whispered to me.

"Only in one sense."

"Actually, I'm an analyst," he said to Salvatore.

"Good to know."

We were greeted at the entrance by one of Tony's top gunmen, Paulie something or other. The main room of the casino was crowded, almost as usual. The evening crowds were a little bigger, but not much. Lots of sailors were there to drink and gamble. This was a lot better than playing poker on board a Navy ship, because they could drink while they were losing here, while the Navy had outlawed alcohol on their ships. Sailors who broke that rule wished they hadn't. A few sailors who had already gone bust were standing in front of the band and ogling the girl singer, who was ignoring them and singing "You'd Be So Nice to Come Home To." More than a few couples were dancing. Time didn't pass in the *Lucky Lady*. It was always eleven P.M.

"The Boss is in his office," said Paulie. "This way."

Bill was wide-eyed at the scope of the *Lucky Lady*'s operation.

"I had no idea there were so many degenerate gamblers in LA," he said.

Paulie just laughed.

"People don't really come here to gamble; they come for the twenty-five-cent turkey dinners."

Tony was behind the desk, going over receipts, but he got up politely and in a friendly way when we walked in. I made the introductions, and we all sat down around Tony's conference table. The chairs were leather, the table was polished mahogany, and the water pitcher and glasses were Waterford. I only knew this because Tony had told me the last time. He didn't rely on his visitors to be able to recognize quality. And, in fairness to Tony, most of them couldn't. In fact, most of them didn't care about it, one way or the other. But they didn't say that to Tony.

Paulie stood by the door, with his hands folded in front of him.

"So," Tony said, when we were all comfortable. "Thanks for coming. This'll be a first for me. Entertaining the Feds."

"It'll be a first for me too," said Bill. I was pleased that he didn't seem overwhelmed or overanxious. He still looked like a kid teacher, but he didn't act like that. I could tell he was going to hold his own.

"So, what're we looking at here? Riley here tells me some bums are planning to knock off one of my cash shipments."

"That's what we think," said Bill. "We can't be sure. But it's obviously best to be prepared."

"We'll do what we need to do," said Tony.

"We're hoping that we could work together on this."

"Could be. What do you have in mind?"

"I've been giving that a lot of thought," said Bill. "Assuming we can work together on this, I think we have a couple of options. First, we could call on the Navy or the Coast Guard and have them station a patrol boat or cutter right along the route of the shipment."

"You could do that?"

Bill smiled and shrugged. "I think so. Even if the thieves were dumb enough to try the heist, there'd be more than enough firepower to drive them off."

"My boys'd be armed, too."

"I figured they would be. In all probability, though, the thieves would see the Navy and abort the whole mission and disappear."

"If they had any sense."

"Right. That's a fine option for you, but it's only a temporary solution. The Navy's never going to agree to stand permanent guard for a shipment of cash from a gambling ship. Even if they wanted to and could afford to spare the men, some civilians would get wind of it after a while and write letters to the editor who would write editorials about taxpayer dollars being used to protect... ah."

"I get it," said Tony. "Protect a bunch of choirboys in shiny silk suits."

"Yes. So that solution is short-term, at best. Once the Navy leaves, you're back where you were before. Same goes for the Coast Guard or even Police Harbor Patrols. Plus there's another drawback: we, meaning the FBI, want to catch these birds, not just scare them away. This isn't just a simple robbery. This is part of a plan to fund espionage activities here in the U.S. by a gang of foreign agents and fascist sympathizers—potential fifth columnists. That's what we think, anyway. So we want to put them out of business permanently. And that means finding out who's behind them."

"Why not just find them and send in a hit squad? Shoot a few, take the rest captive?"

"We don't know who or where they are. We just think we know what they are, and we only have a rough idea of what they're planning."

"So what are they, these guys?"

"We think they're members of the Croatian nationalist group called the Ustache."

"Croatia. Hmmm. That dipshit Mussolini has been looking across the Adriatic like a horny priest with doubts. What he wants with the place is anybody's guess. Those people have never been anything but trouble. But I guess if he was dumb enough to go into Abyssinia, he's dumb enough to want Yugoslavia, or parts of it, anyway."

"I'm impressed," said Bill.

"We read the papers too, you know. Especially the ones from back home."

"But Mussolini's not the only one who's interested," said Bill. "The Germans are playing footsie with the Croatian nationalists, too, and they are playing footsie back. If war comes, and maybe even if it doesn't, the Ustache will be eager to do favors for the Nazis, in return for support for their independence, which is their ultimate goal."

"Sounds like those dipshits never heard the story of King Stork," said Tony. "If that son of a bitch Hitler isn't King Stork in a mustache, I'm Sister Mary Margaret."

"You're right about that. But they don't see it. Or if they do they don't care, because they're desperate to get out from under their own government. But we'd just as soon eliminate these cells before the balloon goes up and they have a chance to do some damage here."

"As a favor to their Nazi friends."

"Yes. If war comes, there's absolutely no doubt that the Germans will try, and probably succeed, in sending saboteurs here. A U-boat could easily drop off all sorts of teams trained to blow up key installations. Power stations and whatnot. But why not also work with groups that are already here? And develop them?"

"What about the Nips?"

"Same story. And we've got people keeping an eye on them too. My assignment is these Croatians. The FBI's job is counterterrorism and counterespionage, so this is right up our alley, but we need to flush these birds out first."

"And our cash is the bait."

"In a word, yes."

"Do you have to catch these bastards alive?"

"Not all of them, although that would be ideal. But we do need one or two to interrogate afterwards. We need to know who's controlling them. Gangs like this never operate independently—unless they're just garden-variety criminals. We don't think these guys are. And frankly, if they were just garden-variety crooks, they'd never be dumb enough to go after one of your shipments. There are other targets that don't bring your kind of retribution."

"You got that right, eh, Paulie?"

"Fuckin' A," said Paulie.

Bill looked at me and I nodded, reassuring him that this was gangster talk for general agreement.

"So what would the Feds expect us to do?"

"Work with us to catch these guys—at least one or two who are well enough to talk afterwards. If the rest end up dead, Uncle Sam's not going to care."

Tony smiled and looked at Bill and me.

"What would they say about all this back in Squaresville, U.S.A. —the FBI working with people that've been wrongly and unfairly called Organized Crime?"

"They'd say we're not interested in the details. We're only interested in one question—did we, or did we not, win? If we did, next topic. If we didn't, who's to blame and who should hang?"

Tony looked over at me and grinned.

"We all know that's how it works," I said.

"Yeah, we do."

"So, if you agree," said Bill, "the next step is to work out those details that John Q. Public doesn't want to know about."

"And for this, the Feds in general and the FBI in particular will become my undying friends?"

"I'm not sure about undying," said Bill. "But I would say in sickness and in health, yes."

"Till death do us part?"

"More or less."

"I like it," Tony said, finally. "What do you think, Paulie?"

"Fuckin' A."

"Okay," said Tony. "I got some things to do before we start the planning. Let's get together again tomorrow, same time, and talk tactics. The sooner we get this taken care of, the better. I don't like having cash piling up."

"Suits me fine," said Bill, happily. "Of course, all this is... ah— confidential."

Tony actually laughed. "Me and my friends and our families, going back a few hundred years, invented confidential. It's called 'omerta.' Maybe you heard of it."

"Yes. I have."

"Good. So then you know if there's any leakage, you know where it ain't coming from."

As we were leaving, Tony pulled me aside and said, in a lowered voice, "I ain't forgetting that you put this together and told me about the heist. You probably saved me a lot of money and a lot of money for the friends who are behind this casino, and I'm gonna let them know about it. You'll get yours, I'll see to it. You also probably saved a couple of my boys who might have been on the wrong end of a shoot-out. I'm gonna let that be known too. You got some new friends."

"Thanks. I appreciate it." And I did, too.

"And if someday you should find yourself in the sack with Catherine, sort of by accident, it won't matter to me, as long as it don't become a habit. You know?"

"Who, me?" I said, looking innocent.

He grinned and patted me on the shoulder. "Yeah. You," he said.

Chapter Thirty-Two

Bill and I chatted briefly when we were back at the pier.

"Happy with the meeting?" I asked.

"Oh, yes. I think if we can work out the tactics, we'll have every right to expect success. What do you think?"

"I think so. But the tactics could be tricky."

"I know. I need to get together with some of our folks this afternoon. Shall I meet you here, same time tomorrow?"

"That'll work."

On the way back to the Garden, I stopped at the Beverly Hills Hotel. The desk clerk said Amanda had not checked out. She had changed rooms, though; she'd moved to the first floor. I remembered that picture of her and Joachim and wondered if she had some phobia about upper floors. I went to her room and knocked on the door.

"Who is it?"

"Rhett Butler."

"Oh. Just a minute, darling."

And it was about a minute before she opened the door. I noticed that the window was open.

"Fresh air?" I said.

"Yes. The maid was in here just before you came, and she stank abominably. It's incredible how some odors just will not go away. Don't these people bathe?"

I couldn't smell anything, but apparently she was more sensitive than I was. Some guy had socked me in the nose during a pile-up in a high school football game, and it hasn't worked all that well ever since. I'm guessing his privates don't either.

She came and wrapped herself in my arms. "How are you, darling?"

"I'm okay. But more importantly, how are you doing?"

"All right, I suppose. It all still seems like a nightmare, but the people at the consulate have been very good. They are bustling around and talking to the police and the district attorney. The tea leaves seem to indicate that things will be worked out. No one seems to want a fuss, legally. Have the papers been awful about it? I haven't read them."

"I took a quick look this morning. The editors seem to have decided to take the tragic-accident approach. Page three, not front page. The fact that you and Freddie are Brits helps. They could have played it either way, but for some reason have taken the high road."

"I think I know the reason. Influence. We English may not be good at some things, but we've invented that game. Strings are being pulled, I'm told. I wouldn't be surprised if Beaverbrook owned one or two of these papers here."

"Who's that?"

"Oh, a big press lord. Frightful man, personally."

"Your version of Randolph Hearst."

"No. Hearst is your version of Lord Beaverbrook."

"I saw Bunny yesterday, and he thought something like that would happen—that it would get worked out with a minimum of publicity and fuss."

"He would know," she said, cryptically.

"Speaking of smells, that's a new perfume you're wearing, or am I wrong?" Even with my sense of smell, I could detect an attractive scent, especially when it was this close.

"You're wrong. You haven't noticed it because I only wear it in the daytime, and you've only been around in the night. It's just a common *eau de cologne*. 4711. Do you like it?"

"Yes, as a matter of fact. Of course, it could just be that you are wearing it."

"Thank you, darling. It's for men too. If you like it, I'll get you some."

"I'm not much for cologne. Bay rum's about my speed."

"Yes, I've noticed. I like it—on you. Most Yanks don't seem to like colognes, although your gangster friend does wear quite a lot, I recall."

"Yeah. Well, some guys go in for it, I guess."

There was a pause and I had the sense that something odd was going on. Amanda was never nervous, exactly. But today she was not quite at ease. Well, I supposed that was understandable, under the circumstances. "How long are you planning to stay here?"

"I don't know. A few more days, at least. They called from the consulate and told me the police were still milling around the house. I can't think why, but there's no sense going back there. I don't want to, anyway. I'm going to have to find some other place to live, unless or until they send me home in disgrace."

"What are the chances of that?"

"Who knows? They don't need me for anything."

"I heard you were actually an official cultural attaché."

"Yes. But I don't do anything. It was just a way to get around some red tape about something or other. To be honest, most of the time I forgot I actually was one. They gave me a check every two weeks to remind me. Not much of a check, but better than nothing. And, of course, I went to parties and events with Freddie, but I suppose I would have done that anyway."

"I'll see what I can find out. They should be finished with the house investigation pretty soon. They're just being thorough, so that their reports will look professional."

"Yes, thank you. In a few days, I may know what I'm doing and where I'm going next. I wouldn't want to leave here... now especially." She smiled at me wanly but with apparent significance. "But I may have no choice."

"Let's wait and see what happens before we start talking about that."

"Yes. That's best. I won't think about it now. Would you mind terribly, darling, if... I didn't ask you to stay? I'm... I'm still out of sorts. I haven't been sleeping. Do you understand?"

"Yes. Of course. I've got things to do, anyway. I'll call you later."

I kissed her and left. I have to admit she did smell good. What was that stuff she was wearing? Something with numbers. These things are always good to know about, especially because when it came to perfume, my knowledge started and stopped at Chanel Number 5. As someone who enjoys the company of women and occasionally wants to buy little gifts for them, knowledge of perfumes comes in handy.

I drove over to Amanda's house. There were two official-looking cars in the driveway. The rental cop, DiMaggio, was loitering around the outside.

"What are you doing here?" I said. "I thought you were working the night shift."

"It's my day off, so I switched with the other guys."

"Anything going on?"

"Just forensics nosing around. I don't know what they're expecting to find. Seems open-and-shut to me."

"Me too. Seen any bad guys lurking around?"

"No, but a Nip gardener came by, raising hell about not getting paid or something. I couldn't make out what he was saying. Kept yammering something about 'I do what she say. Pay money.' I told him to take a hike. No one was home. Then he went inside and was complaining to Foster, the forensics guy."

"Any idea what he was talking about?"

"No. But you can't understand these guys."

"How's your cousin doing?"

He brightened up at that. He was always happy to tell a few lies about Joe Di, as he called him.

"He's having a great year! And he's only 22. We're all proud of him."

"Can't blame you."

I went inside to talk to Foster. I knew him pretty well.

"Hi, Steve. Got a minute?"

"Well, if it ain't Bruno the Dick, and I say that with all due respect. What's up? What're you doing in the fancy part of town?"

"Took a wrong turn. How much more do you have to do here?"

"Not much. It's all pretty straightforward."

"DiMaggio said there was a Nip gardener here earlier. Any idea what he wanted?"

"Yeah, he wanted to get paid for something. And he wanted to get his ladder back. We had kept it to check for prints."

"Were there any?"

"Just his. Whoever used it on the night of the break-in attempt must've worn gloves. But you'd expect that."

"You give him his ladder back?"

"Yep. We were finished with it. It took a little while to check the whole thing. It was one of those extension deals, so there was a lot of surface to check."

"Was it made out of wood?"

"Yeah. Heavy bastard. The little twerp had a hell of a time getting it back on the roof of his truck. But he managed."

"You didn't help?"

"I got an aversion."

"You know, they can cure that now. Did DiMaggio tell you his cousin's hitting .346?"

"Yeah. And my grandfather wrote 'My Old Kentucky Home.' I still get royalties. I only do this job for laughs."

It was getting close to the cocktail hour, so I drove back to the Garden. The usual crowd of slowly deteriorating writers were—or was, if you want to be correct—standing around the pool laughing at each other's adventures in the studio trade. It was all rueful laughter, because none of it was really funny unless it had happened to someone else. It was all like the letters to Miss Lonelyhearts, though not nearly so real. I could hear Hobey saying:

"So then I said to Sol, 'Rhett Butler is really a fag and secretly wants to run away with Ashley,' and Sol says, 'You may be right, but it'll never sell in Peoria. Leave your studio pass with Security and don't let the door hit you in the ass on the way out.'"

This brought a laugh, because the others really couldn't believe Hobey would have been that dumb. Only one or two understood that he really meant it and was only playing his own bitter disappointment for laughs because there was nothing else he could do.

I was about to join them when, on a whim, I dashed across the street to Schwab's Drug Store. There was a beautiful Jewish girl behind the perfume counter. All she needed was a nose job to be the next sultry femme fatale, if that's not redundant. Maybe she was working and saving up for it. Or maybe she figured she really didn't need it. She did, but opinions could vary.

"Can I help you," she said, with a trace of invitation in her voice. Well, who could blame her? After all, I might actually be somebody.

"I'm looking for a certain kind of perfume. I forget what it's called, but it's a number, and it's not Chanel Number Five. Now that I think of it, it's not really perfume; it's cologne. I assume there's a difference."

"Yes, there is," she said, tolerantly. "For men or women?"

"Both, I think."

"Ah. Well, then it's probably this stuff." She turned to a shelf and took down a bottle. "4711."

"That's it." I looked at the label. It said "*Muelhens* 4711, *Echt Kolnisch Wasser.*"

"That means 'Real Cologne Water,'" she said.

"Well, thank you. Let me think about it," I said.

She shrugged and put the bottle back. I had proved to her satisfaction that I was not somebody, because 4711 was not particularly expensive, and if I had to think about it I wasn't anyone she needed to pay further attention to.

"Out of curiosity," I said, "do you know if the word 'cologne' comes from the City of Cologne? Like 'wiener' comes from Vienna, which is Wien in German, and 'frankfurter' comes from Frankfurt?"

"Got me," she said, "but I do know that 'dipshit' comes from the Russian city of Dipshitski."

"Point taken."

I went back to the Garden pool and joined the others. There were two women there—a dumpy brunette and a rail-thin waif who would turn out to be the next big thing in writers. But aside from them, the rest could have posed for a Yale 25th Reunion photo—

they were all well past their physical prime and should have known better than to wear bathing suits. Most likely, though, they were past caring.

Hobey saw me and smiled his lopsided smile, which was a sure indication that he had started well before the others arrived. Hedda was there too, but she was sitting in a chaise longue reading over a pile of letters with what looked to be serious concentration. She was ignoring the revelers.

"Riley, old boy," said Hobey. "Have a drink."

"Thanks. I will."

"I will do the honors." He poured out straight gin over ice in a tall glass and dropped in a wedge of lime. "Dr. Hobey's pick-me-up, sure in the short run to convince you of your genius and in the long run to plunge you into gloom, depression, and the consciousness of utter failure. In short, it is a delayed-action truth serum."

"Sounds like just what I need."

"It is, old chap. It is. Have you discovered the identity of any murderers today?"

"Not yet. But I do have a question for you."

"I deny everything. She was just a friend. I swear it."

"That's not the question. The question is: who is Sir Percy Blakeney?"

"An Englishman. The 'sir' gives it away."

"No. Seriously."

"Seriously? Well, the name is familiar. Let me think. Perhaps a refill will stimulate the little gray cells, as Monsieur Poirot might say."

"They say it actually kills them."

"Do they? Well, what do they know? And even if it's true, I have plenty to spare." He poured himself a generous tumbler full of gin. "Have you noticed Hedda sitting here paying serious attention to her work? She is not worrying about the content of the letters or what advice to give, but merely concentrating on the act of reading. It was not her strongest subject in school. Was it, my dear?"

"Up yours," she said pleasantly, without looking up from her papers.

"Hobey," I said. "Sir Percy Blakeney?"

He sat on the end of Hedda's chaise and thought for a minute or two.

"I feel sure it's a character, not a real person," he said. He thought some more. "Aha!" he said finally. "Sir Percy Blakeney, the Scarlet Pimpernel. A book by some woman with a funny name. Baroness something or other. Made a movie of it a few years ago. 1934, I think. Starred Leslie Howard. And do you know that they're thinking of him for Ashley? A Brit. Well, that would only strengthen my interpretation of the triangle, don't you think?"

"Maybe, but what's the point of the thing? I mean, *The Scarlet Pimpernel*?"

"Oh. Well, it's about this English aristocrat who pretends to be a limp-wristed fop, which may be redundant, who knows? He goes around looking at life through a lorgnette and saying 'Sink me' as his catchphrase. Has a beauty mark and manages to stick it in the same place every day. Wears a powdered wig. Of course, they all did in those days, but he seems to like doing it more than almost anyone else. But all the while and beneath this frivolous exterior, you see, he's this dashing secret agent who sneaks into France and rescues the French aristocrats who are about to have their heads lopped off by Madam Guillotine. Even his wife isn't in on the secret until later in the movie. Or book, if you like. She thinks he's a twit, but he really isn't. *Quelle surprise!* And then she begins to love him even more, because he stops flouncing and starts buckling a swash and doing all sorts of manly and heroic things. The scarlet pimpernel is his calling card, a picture of a flower that he leaves behind. Or maybe a real one. Or something like that."

"Is a scarlet pimpernel a flower?"

"Yes. A red one, as the name suggests. Sounds like some sort of skin disease, but it isn't."

"So that's Sir Percy Blakeney."

"The very man. Why do you ask? Is it a clue of some sort?"

"Might be."

Yes. I was afraid it just might be.

Chapter Thirty-Three

The next morning, I stopped in the office before going to meet Bill at the Pier. Della was there as usual, beclouding the office with Pall Mall smoke.

"Mornin', Chief," she said.

"Good morning, my flame-haired beauty. Any calls?"

"Yep."

It was a running joke. The point was, you had to ask the right question to get the answer you wanted. This according to Della was important, if you were in the detective business.

"Who?"

"Some guy named Joe. Wouldn't give his last name."

"Have an accent?"

"Yes. He sounded like one of those guys in the movies—either the kindly grandfather or the mysterious spy. He said it might be interesting for you to stop by when you had a chance. Said you'd know what he meant. Do you?"

"Yep."

I checked the time. I might just be able to get over to Pedro and get back in time to meet Bill.

"Anybody else call?"

"Yep."

"Who was it?"

"Kowalski. Aren't you going to ask me what he wanted?"

"Nope. I'll call him later."

I ran down to my car and headed for San Pedro.

I was glad to see there were no customers in the bakery when I got there. Joe came out from the back room with a bottle of plum brandy and a coffeepot.

"Which do you want?" he said.

"Brandy, if you please."

I knew that was the proper answer.

"The strudel's not ready yet," he said. "You want something else?"

"No, thanks. But I'll take some to go." I wanted him to know money would be exchanged. "So, what's going on?"

He poured the brandy for me and a coffee and brandy for himself and looked around to make sure we were alone.

"I hear something. I don't call because I don't trust. People listen on phones."

"I understand."

"You know about some people from the old country coming to town this last month or so."

"Yes."

"They are the kind we don't need. Troublemakers. They are troublemakers in the old country, and now they are here to make more trouble. I don't like. Most of my friends don't like it, neither. Everyone here works hard. Obeys laws. This is our country now. We left the old country because of troubles. Always troubles. Here we are doing well. All of us, mostly. We don't need these people here. You understand?"

"Of course."

What Hamlet Said

"But—we don't want no trouble with them neither. So... what I tell you cannot come back to haunt me like a ghost. Not me nor Magda or Nicky. Or any of our friends. You understand?"

"I do. And you have my word."

"I believe. If Mirta trusts you, I can trust you."

That made me feel a little guilty. After all, I was cavorting around with Amanda while Myrtle was playing desert queen out in Yuma. But I was sure of my own trustworthiness as far as Joe and his community were concerned. I had no difficulty making a promise that I intended to keep, like this one. It was the other kind that gave me a little trouble with my conscience.

"So?"

Joe took a swallow of the plum brandy, and I did too.

"I hear these men planning. Two of them sat at that table there and talked. They talk very quiet, but I could hear anyway from just behind the door. They talk in our language. One of them was the boss, you could tell. He said everything was ready, the boat and all, and they were going to hit the shipment tomorrow morning. And he said to get the others together and get ready. Just do everything like they plan."

"He said 'the boat'?"

"Yes. Does that mean anything to you?"

"Yes, it does."

"I thought so. That's all."

"That's enough. Did they notice you?"

"No. I'm pretty sure not. They got quiet when I come out to wait on them. Said nothing more. Just that."

"They weren't the same men who were at that table the last time I was here, were they?"

"No. Those guys work on the docks. Good men. Not like these others, these new ones."

Joe took another quick look around and at the sidewalk in front. "Maybe you should go now."

"Okay." I drank the rest of the brandy and got ready to leave.

"Did you park out front?"

"No. On a side street, two blocks away. I thought..."

"Yes. Good. Go out through the kitchen and the back way. Magda has a box for you."

"That was thoughtful."

"It looks better if you buy something, yes?"

"Yes. And thank you. The people involved in this—our people—will not forget."

"I wish they would forget," he said. "Knowing things means trouble. Like now. Now go, before people come in."

I gave him ten bucks for the strudel and on account. I figured Tony would find a way to reward Joe on the sly, assuming all went well. And there was no reason to think it wouldn't, assuming Bill got his FBI ducks lined up. I went to the car and headed for Santa Monica.

I got to the pier, and Bill was already there. He was excited.

"Had a great meeting yesterday with my boss. He's all in."

"He'd better be, because it's happening tomorrow."

"What?!"

"That's right. I have a very reliable tip that the bad guys are planning to hit the cash shipment tomorrow morning."

"Oh, no. We can't be ready by then."

"Why not?"

"The boss wants to send for some specialists. Some guys from the home office who... who do this kind of thing. Wet work, he called it. And not because it has anything to do with boats."

"What's wrong with the guys in your office?"

"Well... I'm not sure, except he feels none of us have the right experience. Nobody's ever actually shot at someone, let alone hit something. Besides it's a small office. Not a lot of men to choose from."

"Don't you all have weapons training?"

"Yes, but... well, it's not our specialty. We go to the range a couple of times a year and shoot at silhouettes and someone gives us a check mark till next time. If we go after these guys we might botch the whole thing and get ourselves shot up in the bargain. That's what the boss said, anyway."

"Swell. Well, let's go out and talk it over with Tony. He may have some ideas. At the very least, we can cancel the shipments until you guys get up to speed."

Tony was not amused. Not at first. But oddly, he warmed up to the situation when he began to consider his options.

"Ain't that great?" he said. "The government *pezzonovanti* can't put together a decent hit squad, and we have to wait till the wet boys come across country? How long will that take?"

"Probably a couple of weeks. They might be able to fly, but probably they'll take the train. It's cheaper."

Tony turned to me. "Where'd you hear that the hit is tomorrow?"

"A very reliable source. I need to leave it at that."

Tony nodded. He knew I had no reason to mislead him and plenty of reason not to. He had to act on the assumption that my information was good. If it was wrong, he lost nothing. If it was accurate and he did nothing, he stood to lose plenty. So the source of my information was really irrelevant.

"So, I got two choices. I can cancel all my shipments for the next two weeks and let my cash build up in the strongroom, or I can take care of this myself."

"Cancelling the shipment might scare them away," said Bill. "If we don't send regular boats in to shore, they might get the idea someone is on to them, and they could disappear or switch to some other target."

"I like how you say 'we.'"

"Sorry. I meant you."

"You know if these bums do smell a rat and call it off, that's bad for you boys, but it's no skin off my ass, 'cause I still got my money."

"I see the point."

"But two weeks of cash takes up a lot of room, and I ain't got the secure space to house it all."

"Someday I hope to have your problems," said Bill, with a sheepish smile. Personally, I thought what Tony said made no sense. Surely the *Lucky Lady* had enough room to store cash while the FBI was trying to get organized. But I figured he had his reasons. Which he did.

"So," said Tony, ignoring Bill, "my other choice is to send the boat tomorrow as planned—without the money, but with some of my boys—and we do your job for you. Because take it from me, my boys don't have to ask what you mean when you say 'wet work.'"

"Maybe they'd like to talk to me about a career in the FBI." I had to hand it to Bill; he had a gutsy sense of humor.

"I don't think so. This business pays better. Way better. Although I will say that you guys have opportunities, if you keep your eyes open and play it right."

"I don't think Mr. Hoover would approve."

"Hoover, my ass! The head *pezzonovante*—and the word is, he's a pansy. But let's get back to the point. Those are my two choices. So, Mister FBI, what do you think I should do?"

"Send the boat with no money but with some of your best men. And me."

Tony smiled tolerantly and Paulie, standing by the door, laughed.

"You? Why do I need you?"

"To make it official. Sort of like when the town sheriff deputizes the town... ah..."

"Crooks?"

"I wasn't going to say that."

"Good. It would not have been polite. How about you, Riley?"

"Your call, Tony. But if it were me, I'd wait and let the Feds do the work, whenever they get here."

"That's the smart call. But I figure there's another angle. Let's say I agree to be deputy dog in this deal. Seems to me that I should get some brownie points that go way beyond the 'for better or worse' you promised me before. I figure those brownie points could come in handy for me and my friends sometime in the future. Like Tonto says to the Lone Ranger: who knows?"

"Is that what Kemo Sabe means?" I said. "'Who knows?'"

"Why not?" He smiled. "Who knows?"

I had to admire Tony's rich mixture of metaphors and references —and the fact that he actually seemed to be enjoying the situation. Because he was. Plus, he knew his business, and he knew his friends and the extent of their business, and he had a keen appreciation of the value of having friends in government in general and the FBI in particular. After all, he and his friends had built little empires by cooperating with—and sometimes coopting—state and local governments. Now he was just taking a step up. Same game, larger arena. So he saw this situation not as a problem to be solved, but as an opportunity. Most likely, it would also be a feather in his cap within his own organization. He had bosses, of course. And no doubt they would approve if he provided new levers of influence. And I had to wonder whether he had planned it this way all along, knowing that it would take the FBI a little while to get their act together. The longer-than-expected two-week delay only made it that much easier for him to sell the plan he'd had all along. Maybe I was giving him too much credit for being devious, but I don't think so. In fact, the thought was laughable.

"What do you think, Paulie?" asked Tony.

Paulie was ready with his answer. Had he been briefed? Probably.

"It depends on how we go about it," he said. "If we wait for them to make the first move, then we're just sitting ducks. The boys wouldn't like that. Me neither. But if we ambush them, shoot first, ask no questions, then that would be a piece of cake, and I say let's do it."

"I agree to that," said Bill. "As long as I'm along to make sure it's not a boat full of church ladies on an outing. Plus we need at least one of them alive."

"There's something else," said Paulie. "We should do it now, because if we wait for the Feds, we might have to do it all over again once they fuck it up, and by then it'll be that much harder. You know these guys, whoever they are, would try again. The money's just too good to pass up. And the next time, they'll come harder."

"Okay," said Tony, with a smile. He was happy because things had worked out the way he wanted and expected them to. "Now, how many guys do we need, not counting Junior, here? Paulie?"

"I'd say three with Tommy guns would do it. I'll take Vito and Sonny the Gherkin."

"You sure you want a piece of this, Paulie?"

"Wouldn't miss it."

"Good."

"But..." said Bill, suddenly nervous. "How will I get one of them alive?"

What Hamlet Said

"Why, that ain't no problem," said Paulie. "We'll watch 'em coming up to us real careful and we'll pick out one for you to shoot at. Odds are he'll make it through okay."

Tony and Paulie laughed at that, and I admit I had to smile too. Even Bill grinned. A little. But I had to admire his guts. He was signing up for a guaranteed gunfight. It was a far cry from his office full of research materials. If things went according to plan, the shots would be going in only one direction; but things almost never go according to plan, and everyone in the room knew that. Except maybe Bill.

I wondered if Tony had already drafted a list of favors he wanted from Director Hoover once this little operation was complete. I was sure of one thing—he had already thought of a few.

Chapter Thirty-Four

The meeting was over, and Bill and Paulie left. Tony signaled for me to stay behind.

"This information—how'd you come by it?" asked Tony.

"From people who got it by accident. Civilians. Good people. I promised not to say anything more. But I think we should maybe do a little something for them."

"A quiet envelope of cash?"

"Something like that. They didn't ask for anything. But it's the right thing to do."

"Okay. I understand. You want to go on the party boat tomorrow?"

"Would you think less of me if I said 'not really'?"

"Nope. You'd just be in the way, like our G-Man. But he has to go, like he said. You don't."

"Are you going?"

"Why? Paulie can handle it, believe me. Him and Vinnie and Sonny."

I thought about asking Tony why they called Sonny "the Gherkin," but really, what was the point? Besides, what else could it mean, anyway?

What Hamlet Said

Bill and Paulie were waiting for me at the ship stairway. Tony's speedboat was alongside, waiting.

"Are you going to use that boat tomorrow?"

"No, we've got a bigger launch that carries the money. More room to hide." Paulie slapped Bill on the shoulder. "See you tomorrow, Sheriff. Bring a gun that shoots straight."

Bill grinned, kind of. And we got into the boat and headed for shore. Bill was quiet on the trip back, probably like a soldier who had volunteered for something and now wished he hadn't.

When we got to the landing, he said "I'm supposed to be here at seven in the morning. Are you coming?"

"Not on the cash boat."

"Good. It's best if you don't go with us. This is no job for civilians." He said it with a devil-may-care tone. It was a pretty good imitation.

"What about your boss? Won't he have something to say about all this?"

"I'll tell him afterwards. There's an old Spanish expression: 'What the eyes do not see, the heart does not feel.'"

"Where'd you hear that?"

"From an old Spanish guy. Anyway, when I make the collar, as the cops say, everything will be fine. It's government work. The only real crime is failure."

"You're awfully young to be a cynic."

"I'm older than I look."

I felt myself hoping that tomorrow night he'd be yet another day older than he looked.

"I'll be here in the morning and go with you out to the *Lucky Lady*."

"Okay. Maybe you'll be able to see the action from the ship. See you tomorrow." He waved and drove off in his government-issue green Chevy.

I went back to the office. I needed to call Kowalski back. I had debated with myself about telling him about the FBI operation, but decided it really wasn't my business to do it. If Bill had wanted them involved, he would have told them. Besides, I wasn't sure the LA cops had any jurisdiction on the sea. After all, that was the reason the gambling ships were anchored where they were, out beyond the three-mile limit. So I figured I'd let things play out without any more participation from me.

Kowalski answered the first ring.

"Where you been?" he asked. "Or is that a silly question?"

"Client meeting."

"Yeah? Blonde or brunette?"

"Brylcreem. What's up?"

"I thought you'd like to know that your girlfriend, the nun, is going to walk. The D.A.'s going to treat the whole thing as an accident, which is a very generous definition of the word, since she aimed at the guy, pulled the trigger, and nailed him above the eyebrows. Some accident."

"Well, I suppose it's a matter of semantics. The point is, she didn't mean to shoot *him*."

"Semantics, my ass. What we have here is the absolute definition of manslaughter, maybe justified, but it was no accident. But my opinion doesn't matter. Calls were made, pressure came down, and she walks."

"That was fast."

"Like I said, calls were made. Your Champagne will taste good tonight, along with anything else. No one's told her yet. But it'd be okay if you let her know. It's official."

"You could be right about the Champagne." Frankly, I was not surprised. But it was good news nonetheless. "Anything on Jimmy Hicks?"

"Still missing."

"As in 'still dead'?"

"That'd be my reading, but I've been wrong before."

"Did you ever get anywhere on the Hobart Smith shooting?"

"Smitty? Nope. You can tell we're having a hell of a lot of success around here. It's a good thing cops don't have to run for office. Keep in touch."

He hung up.

I had thought about telling him about Jessie at the diner—that she more or less identified Freddie as having met Smitty on at least two occasions. Maybe I should have mentioned it, but it was still rattling around in my mind, creating confusion. When I had it sorted out a little better, maybe that would be the time to bring it up. And at this stage of Amanda's situation, it might have muddied the water. In fact, I was pretty sure it would have muddied the water.

While I was thinking about Freddie and wondering what he had really been up to, something occurred to me that should have occurred long before this: if Freddie was really a spy, he was obviously working for some governmental agency. They would know what he was doing and why. They would certainly not tell me, but maybe there was a way to find out at least who they were, and maybe that would lead to something else. It was worth a try.

I knew the most logical place to start. I headed to Westwood. It was time for more coffee with Bunny.

Luckily, he was still in his office.

"Greetings," he said. He was a little cheerier than the last time, but still not up to his usual standard of upper-class insouciance.

Freddie's death seemed to have bothered him more than he'd like to let on. At least that's how I interpreted things. "To what do I owe the pleasure of this visit?"

"I had an interesting talk with Hobey."

"I'm not surprised. He's an interesting man. You know, I think someday he will be recognized for the excellence of his writing. I hope he's around to enjoy the accolades. But the way he is going, I rather doubt he will be."

"I know what you mean. He's not alone, though. The dissipation stakes are run daily out at the Garden of Allah. Hobey's always the favorite, but there are others running too."

"Too bad, really. But please excuse me, I interrupted you."

"I asked him about Sir Percy Blakeney."

"Ah. So the secret is out."

"About the Honorable Freddie, yes. Or at least the secret is peeping out from under the bed."

"And you want to know...?"

"Who was he working for? What was he doing? Something tells me you might know."

"Ah. What was he doing? Well, I can't really tell you that, because I don't know for sure. And if I did, telling you would be indiscreet, to say the least. Not that I don't trust you, old boy."

"But you can make an educated guess."

"I wouldn't like to do even that. I simply can't go into specifics. But I can tell you in general how the British go about this sort of thing. What I'm about to say is nothing more than common and public knowledge, you understand. If you can draw useful conclusions from that, all well and good."

"Understood."

"Let's assume that Freddie was working for the British secret service. I don't say he was, you understand, but he might very well have been. The secret service has at least two divisions: MI5 and MI6. MI5 is responsible for intelligence and security within the U.K. MI6 handles the same sort of thing outside our borders. Think of them as one being domestic and the other international."

"So if Freddie was a spy, he would have been working for MI6."

"Yes."

"And what would he have been working on, do you think?"

"Oh, I couldn't possibly say. But you might take a look at the morning and afternoon papers and draw your own conclusions. Who are Britain's most active potential enemies? Germany, of course. Italy, probably, too. And although people tend to discount them simply because they're Italians, they sit right astride the Mediterranean with our base at Gibraltar on one end and the Suez Canal on the other—the vital link between us and India. Then there's our Malta right in the middle. And the Italians have a very decent navy. So they're perfectly positioned to cause trouble in a very important part of the world for us. And it's plain that Hitler hopes he can rely on the Italians to keep his back door secure. Whether he can or not remains to be seen."

"You sound like you're expecting war."

"I'm afraid so. One would like to be optimistic, but it's very difficult these days. And unrealistic. Besides, you know the old expression: plan for the worst, hope for the best."

"I've also heard that Italy is interested in the Balkans."

"Yes, which means that we should be too, although I'm not sure we're giving them the proper attention. And when I say 'we,' of course I'm talking as an Englishman."

"But how is all that relevant to a cultural attaché in Los Angeles?"

"Well, one intelligence officer here is only a single part of a huge picture. There are hundreds of Freddies and other agents scattered all over the world, not just embassy and consulate personnel, but individuals, including locals we've hired, one way or another. As for being here in Los Angeles, don't forget that there's one more potential bad guy on the loose."

"Japan."

"Right. They're not just a worry for you. They're a worry for us with our interests in Asia in general, and our colonies in particular —Hong Kong and Singapore. Also, our friends the Dutch are very concerned. They feel quite rightly that the crafty samurai have their eyes on the Dutch East Indies' oil. So, needless to say, there's a lot to observe and report at the various consulate parties, to say nothing about trying to keep a finger on more nefarious doings and comings and goings beneath the surface."

"Even here?"

"Even here."

"And that's what Freddie was up to."

"That would be my guess. Strictly a guess, of course."

"I ran across some funny information the other day."

"I could use some."

"It's not that kind of funny. It seems that a guy who looked a lot like Freddie was having lunch with a dodgy character named Hobart Smith."

"You mean Smitty, the photographer who was murdered?"

Although nothing Bunny said should have surprised me, this did. "You're very well informed," I said.

"I read the papers. Nothing more than that. What's this about Freddie, though?"

"Just that the two of them met. It seemed odd to me. Then Smitty turns up dead, and now Freddie."

"It is an odd coincidence, I agree. And people say coincidences only happen in a Dickens novel. But Freddie could have been talking to Smitty about any number of private assignments, given the kind of things he was probably up to. But I can't imagine anything connecting the two deaths. Can you?"

"Only that Smitty took the photos of Amanda and Joachim Embs that were part of that blackmail scheme Amanda told you about."

"Really? Well, that's an even odder coincidence. But are you suggesting that Amanda or Embs might have had something to do with Smitty's murder?"

"Not really, I guess," I said. "I can't see that there was anything like a motive."

"I can't see one either. Neither Amanda nor Embs cared much about those silly blackmail letters. Embs didn't care at all, in fact. And Amanda was on the verge of leaving Freddie, anyway. The blackmail was nothing more than an embarrassing annoyance, which is why she came to you. If it could be made to go away, so much the better; but if not, no real harm done. Just some red faces and tittle-tattle, but you know blushes and gossip do tend to fade rather quickly. If anything, the photos could have given her a welcome final push toward separation. You of all people can understand how she felt, I should think."

"Well, what do you think about Freddie's death?"

"In what way?"

"In any way."

"I think it's a damned shame, really. He was quite a good chap, you know. Played his role very well."

"The Scarlet Pimpernel?"

"In a way. Far less dramatic, of course."

"Do you think it was an accident?"

"No. I think it was a very sad mistake. But I don't think 'mistakes' are a legal term. The authorities will have to decide if it was an accident or manslaughter. If it's manslaughter, Amanda will have a bit of a rocky road ahead. Grand jury and so forth."

"I just heard Amanda's going to get off with no charges. They're saying it was officially an accident."

"Really? Good. I'm glad. But I'm not surprised. Are you?"

"I guess not. It's good to have friends in high places."

"It's the way of the world, old boy. Care for some coffee?"

Chapter Thirty-Five

After coffee and a chat about nothing, I left and drove east on Sunset Boulevard. It was another lovely Southern California day. Did the natives ever get bored with it, I wondered? I know I never did. The Beverly Hills Hotel was on the way, and, beyond that, a little further, the Garden of Allah. I figured I might as well stop and give Amanda the good news, although I was always a little wary of dropping in unexpectedly, not just on Amanda, but on any woman I was friendly with. It seemed to be good manners, and also a way of avoiding nasty shocks to my ego. Not that my ego was that tender, but no man is entirely invulnerable that way. Even Achilles had a bad foot. It was true that I'd stopped by unannounced at Amanda's room just the other day, and it had seemed okay, but I did have the feeling she had not quite been herself, for some reason. She was nervous in a way that was unlike her, but that was entirely understandable, if you felt like being understanding.

I called her room from the hotel lobby, but there was no answer. I knew the doorman, an actor named Fuzzy who regularly auditioned for roles as the sidekick in westerns. Fuzzy was not his real name. He thought it was a good, self-deprecating, ironic joke, because he had neither hair on his head nor beard on his face. No one else thought of it that way, though. No one else thought of it at all. He was still waiting for his break.

"You know Amanda Billingsgate, don't you, Fuzz?"

"The lanky English blonde?"

"Yeah. Reminds some people of butterscotch. Have you seen her?"

"Yeah. She went out around lunchtime. Didn't check out. Just went off like she was going somewhere."

"As opposed to wandering aimlessly?"

"You could say that. I noticed that she smelled really good. But those classy broads always do."

"I've noticed that too. Anyone with her?"

"Not that I saw."

Well, I wasn't going to worry about giving her the happy news. No doubt, someone from the consulate or the cops or the D.A.'s office would get hold of her sooner or later. I drove back to the Garden in time for cocktail hour. But then cocktail hour was pretty much anytime, so it was hard to miss it. It was one of the reasons I liked the place.

Sure enough, Hobey was in his accustomed spot by the pool, and Hedda was there right next to him. She was lying on her back, sleeping. Some people look good while they're sleeping. Others don't.

"Ah!" he said gaily. "Here comes our modern Diogenes. Looking for an honest man?"

"Just the opposite. Is there any gin left in that bottle?"

"Not only in that one, but in its twin, which is hiding under Hedda's chair." He focused on me with only a little difficulty. "'What can ail thee, knight at arms?' If not for your suntan, you'd be pale and wan."

"Hard to say. Things just don't seem quite right. I can't put my finger on it. Lots of pieces, but none of them want to fit together. Or if they do fit together, I don't like the picture."

"Good. I detect a story. Let's have it. Perhaps the Japanese will figure in it, after all."

"You really interested?"

"Silly question."

So I poured myself a stiff gin and no tonic and sat back on a chaise and told him what I knew about Freddie and Amanda and Smitty and the blackmail letters—the whole situation. I left out all the stuff about the Croatians, the *Lucky Lady,* and the FBI. That was a different problem. At least, I was pretty sure it was. Telling Amanda's story took a little while, but Hobey was a good listener. And when I finished, he smiled and nodded.

"Well, old sport, the thing is as clear as the gin in my glass. Amanda's a German spy."

I wasn't surprised. Hobey liked stories that operated as much below the surface as on it.

"You really think that?"

"Yes. It's the only explanation that covers all the facts."

"How so?" I pretty much knew what he was going to say, because, frankly, I had been thinking along the same lines. I just didn't want to face the ramifications.

"Start with the fact that Amanda is chronically short of cash," he said. "Agents are often recruited for money alone. No political ideals, no sense of patriotism or any of that stuff. Cash only. Of course, it takes someone with a certain cynicism or sophistication or world-weariness or all-around contempt for society to take money for spying. Would you say that Amanda might, just might, qualify there somewhere?"

"Maybe. But I had the impression from Bunny that both Amanda's and Freddie's families were at least fairly comfortable."

"How much is enough? That question has different answers depending on the person. And for someone with good family connections, she made a lot of comments about being stony, which is Brit for broke."

"I suppose she did."

"Then there's the fact that Freddie was an MI6 agent in fool's clothing. Did she know that when she married him?"

"I doubt it."

"So do I. Amanda approaches you because she is being blackmailed in the form of a very spicy photograph and some letters cut from newspaper headlines. She wants you to handle the problem. You find out that Freddie met Smitty the photographer and hired him to 'do a peeper,' as they say, on Joachim and Amanda. There's no doubt that they were having an affair."

"None at all, although it's hard to say how serious."

"And equally hard to say how casual. Perhaps Joachim recruited her during pillow talk, or perhaps she was already on board the good ship Adolf when she came to LA and met a kindred spirit in Joachim. How and why she was recruited doesn't really matter, does it?"

"Not really. But she did say that she thought the Nazis were…"

"What? Déclassé? What do you think she would say?"

"Yes, of course." And she did not say that they were power-mad, dangerous totalitarians. She only said Himmler had a bad case of halitosis. And he probably did.

"So Freddie now has the goods on Amanda's infidelity, and sends her the photo to prove it. But he does not know that she's a foreign agent. He just thinks she's a cheating wife. And about this time, he goes off on some assignment for a few days. Where he went probably doesn't matter. At that point, she begins to get the blackmail letters—composed, mind you, of newspaper cutouts."

"That are untraceable."

"Yes. Clearly, she has sent them to herself to establish some sort of alibi that she's a victim and to lay the groundwork for the plans she and Joachim are developing. Who knows what they might be? But the fly in the ointment is Smitty. She doesn't know what else he may have on her. And we don't know where she was going and what she was doing all the time. But once she gets the first photos, she begins to worry that Smitty has been tailing her around, shooting pictures of clandestine meetings with various suspicious characters. Maybe she even spotted him one time."

"It's possible. I remember that one of Smitty's friends said he was tailing her but got nervous when he thought she saw him."

"There you go."

"But how did she know that Smitty was the one who took the original pictures?"

"Good question. It's entirely possible that Smitty approached her and threatened her with exposure, no pun intended. Or maybe Joachim's network of underground contacts fingered Smitty."

"That's more likely." I thought about the connection to San Pedro and Blinky Malone and his connection to the mysterious gang of Ustache. I had already come to the conclusion that Joachim at the very least knew about the Ustache. He could very well be managing them.

"I admit, that part of the scenario isn't clear," said Hobey. "But if you assume that they somehow got wind that Smitty was the photographer, the next logical step was for one or both of them to go to Smitty's apartment. Maybe he wasn't even there when they broke in. It's a crummy old hotel where no one pays attention to anything that's going on. They ransack his darkroom, looking for anything that he might have taken other than the blackmail photos. They steal everything. And just as they're about to leave, Smitty walks in. Bang. No choice. Was it a thirty-eight, or a nine-millimeter? Hard to say. Bullet too deformed. The job may well have been done by Joachim alone. Amanda might not have even been there."

"I'd prefer that version. Besides, it seems more likely."

"Okay. Let's go with that."

"Okay. But if Amanda was sending herself the blackmail letters, what about the break-in at her house?" As soon as I asked it, I knew the answer.

"There wasn't one. Amanda borrowed the gardener's ladder and leaned it against the wall."

"It's possible. The Jap gardener was around claiming she owed him money for something or other."

"I knew they were involved somewhere! So Amanda sets up the supposed break-in. She fires your gun against the window frame and shatters it. And the glass. But was anyone really there? Did anyone ever find any fingerprints of an intruder? They figured he'd worn gloves, of course. But was there any blood anywhere? Did anyone ever see or hear of a man doing a Van Gogh imitation? Doctors? Hospitals? Nosy neighbors? Anyone?"

"No. But if the wound wasn't too serious, he would have been able to dress it himself. Or one of his gang. They wouldn't have gone to a doctor or hospital. Gunshot wounds get reported."

"Yes, you're right about that. But still the fact remains that the earless assailant disappeared, apparently into thin air."

"She might have missed. Maybe she just thought she'd hit him."

"It's possible, I admit. But if you assume there was no intruder, that the whole thing was staged, what does that tell you about Freddie's unhappy demise? Hmmm?"

"That maybe it was all a setup."

"And the motive?"

"Getting rid of Freddie and, as importantly, covering up espionage by Amanda and Joachim."

"And not only in the here-and-now, but back in jolly old England, once Amanda went home. There she'd be in diplomatic circles, well placed to gather and pass information along to Joachim, wherever he might be. Or to German intelligence."

"But she'd be a pariah, socially."

"Beautiful aristocratic women like Amanda do not remain pariahs for long."

"She'd be a traitor and a murderer, though."

"Who would know? As for being a traitor, she wouldn't think of it that way. There's no war on, you know. Not yet. And there very well might not ever be. She and a lot of people who think like her might feel they were doing their bit to prevent a war. Doing the right thing for king and country. There's a lot of that kind of sentiment in England these days. This guy Sir Oswald Mosley is leading torchlight parades in front of his small army of blackshirts, who are mirror images of Hitler's crowd. Lots of Brits think Hitler's the berries."

"But surely if Freddie felt he was on to something, he would have reported it to his superiors."

"Maybe. But maybe he didn't feel he had enough yet. After all, she was his wife, and he would really look like a fool if he accused her and got it all wrong. People would say he was just a jealous cuckold. If he really suspected he was married to a spy, he'd want to be absolutely sure before exposing her. And we have to admit something else: it's possible that he was actually fond of her."

"She does have her points, as our friend Catherine might say."

"Yes. Anyone can see that. But if you accept all this, you have to arrive at the unhappy conclusion that shooting Freddie..." Hobey waited for me to finish the sentence.

"Was no accident. It was murder."

"Yes. And damned cold-blooded and premeditated. But she may have felt that there was no other way out. It wasn't as though she liked Freddie, although I admit it's a giant leap from there to a decision to kill him. She must have been made desperate by something. Maybe it was fear of discovery and scandal. Maybe it was passion for Joachim. Maybe she hated Freddie and wanted out any way she could. Maybe she was a true believer in the Cause. Maybe it was all of that. After all, people do things for multiple reasons. It's often the combination that makes the act irresistible."

"And Freddie made it easy for her by getting drunk and barging into her bedroom."

"It would seem so. I mean, it's perfectly possible that she and Joachim had already decided to do away with Freddie. Freddie just provided the opportunity. She took it. Maybe it was a split-second decision. Or, maybe in the first moment when she was terrified and reached for the gun, she really *didn't* recognize him. Maybe she recognized him at the very moment she pulled the trigger. Maybe she's able to tell herself that that shooting really *was* an accident. She and Joachim may have planned to get rid of Freddie, but Freddie's blundering made it all unnecessary. I doubt we'll ever know. I almost doubt that Amanda herself knows."

"And what about... Amanda and me?" Had I really spent all those delightful hours in bed with a murderer? Was she really that good an actress?

"Oh, there's nothing to say it's not genuine affection on her part. You would be the best judge of that. But at the risk of hurting your pride, I will say that an affair with you would be an ideal way to disguise a more complicated relationship with Joachim."

And at that moment I remembered a nervous woman, an open first-floor hotel window, and the smell of *Muelhens* 4711 *Echt Kolnisch Wasser*—"a refreshing cologne for men or women."

"Of course, this could all be a fairy tale," he said, like a satisfied writer who was just finishing his draft for the day, knowing he could repair any mistakes or plot errors tomorrow. "It all could be exactly as it appears on the surface: a sad accident and an innocent woman. But I like my story better. I may turn it into a movie treatment. I keep coming back to the thorny question of who killed Smitty, and why. It only makes sense if you tie in Amanda and Joachim."

"Unless it was someone completely unrelated to this case. An unpaid gambling debt. A homicidal ex-wife."

"Could be. Or even a homicidal *current* wife. If I didn't send money for dancing lessons, my life wouldn't be worth a plugged nickel. It's possible to be nagged to death, you know. Why do you think Jason abandoned Medea?"

"For another woman?"

"That's the conventional reading. I like my interpretation better. My good lady's on the East Coast, and I often feel it's only geography that protects me. Too much bother coming cross-country."

"Are you guys still yakking?" asked Hedda, coming out of her semi-coma. "What time is it?"

"Cocktail hour."

"Before or after dinner?"

"Before."

"Good. I gotta get through this new pile of whiners."

"You will get your reward in Heaven, my angel."

"I'll settle for a regular paycheck. Hey, listen to this one. 'My husband drinks too much and makes a fool of himself in front of my friends. Should I divorce him? Signed, Fed Up.' What should I tell her?"

"Tell her 'Yes! Divorce him, by all means, and the sooner the better. It will be a profound relief... to him.' Ha!"

"Should I put in the 'Ha!'?"

"Why not?" He turned to me with a lopsided grin. "How about a refill?"

Chapter Thirty-Six

After a few more drinks, I went to my cabana. The gin wasn't having its hoped-for effects. I felt pretty depressed. Well, that can be the downside of gin. But the real cause was Hobey's interpretation of the story. It was too plausible for comfort, and, even worse, I had to admit to myself that it was something I had been thinking about, myself. Maybe thinking isn't the right word. But something along the same lines had been wandering around in my head amidst all the other confusions and uncertainties about the case. I hadn't worked it out so thoroughly, probably because I didn't want to. But I had to admit, it all made a certain amount of sense. Maybe more than a certain amount.

I didn't feel like having dinner, and before I turned in I tried to call Amanda's room. But she wasn't there. It wasn't very late, so there was no reason why she should have been in. Maybe she'd gotten word about the D.A.'s decision and was out celebrating. Who with, I wondered? Well, it didn't matter in the grand scheme of things. Of course, in the grand scheme of things what really *did* matter? Or does?

I had an early morning coming up, so I turned out the lights and put the day out of its misery.

Driving to Santa Monica the next morning, I thought about Hobey's theory. I didn't like it any better in the morning light, but I couldn't see many holes in it. I don't know why it depressed me. Maybe I had become a little too attached to the lady and hadn't even realized it. It happens. Well, I had to put it out of my mind for the immediate future. There was a job to do today. So as far as the case of the Honorable Amanda was concerned, I would think about it later.

It was seven when I got to the pier. Bill was already there. He was wearing his old navy clothes—khaki shirt and pants, and a blue baseball cap. As I learned later, he had come to the FBI after doing his required four years of active duty following Annapolis. If I had known that then, I would have felt better about his upcoming shootout. He was carrying a long gun case and seemed to be in good spirits.

"Whatcha got in the case?" I asked.

"Twelve-gauge pump. Finest riot gun ever devised. The boys are at the boat. We were just waiting for you."

"Let's go, skipper."

Paulie, Vito, and Sonny the Gherkin were waiting in the *Lucky Lady*'s speedboat. The plan was to run out to the ship, gear up there, and switch to the larger cash boat. I had put my snub-nosed police special in my pocket. I don't know why. It wasn't very accurate, but I figured it was better to have it than to wish I did. There was an old cowboy saying about that. I had no plans to go along on the mission, but you never know when a sudden burst of stupidity will hit you.

"Nice day for a gunfight," said Paulie, grinning. The other two gangsters didn't seem so sure, but they weren't visibly nervous either. It was business and they were businesslike. Bill was feeling his oats. He was finally getting some field action. I guess I was the only one who wasn't even a little bit enthusiastic, but that could have been a holdover—or hangover—from yesterday.

We would get to the *Lucky Lady* in no time. The sea was calm, and that seemed like a good omen. The boys would have a stable shooting platform.

"Have you thought any more about how you're going to get one of these mugs alive?" Paulie asked Bill as we sped through the calm water.

"Yes. And I think trying to do it is not worth the risk. I figure if there's six of them, one or two might survive. But if not, so be it."

"Fuckin' A," said Paulie. "That's using your melon. We were going to do it that way all along, but it's good you see it that way too. We was afraid you'd be disappointed. Ha!"

"You know, I always wanted to work for the FBI," said Vito. "Until I seen what they pay. You guys don't get proper respect moneywise."

"Tell me about it," said Bill.

"My old man was with the FBI for a while," said Sonny the Gherkin.

"Really?" said Bill. "When was that?"

"When I was a kid. He was with 'em, till they let him go. Lack of evidence. Ha!"

They all laughed, even Bill. Comrades together. I wondered if this was going to spoil Bill for office work forever. Probably.

"Hey, Sonny," said Vito. "Since you're making confessions, tell these civilians why they call you The Gherkin."

"Because Italians like what you call irony," said Sonny, grinning. "Same reason some call you Handsome Vito."

"*Vaffanculo!*"

It went on that way till we reached the ship. Tony was waiting for us at the top of the companion ladder. Behind, inside the main

Terry Mort

salon, the gamblers were hard at it. There weren't quite so many as there would be later, but there were enough, and even the girl singer was hard at it, belting out "Let's Misbehave."

"Well, if it ain't the pirates of pissants," Tony said. He was dressed for the day—dark suit, dark short matching tie, shiny shoes, and shiny hair. He was perfection of the type, and he was smiling through a cloud of cologne. "The cash boat's ready to go. Instead of cash in the bags, we filled them with sand. Some sort of cover might come in handy."

"Good idea," said Bill.

"The Tommy guns are in the boat, loaded and ready. What's that thing you got, Bill?"

"Twelve-gauge."

"Yeah, boss," said Paulie. "He come to his senses. Not going to try to wing one of them. Somebody lives through the ambush, it'll just be luck. I wouldn't bet on it, though."

"Good. Did you see any likely-looking boats on the way out?"

"No. But that don't mean nothing. They'll come fast, figuring we won't be expecting anything."

"All right, then. Off you go." Tony turned to me. "Change your mind?"

I thought about it for a second. I had a feeling this would happen. "Yeah. Why not?"

The others laughed.

"Okay," said Tony, grinning. "I figured you might. There's an extra scatter gun in the boat."

We got in the boat and headed for shore. Paulie was driving, and the rest of us hunkered down with just our heads barely showing above the gunnels and sandbags. Now that we were under way, the banter and lightheartedness disappeared, certainly in my mind, not that there was much of it there to begin with.

292

What Hamlet Said

"Remember, guys," said Bill. "You've all got to wait till I give the word to fire. We don't want any accidents or innocent casualties. I'll take the responsibility. If there's a screwup, it'll be my fault."

The three gunmen nodded. They knew what they were doing.

The sea remained unusually calm. The Pacific was like a lake, and there was no breeze. All in all, it was a beautiful day for a boat ride. There were a few sailboats here and there, their sails hanging limp in the calm. A motorboat or two were in the distance, creating creamy wakes behind them. One was hauling a water-skier. We went a bit slower than usual with the cash boat, just to give the hijackers every opportunity. But there was no sign of a fast boat capable of carrying six men.

And, in the event, there never was.

"What the fuck?" asked Paulie, as we approached the shore and it became obvious that nothing was going to happen, not this morning, anyway. "What happened to the bad guys?"

"Chickened out, maybe," said Vito.

"Goes to show you can't trust foreigners," said Sonny. "Never around when you want 'em."

We arrived on shore where the Brink's truck was waiting, tossed around a few bags to make it look like we were offloading money, and then Vito and Sonny got in the ship's car and followed the empty Brink's truck, the way they always did, just in case people were watching.

"Well, all dressed up and nowhere to go," said Paulie. "You want I should drop you at the pier?"

"I guess," said Bill. He was dispirited, and the adrenalin he had been feeling in anticipation of a fight had all drained away. "I don't suppose they'd try anything on the way back."

"For what? But maybe tomorrow. Something must've messed up their plans. I don't think they made us."

"No. Everything was the same as always. Maybe they got cold feet."

"Could be."

We motored the short distance to the pier, and Bill and I got out. Paulie went back to pick up the others.

"Ahoy, maties," said Paulie, as he was leaving.

"I'll call you later," I said to Bill.

"Okay." He was pretty disappointed. I wasn't sorry to miss a gunfight, but I did worry a little about my credibility with Tony. Well, there was nothing to be done about that now, and I went to my office to make some calls. Paulie would fill Tony in.

Della was there at her usual spot.

"Mornin', Chief. I've seen you looking chippier."

"I've *been* chippier. Any calls?"

"Nope."

It was still morning, and I was surprised when Amanda didn't answer her phone. That only deepened my suspicions. Of what? Just about everything.

Then I called Kowalski. It was more or less a routine call. I didn't expect much, but I was wrong for the second time that morning. And it was only ten-thirty.

"What's up?" said Kowalski in answer to my question. "I'll tell you. Big doings down south. Six men knocked over the cash truck at Del Mar."

"The racetrack?"

"Yep. Pretty classy operation, if I do say so. The heist, I mean."

"How many?"

"Half a dozen. Plus a guy in a boat."

"How much did they get?"

"Seven figures."

"Wow."

"Yep. The track adds up all its takings after the last race, of course, and that takes a while. By the time they're through, the banks are closed, so they make their deposit run first thing in the morning."

"Brink's truck?"

"No, they have their own. I guess they figure over time, the thing pays for itself. Goes to show how wrong smart people can sometimes be."

"Words to live by. How'd it happen?"

"Slick as you can wish for. The truck pulled out on Highway 101 and started south toward Wells Fargo in San Diego. Right where the road is practically on the beach, a car pulled in front and another behind, and they used the old hijackers' maneuver. The cars were stolen, of course. Anyway, the guy in front went bumper to bumper and slowed to a stop. Forced the truck to stop. Guy in the back closed up so the truck couldn't reverse or even swing out wide. Three guys came out from each car, started shooting up the truck. There were only two guards, and the truck wasn't armored or anything, so they both got nailed. One of them did manage to get a shot off and hit one of the thieves. Hit him in the throat. No more opera for him. Then the other five stood around for a second, wondering what to do about their man, but they heard a shout from the beach to hurry up and leave the dead guy. See, there was a guy in a speedboat waiting at the water's edge. He seemed to be in charge, and he yelled at them to come on and bring the money sacks. He kept yelling something that sounded like 'birdso' and 'shnell'. Mean anything to you?"

"Yep. 'Fraid so. '*Brzo*' is Croatian for 'quickly.' As in move your ass."

"I guess you would know, what with your actress girlfriend."

Terry Mort

"Yeah, I would know." Actually, I had picked up the word from Joe. He was constantly yelling at his son Nicky back in the kitchen to do something faster.

"What about shnell?"

"'*Schnell*' means pretty much the same thing, in German."

"Really! Interesting."

"I'll say."

"The crook who got shot must not have been a close relative, because they left him there beside the truck along with the two guards, and they grabbed the cash and ran across the beach and jumped in the boat and took off into the morning mist. Not a trace of them since. Maybe they headed south to Mexico or met up with a bigger boat out to sea. They could be miles on their way to Hawaii by now. Or just about anywhere."

"How'd you get all this?"

"There were two witnesses—a guy and his girl were playing hide the salami on the beach between two sand dunes. Some people like the mornings. I wouldn't know. Lucky for them, the crooks didn't see them. They saw and heard the whole thing."

"Any ID on the dead guy?"

"Yep. A passport. John Smith. Might as well have been John Doe, cause that's what his toe tag should say. The passport was one of Blinky Malone's poorer efforts. Looks like it was rushed."

"You know Blinky?"

"Doesn't everyone?"

"You say they got seven figures?"

"Yep. Can you imagine how much cash a race track handles in a day?"

"Yeah, I can. About the same as a casino, I'd guess. Just a tip: you might want to call Bill Patterson at the local FBI office. He'll be interested in all this, and he might have some stuff for you too."

"Feds? You been holding out on me?"

"No. Just making new friends."

Well, even though there were three dead guys and a million or more missing, I felt better. At least my tip from Joe had been a good one. We just figured on the wrong target. It was the Croatians, most probably the newly arrived six plug-uglies, which meant it was also no doubt the Ustache. And a boat was involved, and they did hit a "shipment," just not from the *Lucky Lady*. And it seemed very much like there was a German in the woodpile. Joachim? Maybe. Or maybe he'd sent one of his assistants or soldiers. But you'd have to be pretty naïve to think he didn't have his fingerprints all over this operation. Hell, there might even have been a U-boat offshore waiting to pick them up. As for the three dead guys, one of them was no loss, and I didn't know the other two, anyway. So, yes, I felt pretty good about the news.

I drove back to the pier. I wanted to go back to the *Lucky Lady*.

Perry was handling the noon-to-eight shift.

"Mornin', Chief," he said.

"Mornin', chief. How about a ride out to the *Lucky Lady?*"

"Cost you a quarter. Friendship only goes so far."

"Not as far as the *Lucky Lady,* it seems."

"Times is hard. Say, did you hear about that heist down in Del Mar?"

"Word travels fast. Yeah, I heard."

"I listen to the police radio in my spare time."

"Seems your buddy Blinky supplied the crooks with passports."

"Really? Imagine that. And just last week I sat next to him in church. Life sure is full of surprises."

Chapter Thirty-Seven

"Don't take it hard," said Tony. We were in his office having an early lunch—*fruiti de mare*, a loaf of *ciabatta*, and red wine. There would be fruit for dessert. Tony had his napkin tucked in his collar to avoid spatter on his shirt and tie. I followed his lead. "You got everything right except the target, and I for one ain't too unhappy about that. Naturally, I'd like to help our new friends, the Feds, catch some bad guys; but the way I figure, it's even better to get some credit just for trying—lots better than getting my boys and my boat shot up. It's like with Catherine. I tell her 'Honey I was going to buy you a diamond necklace, but when I got to the store they were out, so I got you this nice leather wallet instead.' She don't buy it, of course—not all of it, but she's gotta admit that at least I was thinkin' of her, and everybody says it's the thought that counts. Am I right?"

I nodded. Both of us knew what Catherine thought about Tony's gifts.

"I guess you are," I said. "The fact is, I wasn't too disappointed about missing the gunfight."

"No one with any brains would be. You wanna shoot some guy, you do it when he ain't expectin' it, or lookin'. Not when he's comin' at you in a boat with a load of gunmen. This was kind of a last-resort operation, plus something to sweeten my reputation with

Hoover's boys. That's worth a risk or two. So, what do you think? They gonna make another try at us?"

"I doubt it. Seems to me they got enough on this one job to finance whatever they had in mind, whether in this country or even back home. A million bucks or more buys a lot of weapons and politicians. Plus, the heat's going to be pretty intense after the two killings. And everybody who moves money is going to be on the alert."

"That's the way I see it too. But just to be on the safe side, I'll beef up our cash runs. Send the speedboat alongside with a couple of boys with Tommy guns visible. That won't blow our cover any more, 'cause like you say the heist in Del Mar's going to make everyone more careful. How's your pasta?"

"Never had better." Truth was, I don't think I ever had it. Spaghetti and pizza were about my top speed when it came to Italian food. But I was learning.

Tony looked at me and smiled, appreciatively. Almost affectionately.

"Word is, you're shackin up with Yvonne Adore." That was Myrtle's film name. I knew that Tony was a little star-struck. After all, that was the reason he'd pursued Catherine—because she looked so much like his former girlfriend, now deceased. Minnie David had been a big-time movie star, and she was the one he'd left in the motor court in Joshua Tree. The story was, he'd had tears in his eyes when his man drove him away. Minnie was also producer Manny Stairs's wife at the time, which is why he'd pursued and married Catherine. Catherine got a lot of mileage out of the resemblance.

"Well, when she's in town," I said, "we do see a lot of each other."

"From head to toe. Ha, ha! Man, I envy you that view."

"Yeah. Botticelli."

"On a clamshell. But I also hear you been nailin' that English broad, while Yvonne's been out of town. That right?"

Well, there was no sense denying it. It certainly wouldn't damage my stock with Tony. "Yes. I guess you could say that, too."

"Nice. I seen her out here a few times with that Kraut she used to bang. She sort of reminds me of butterscotch, for some reason."

"I know what you mean. It's her coloring, I guess."

"She's a good-lookin' woman. Too bad she cost me a lot of money."

"Really?" Uh-oh. Something new was coming my way. I didn't know whether Tony was dropping this casually, or whether he intended it. You never did know with him, although it was always safer to assume that whatever he did, he had a reason and had thought it out in advance. "How'd she cost you money? If you don't mind my asking."

"No, I don't mind. When she shot her old man. That limp-wristed bastard loved blackjack and was lousy at it, which is just how we like 'em. But how we don't like 'em is when they run up losses to the limit of their credit and then don't come around when it's time to pay off. He was into me for fifty grand. I figured because he went by The Honorable, back in the old country he was some kind of *pezzonovante*, which means 'big shot' in Ohio where you come from. Plus he was workin' for the government here. So I figured he was good for it. Maybe he would have been, though I sorta doubt it now. But I can't do nothing about it, now he's headed home in a box. Can't collect from his old lady."

"I'm pretty sure she doesn't have that kind of money."

"Well, it ain't her debt, anyway, even if she did. What do you think? Was it really an accident, or was she just tired of the *cazzo*? Which, for you Presbyterian boys, means 'dick'."

What Hamlet Said

"An accident? To tell you the truth, I just plain don't know."

"Well, do me a favor. Next time you're taking a break, sipping Champagne and waitin' for your *salsiccia* to point north again, ask her. I'm just curious."

"Think she'll tell me?"

"Who knows about women? You can never tell what they're gonna do. Can't hurt to ask."

I planned to. Ask her about that, I mean, and a few other things.

When I got back to the office, I called her at the hotel. I didn't expect to find her there, but she answered on the first ring.

"Oh, Rhett! Hello." She sounded surprised it was me.

"Expecting someone else?"

"No. I just thought you'd be... working this time of day."

"I am, honey. What are you doing for dinner tonight?"

"Why, darling, didn't you know? I'm having it with you. What would you say to a little room service, here?" She actually giggled at the straight line.

"I'd say, I'll be there at seven."

I called Kowalski to see if there was anything new about the Del Mar heist, but there wasn't. The Coast Guard had joined the search for the escape boat, but everyone figured by now it was tied up and abandoned in some little inlet in Mexico. The gang was long gone, most likely scattered and headed for parts unknown.

"Any news on Jimmy Hicks?"

"Still dead."

I went back to the Garden to shower and change for dinner. Hobey and Hedda were out by the pool. I thought about having a quick drink with them before changing.

"What ho!" said Hobey as I walked over. "Come and join us. We're celebrating."

301

Only Hobey was celebrating. Hedda was reading her stack of mail and was paying no attention to him.

"Good," I said. "I'd like to hear some happy news."

"Yes. I've been hired for another screenwriting assignment."

"Really! That *is* good news. What's the deal?"

"Tahiti. You know those ten-minute shorts they show before the main picture comes on? Well, one of the producers just got back from there, and he took some home movies which we'll turn into a travelogue. I'm to write the narration. Tahiti—land of something or other. Exotic flowers. Bare-breasted women. Gauguin. I haven't quite decided yet. But it's early days."

He was pretty drunk, and I could tell this new assignment had depressed him by its utter insignificance.

"Well, that doesn't sound too bad. Do you get to go there for background?"

"Not exactly. I get to go to the Los Angeles Public Library and read up on the subject and then scatter my word pearls accordingly. I'm to have the script ready the day after tomorrow. Two pages, double-spaced. Three at the most."

"Ah."

"By the way, any progress on the great spy mystery?"

"I don't think so."

"Hey, listen to this…" said Hedda.

"Sorry," I said. "I've got to run."

302

Chapter Thirty-Eight

"That was lovely, darling," she said, breathlessly. "Was it enough to make you hungry again?"

"I'd say so. In a while or two."

"While we're waiting, will we have time for dinner? I'm starved. It's good the lobster is cold, and so is the Champagne. Are you hungry for that too, darling?"

"As a matter of fact, I am."

"Good. Let's stay starkers."

We sat in bed and ate off the tray and finished one bottle of Veuve Clicquot and started another.

"This is fun," she said.

Well, there was no denying that. But at the risk of breaking the mood, it was time to change the subject. "Can I ask you something?"

"Anything. I don't promise to answer, though. A woman's prerogative."

"Did Freddie know about the blackmail letters?"

"Oh, dear, we are turning serious, are we?"

"I suppose so."

"Do you really want to know?"

"Yes."

"Well, yes. He did."

"How did he react?"

"To be honest with you, they made him almost frantic. He was so afraid the pictures would become public."

"Because of the scandal?"

"In a way. But you see, he didn't really care so much about *my* reputation. We were pretty much finished anyway. But he was terrified for *his* career, because there I was, the wife of a British agent, having it off with a German officer. And even though you couldn't see Joachim's face, Freddie was convinced the photographer had others that were even worse—others that the guy had kept to extort money from Freddie. He might have even been trying already. I don't know about that."

"Freddie was a British agent? You knew?"

"Well, of course I did, darling. Didn't you? I assumed that Bunny mentioned it to you in confidence. Bunny knows all."

"Well, he did say something about Sir Percy Blakeney."

"Yes, he would say it that way. Nothing direct about our Bunny. Anyway, the letters made Freddie terribly nervous. So nervous that he was trying to find a way to pay the blackmail. He couldn't see any other way out, even though we were stony broke. And the worst part was, he had no clue who was behind it. He even wanted me to get the money from Joachim, who's swimming in the stuff."

"Did you ask Joachim for a loan?"

"Well, no. But Freddie kept after me about it. I was almost tempted. But then... things changed... that awful night."

"Did you know Freddie was a gambler?"

"You mean with cards and things? I knew he liked to do card tricks. That was part of his cover as an upper-class twit. But I don't think he ever gambled for money the way Joachim does." She paused and looked at me with apparently sincere questions in her eyes. "Did he?"

"It's possible."

"Oh, no! Did he owe money?"

"Also possible."

"A lot?"

"I think so."

"Oh, dear. That does change things."

"It might."

We drank the rest of the second bottle in silence. Amanda was thinking over the significance of this new information—if it was new.

"Darling," she asked, "do you think it's possible... that Freddie..."

"Sent the letters?"

"Yes."

"Do I think it's possible? Yes, I do."

"As a way of getting me to get the money from Joachim?"

"That would be my guess, yes."

"To pay off gambling debts."

"He was in pretty deep. Fifty thousand, to be exact."

"Fifty thousand! How awful! How... common and vulgar." It was hard to tell what bothered her more, the size of the debt or the fact that Freddie was such a contemptible loser.

She was quiet again for a few minutes, and I let her think.

"Do you think that the people he owed the money to will... come after me for it?"

"No. I know them, and I'm quite sure they won't. They told me so."

"Was it that gangster on the gambling ship? The one with too much cologne?"

"Yes. You needn't worry. I'm quite sure of that. He and I are... friendly."

"That's good."

She thought some more and gradually began to relax. There was nothing to do about any of it. No use to worry. She was remarkably resilient. Well, from her point of view, she could afford to relax. She was out of it now.

"Well," she said finally, "if it is true, there's one silver lining: there's no horrible blackmailer out there lurking around. Do you suppose Freddie hired that awful Caliban to frighten me? I guess he must have."

"If he sent the letters, he sent the Caliban."

"Oh, dear. How frightful of him. I mean, we weren't getting along, but to do that.... I might have killed the man. And he was probably no more than some vagrant Freddie hired and told to climb up the ladder and grin at me. It's too bad, really too bad."

"That's the way it looks."

She was quiet for a few more minutes, but then seemed to gather herself again.

"Is that all you need to know about Freddie? That's really all I can tell you. I mean, that's all I really know about any of it. In fact, you seem to know more about things than I do."

"I guess so. I mean, that's all I really need."

"Why did you want to know?"

"It's all tied up with a case I'm helping the police with. Nothing to worry you."

"That's good." She snuggled against me and whispered "Have you had enough?"

"Enough lobster, yes."

"Is there any butter left?"

Around midnight, she rolled over on her side and said "I almost forgot. I have a present for you." She got up from bed and walked seductively to her bureau and got something from a drawer. "Here, from me to you."

I opened the small package.

It was a bottle of 4711 cologne.

"To remember me by," she said, sliding back to bed.

"Remember you by?"

"Yes. I didn't want to tell you until we'd finished our lovely dinner and our lovely time in bed, though that might not be completely over. But, you see, they're sending me home with Freddie's body."

"Oh. I'm... sorry to hear that." And I was, too. And very surprised.

"Are you, darling? I'm glad you feel that way. Freddie's to be buried in the family plot, as you'd expect. After the funeral and whatnot, I'm to have a new assignment. I think the Foreign Office is being nice to me and giving me a job so people will believe the story about Freddie's accident. Which they should, of course. But you know how people can be, sometimes."

"A new job? Where? Here?"

"No, unfortunately. In Berlin. At our embassy. If it's still open by the time I get there. With any luck, there won't be a war, though, and things will be jolly despite the gloomy old Nazis marching around being tiresome."

"Tell me something, Scarlett."

"Anything, Rhett, darling."

"Are you a spy too?"

She laughed.

"Heavens, no. I couldn't keep a secret from anyone. Besides, don't you remember, I'm writing a book on what's done and not done, and if there's anything that's not done, it's snooping around in other people's business. Freddie and I always argued about that. The point is that you should simply not care—about almost anything, and certainly not about politics. Too grubby for words. That's the foundation of my whole worldview. Indifference. Not giving a damn about anything. So I'm going to the embassy, and I'll go to parties and stand around looking glamorous and letting myself be breathed on by fat little Germans in those awful uniforms. But that will be all I do. In the daytime, they'll have me licking stamps or something meaningless. And the funny thing is, Joachim is leaving here too. Going home."

"Really!"

"I suppose his work here is done, whatever it was."

"Yes. I imagine it is."

Did I believe her? With my arm around her bare shoulders and my hand cradled around her breast and her legs moving seductively against mine and the hunger returning on cue—did I? Well, yes, I did. I believed her.

And later I said "I suppose you'll be able to see a lot of him."

"Who?"

"Joachim."

"Yes, I suppose so. Do you like your present, darling Rhett?"

"I'm not much of one for cologne."

"I know. But just open the bottle now and then and the scent will remind you of me and our fun times with Champagne and lobster and eating starkers and you quoting Shakespeare."

"Sure. I will do that. And thank you. It was very thoughtful."

Now that I pretty much believed her story—that she wasn't a spy, that she hadn't killed her husband on purpose, and that Freddie had sent the blackmail letters to try to extract money from Joachim through her, now that she was just the lovely and desirable woman that she seemed to be—I found myself suddenly caring a bit more than I would have thought possible. And now, of course, she was leaving. That made it worse, because I did believe her story. Most of it, anyway.

"When are you leaving?"

"Tomorrow. On the ten o'clock train. Do you want to come to see me off?"

"No. I'll pass on that, if you don't mind."

"Oh, darling, don't look so unhappy," she said, curling up next to me.

"I'm not." Fact is, though, I was, a little.

"You didn't think there was really anything between us, did you? You didn't think it meant anything more than just a fun bit of shagging? Did you?"

Did I?

No, I guess I didn't.

Chapter Thirty-Nine

The next morning, I went to the office. Della was there, working on her novel. Or something.

"Hiya, Chief. Say, you look worse than usual."

"Long night. Any calls?"

"Nope."

I called Kowalski. "Any news about the heist?"

"Nope. They got away faster than Jesse Owens with a rocket up his ass. By the way, I called your buddy at the FBI. Nice fella."

"He have anything?"

"Between the two of us, we got a Gershwin song—plenty of nothin'. You hear anything?"

"No. Say, out of curiosity, what sort of weapon does a British secret agent carry?"

"Damned if I know."

"Any guess?"

"Well, if I had to guess, I'd say they'd use a Webley, which is a British manufacturer. They make sidearms for the army. Forty-fives. But they also make a smaller, short-barreled model that would fit in a shoulder holster. They call it the Bulldog."

"What calibers?"

"The usual."

"Thirty-eight?"

"Yeah, I think so. Why?"

"Just curious. Any news on Jimmy Hicks?"

"No. And here's a news flash for you: I don't think there's going to be."

"I'm afraid so, too."

"By the way, you can pick up your thirty-eight down here whenever you want to. We're finished with it."

"I'll stop by. Thanks."

The following Saturday, Catherine gave another party at her beach house in Malibu. The usual crowd of movie people were there, the men smoking cigars and talking business, the women looking gorgeous and knowing it. But Catherine had invited her special friends too.

It was another perfect California evening. The patio was lighted with overhead Chinese lanterns, and the sun was setting gorgeously over the Pacific. The water was as smooth as a millpond. Three massive and elegant yachts lay at anchor, and they were hardly moving in the calm water, their gleaming white hulls reflected almost perfectly. There was a small musical combo in the patio corner opposite the bar, and a girl singer was standing at a mike, almost whispering "What'll I Do When You Are Far Away." She was pretty good and added just the right touch to a nearly perfect scene. If there were war clouds in the news, there weren't any clouds here, and the colors and the scented air and the music all told you that nothing could ever go wrong. Not here, anyway.

I arrived when everyone else was already there—everyone but Ethel, who was off somewhere for the weekend. She had sent me a note saying only "Wednesday? Number 66." Once again, I wondered just how many there were, but I supposed I would find out, eventually.

"Hello, Sparky," said Catherine as I walked around the house to the patio. "Do you like my dress?"

"I like what's in it. You look like you smell good all over."

"Smooth talker. And you know what? I do."

"Come closer. Let me check."

"I would, but Manny's here. He's talking money with his friends, but he watches out of the corner of his eye."

"And who could blame him?"

"I know. You know, Tony said he really likes you. That's not a bad thing for a man in your business."

"I realize that."

"I don't think he'd even mind too much if you and I had a little fling now and then. Want to?"

"Desperately."

"Good. It's all good clean fun, isn't it? Especially in the shower."

"You are my heart's darling."

"I know that too."

"Nice party. Who else is here?"

"Hobey and Hedda and Bunny with a new girlfriend. Will you do me a favor and ask Hobey not to play those funny songs?"

"I'll try."

On cue, Hobey and Hedda came over, and Catherine went off to be admired.

"Hello, old sport. How's the mystery business?"

"So-so. How'd the Tahiti project go?"

"Ah! As easy as a shark swallowing a native. I gave them two pages of delightful narration, and they loved it, probably because of its utter banality. I didn't have time to make it into anything meaningful."

"No romantic egotists in Tahiti? No love triangles?"

"That's right. They liked its pedestrian nature so much, they gave me another one to do—this time on Madagascar. Have any idea where that is?"

"Vaguely."

"I'll have to look it up. But it's another payday and more dancing lessons for the missus. This might be the opening of a whole new career."

"I'm really glad to hear it. How's the lovelorn business, Hedda?" She was wearing a wildly inappropriate flowered dress.

"Real good. It's fun being a journalist. Beats selling ladies' hats in Flatbush, like I used to."

"I'll bet."

"Plus, it's a chance to do some good for people. You know?" Her laugh was utterly insincere and not very flattering. More like a cackle.

"How about a drink?" said Hobey.

"Sounds good."

"I'll bring you one."

He went to the bar, and Hedda drifted off. I noticed Bunny standing to one side, talking to a stunning woman. Well, that was not surprising. He never seemed to talk to any other kind. But he saw me and left her for a moment and came over to me.

"Hello, Bunny," I said. "That's a beautiful woman you're with."

"Yes. She's lovely. She mispronounces 'mauve,' though. That sounds trivial, I suppose. But with so many beautiful women around, one shouldn't have to compromise. How goes it with you?"

"Not bad. A little dispirited. Too much... something or other."

"Yes, I think I understand. Speaking of that, I saw our girl Pansy off on the train yesterday. Or I should say 'Amanda.' I was a little surprised you weren't there. Don't like good-byes?"

"I don't mind them in general. Just not that one."

"I understand. Was it Cole porter who wrote 'I've Got You Under My Skin'?"

"I believe so."

"Apropos?"

"A bit.... Tell me something, Bunny."

"If I can."

"She's a spy, isn't she?"

"Yes."

I nodded. "I figured. She hides it well."

"Yes, again. But that's the name of the game, isn't it?"

"I suppose it is." I paused and then asked the question he probably knew was coming. "But which side is she playing for?"

"Ah. Well... you're a self-educated man."

"So?"

"So you undoubtedly know what Hamlet said, just after he said 'To be or not to be.'"

As a matter of fact, I did know. I read a lot.

THE END

About The Author

Terry Mort

Terry Mort is a novelist and historian. His non-fiction includes two books about Ernest Hemingway's activities in World War Two, a history of the origins of the Apache wars and a history of George Custer's 1874 expedition into the Black Hills of Dakota. Both Hemingway books were selected as Amazon Best of the Month and both western histories were selected by all the major book clubs. His work has been translated into French, Czech, Greek and Russian and has been published not only in Europe and North America, but throughout the British Commonwealth.

In his fiction he has written novels in various genres, including westerns, sea stories and noir mysteries, in all cases to critical acclaim. As the *Wall Street Journal* wrote: "Mr. Mort's lucid, beautifully written books are a pleasure to read."

He is unique in having been favorably compared to both Raymond Chandler and Francis Parkman—a comparison that underscores his versatility and wide ranging interests.

He has also edited collections of Mark Twain, Jack London and Zane Grey, and written a book on fly fishing.

He has degrees in literature from Princeton University and the University of Michigan. After graduate school he served as an officer in the US Navy. He has travelled to over thirty-five countries and now divides his time between Sonoita, Arizona and Durango, Colorado. His website is Terrymort.com.